Waiting for Tom Hanks

Waiting for Tom Hanks

KERRY WINFREY

JOVE

New York

A JOVE BOOK
Published by Berkley
An imprint of Penguin Random House LLC
penguinrandomhouse.com

Library of Congress Cataloging-in-Publication Data

Names: Winfrey, Kerry, author.
Title: Waiting for Tom Hanks / Kerry Winfrey.
Description: First edition. | New York: Jove, 2019.
Identifiers: LCCN 2018058330 | ISBN 9781984804020 (pbk.) |
ISBN 9781984804037 (ebook)
Subjects: LCSH: Romantic comedy films—Fiction. | Man-woman
relationships—Fiction. | Women writers—Fiction. | Motion picture
industry—Fiction. | Hanks, Tom—Fiction.
Classification: LCC PS3623.I6444 W35 2019 | DDC 813/.6—dc23
LC record available at https://lccn.loc.gov/2018058330

First Edition: June 2019

Printed in the United States of America
3rd Printing

Book design by Elke Sigal

For Lauren Dlugosz Rochford, first and best reader

ACKNOWLEDGMENTS

I could never have written this book without the help and support of many, many people.

Thank you to my amazing agent, Stephen Barbara, for believing in this story and working so hard to find it the perfect home.

Thank you to the entire team at Berkley, most of all my brilliant editor, Cindy Hwang, for making this book the best it could be. Thank you to Angela Kim for all your hard work and to Farjana Yasmin for this absolute stunner of a book cover. Thank you to Jessica Brock, Fareeda Bullert, Elisha Katz, and Brittanie Black for going above and beyond (and responding so quickly to all of my many, many e-mails).

Thank you to all my friends and family for coming to my events and caring about my books. Special thanks to Lauren Dlugosz Rochford for reading everything I write and always knowing exactly what to do to make it better. Emily Adrian, thank you for reading an early draft, for reassuring me that it wasn't terrible, and for being willing to talk about the minutiae of publishing. Dr. Catherine Stoner, thanks for recommending my books to the vets and for listening to the boring details of writing! Thanks to my pizza sluts for inspiring the friendship between Annie and Chloe.

Alicia Brooks: your never-ending hatred for "Escape (The Piña Colada Song)" inspired an entire scene in this book. Thank you for your tireless efforts to make sure everyone realizes how weird that song is.

Thank you to the booksellers and librarians I've met on my writing journey. I appreciate your enthusiasm and hard work so much. Special thank-you to Cover to Cover in Columbus and Joseph-Beth Booksellers in Cincinnati for being so supportive of me and my career. And, of course, thank you to the Book Loft for being a great place to set a fictional scene of sexual tension.

I'm so grateful for everyone who read my Tumblr, A Year of Romantic Comedies, and messaged/e-mailed/tweeted me to recommend a movie or talk about Tom Hanks. Even when people swore the rom-com was dead, we knew it could never really die.

Thank you to Nora Ephron for all the joy you brought to the world and how well you understood sadness.

Thank you to Harry for occasionally taking naps so I could write this book. Thank you, as always, to Hollis, especially this time for being my fact-checker.

And, of course, thank you to Tom Hanks. It's an honor to name a book after you.

Chapter One

I JUST THOUGHT I WOULD'VE MET TOM HANKS BY NOW.

Not *real* Tom Hanks, the beloved actor. After all, he's married to Rita Wilson, and I'm not the sort of monster who would want to break up what is perhaps Hollywood's one truly perfect union. And anyway, I'm twenty-seven, so he's a little bit old for me (no offense if you're reading this, Tom).

The Tom Hanks I thought I'd meet is the Tom Hanks of romantic comedies. The Tom Hanks who starred in Nora Ephron films. The one who wrote about bouquets of sharpened pencils or told call-in radio show hosts how much he missed his wife. The one who lived on an unbelievably luxurious houseboat or called Meg Ryan "Shopgirl." The man with a heart of gold, the one I was meant to be with even if we lived on opposite coasts or owned competing bookstores.

I should have run into him by now, while I'm carrying a large, unwieldy stack of books and he's hurrying to some important business meeting. Or maybe I should have tripped over my own feet and fallen right into his arms (note to self: start wearing more impractical footwear). Or maybe I should've bumped into him while Christmas shopping, when both of us spotted the very last fancy scarf and we each desperately needed to buy it for our own fancy-scarf-wearing relatives. And we would fight and get angry and hurl insults that neither of us really meant, but that underlying passion would translate into some fantastic flirty banter, and then that scarf would get written into our wedding vows in a hilarious-yet-touching surprise that wouldn't leave a dry eye in the house.

Not that I've spent a lot of time thinking about this, or anything.

It's just that I've seen a lot of romantic comedies, and I can't even blame that on Tom Hanks himself, as much as I would like to pin all my problems on a celebrity.

No, I blame my mother.

She's the one who indoctrinated me into the Cult of Ephron, the one who showed me *When Harry Met Sally . . .* when I was only nine years old and way, way too young to understand what Sally was imitating in that deli scene. She's the one who spent Saturday nights sobbing over the end of *Sleepless in Seattle*, showing me that true love sometimes involved a little bit of light stalking and a lot of encouragement from Rosie O'Donnell. She's the one who introduced me to the charms of Rock Hudson and Doris Day sharing a phone line and being incredibly deceptive in *Pillow Talk*.

And yes, only one of those films actually stars Tom Hanks, but that's not the point. Tom Hanks isn't a person so much as he is a representation of the kind of man I deserve, as my mom told me over and over. "Don't settle for someone who doesn't adore you," she told me. "My favorite thing about your dad was that he worshipped the ground I walked on."

She was kidding, but only sort of. Anyone who saw a picture of my dad and mom together would know that they were one of those golden couples, the ones who get together and stay together and end up like those old people talking to the camera in *When Harry Met Sally . . .* about how they met. And they would've been, if he hadn't died when I was just a baby, before I even got a chance to remember him.

My mom died much later, of a heart attack. I have a theory that you can react to tragedy in one of two ways: you either distract yourself from your pain with over-activity, or you make yourself a home inside your pain cocoon. In high school and college, my coping strategy was the former. Instead of thinking about how much I missed my mom, which could easily have been a 24/7 extracurricular, I threw myself into activities, clubs, and projects. I was valedictorian in high school and graduated summa cum laude in college with a degree in film studies. I studied movies, watched approximately one million of them, and dreamed of someday writing my own Nora Ephron–style romantic comedy.

But after college, after I was done crossing off every item on my to-do list, my over-activity ground to a halt. I couldn't bear to leave my childhood home, which my uncle Don moved into after my mom's death so I wouldn't have to change schools. I didn't have anything to do after I hung up my graduation robe in the closet, but I knew one thing: Tom Hanks would be able to solve this.

Again, not Tom Hanks himself, although he does seem like a very smart man, and I'm sure that if he can write a short-story collection or direct the film *That Thing You Do!* then he could probably figure out a way to fix my life. But in most romantic comedies, the female lead is floundering. Maybe she's adrift, maybe she's lonely, maybe she's a workaholic who needs to learn how to love! But no matter what, she has some sort of dream she's working toward, and she just can't figure out how to get there. But then she meets him—Tom Hanks or Rock Hudson or the rapper Common in the *way* underrated basketball rom-com *Just Wright*—and it all clicks into place. She figures it out. She gets stronger and smarter and she achieves her dreams, plus she finds love.

But I'm starting to think that the movies I've dedicated my life to may have lied to me. Nora Ephron herself may have indirectly lied to me. Tom Hanks, as much as I've trusted him, may have lied to me.

Because I have it all: the sympathetic backstory, the montage of humiliations minor and major, unrealized career aspirations, the untamed pre-makeover hair. But still, I wait. Single, lonely, Hanksless.

I can't help but think that a large part of my current state of Hankslessness is due to the fact that I'm a twenty-seven-year-old woman who shares a Victorian house with her uncle.

I let myself into the house as quietly as I can, slipping off my boots to avoid tracking slush through the house. It's the middle of January, and the Columbus snow long ago ceased to be the sparkling, magical holiday treat it is in so many Hallmark Christmas movies. Now it's just gray and gross, and it's depressing to look at it and know there are months left of this. Ohio winters are an endurance test, not necessarily in how much snow you can handle but in how many gray, sunless days you can take before you flee to a warmer climate.

I hang up my coat and try to creep through the living room and upstairs without being noticed, but then I hear Uncle Don's voice ring out. "Annie!"

I turn to my right, where four fifty-something men are crowded around our dining room table.

I wave and step into the dining room, which is lined with dark wainscoting and the same red floral wallpaper my mom installed when I was a baby. "Hey, guys."

This is Uncle Don's Dungeons and Dragons group. Every Thursday night they meet to—well, honestly, I'm not 100 percent sure what the game entails. I hear snippets—stuff about orcs and werewolves and ice lords—but personally, I wouldn't know a wizard from a warlock, so I figure this is Uncle Don's version of book club and try to stay out of it. Mostly I think it's kind of sweet that these four men have been getting together almost every week for going on twenty years. And other than his part-time job at the gaming store, the Guardtower, Uncle Don doesn't really get out much, so it's nice that he has some built-in socialization.

"How was the library, sweet pea?" Uncle Don asks, ignoring the glare from his friend Rick. Rick is the Dungeon Master, aka the boss of the game, which you would know if you saw the shirt he wears every Thursday that proclaims, "When the Dungeon Master smiles, it's already too late." I have no idea what this means, but since Dungeon Master Rick hates distractions, I've never asked for an explanation.

"Good," I say. "I got a lot done."

Even though I've been attempting to write my own rom-com for years, right now I'm working as a freelance writer. Well, that makes it sound a little more glamorous than it is, seeing as I write "web content" with titles like "The Five BEST WAYS to Unclog a Toilet" and "Ten of Jennifer Lawrence's Hottest Hairdos!" I may not be winning any awards anytime soon, but it pays (and you'd be surprised how often you use that toilet-unclogging advice when you live in a house with old pipes).

"What did you write about today?" asks Earl.

"Is It Expired? What to Keep and What to Throw Out!" I say with wide eyes and jazz hands, trying to mimic the excitement of the headline.

"Did I ever tell you guys," Paul says, wiping his glasses on his shirt, "about that time I accidentally ate a yogurt that expired in 2007?"

"Ugh!" I say as Don asks, "What happened?"

Paul shrugs, putting his glasses back on. "Well, I'm still here, aren't I?"

"But he did throw up for the better part of three days," says Paul's husband, Earl, who rounds out their gaming foursome. The two of them met through D&D, which would be a great meet-cute for a rom-com if I knew enough about D&D to write it.

"Excuse me," says Dungeon Master Rick. "But unless the evil gnome that's currently trapping your party in a cave can be vanquished by dairy, I don't really want to discuss yogurt right now."

"Fine, fine, fine," Paul says. "See you later, Annie."

Uncle Don waves, rolling his eyes at Dungeon Master Rick, who's already describing the various gnome inventions scattered throughout the cave.

I smile and head upstairs to my room, the same one I've had since I was a child. Although it's changed a little—now I have soft pink walls instead of kitten wallpaper, and framed photos of my parents (and, okay, one of Nora Ephron, too) instead of posters of whatever guy I thought was cute at the time. But other than that, it's pretty much the same. My twin bed, my refinished antique desk, the green glass lamp that used to belong to my grandma.

In other words, this isn't the kind of bedroom you can bring a man back to. Other than the regrettable sex I had with my high school boyfriend right after my mom died in the hopes that it would make me feel better (spoiler alert: it did not!), I've never even had sex in this room. I mean, how would that even *work*? Would I introduce a dude to all the D&D guys, then excuse us with a line like, "Well, I'm going upstairs to try to bone this guy as quietly as possible, but everything in this house squeaks because it's a million years old, so sorry, I guess!" I don't even know how a full-size man would fit into that twin bed; his feet would probably hang off the end.

But I haven't done anything to change my situation, and that's because I'm still waiting for Tom Hanks. And sure, he hasn't found me yet, but it's okay, because I'm just at the beginning of my rom-com, the part with a montage that demonstrates how sad, lonely, and down-on-her-luck our leading lady is.

My Tom Hanks is out there, and I'm not going to settle until I find him.

Chapter Two

"I'M NOT SAYING YOU HAVE TO SETTLE," MY BEST FRIEND, CHLOE, SAYS as she sits down across from me at the wobbly table. "I'm just saying you should give some of these guys a chance."

Nick's coffee shop is the perfect place to get some writing done. It's within walking distance of my house, there are plenty of outlets to plug in my laptop, and the ambient noise of people talking and cups clinking is the perfect soundtrack for working. I guess what I'm saying is that it *would* be the perfect place to work if Chloe wasn't a barista there and we didn't spend most of my work time talking.

Well, *she* calls herself a barista. Nick Velez, the owner, simply refers to her as an "employee" because words like *barista* and *latte art* make him cringe. Nick's other employee, Tobin, is a college student who rarely, if ever, shows up on time and usually drops more cups than he serves, but he has a good heart, and Nick keeps him around, despite always threatening to fire him.

"I give every guy I go out with a chance," I say, "but the last guy I went out with smelled like Funyuns."

Chloe wrinkles her nose. "You mean onions?"

"No," I say. "That would've been better. He smelled specifically like the snack food Funyuns."

Chloe rolls her eyes. "Okay, well, what about that guy?"

She points to a dude in his late twenties wearing headphones and sitting at a table in the corner. I shake my head.

"What's wrong with him?" she asks, exasperated. "He's cute!"

"First off, he doesn't give off 'lives on a houseboat with his young son' vibes," I say. "And secondly, he's just . . . sitting there. Big deal."

Chloe stares blankly at me.

"Where's the intrigue? The mystery? The part where we're secretly pen pals but also own rival businesses?"

Chloe shakes her head. "I always think you're exaggerating, but you're literally in love with a fictional man. You know those movies aren't real, right? They're made up! I've watched about ten thousand more rom-coms than I ever wanted to see because of you, and I can definitely say that they're all bullshit."

"They aren't!" I start to protest, but Chloe cuts me off.

"I'm not trying to insult them, because I know you love them and I'm sure the rom-com *you* write is going to be a cinematic masterpiece, but you can't live your life by their rules. I mean, I don't let what I watch affect my life."

"That's because you mostly watch documentaries about murder," I point out.

"True. And I guess I have changed a lot of my actions. I don't wear a ponytail anymore, that's for sure. Makes it easier for some guy to yank it and pull you into a darkened alley," she says, pulling a pretend ponytail.

"Just because I'm looking for what I know I deserve doesn't

mean I'm being unrealistic," I say primly, as if this is all a joke for me, but really it isn't. I have so little of my mom, but this—her movies, her insistence that I not settle—is what I remember.

"Join the rest of us here on planet Earth," Chloe whispers, grabbing my hands. "We get free drinks from men and enjoy commitment-less sex. It's great."

"I'm not interested in meaningless sex," I say, trying to focus on my laptop. "I want a connection."

"Re-download Tinder and I can help you find a connection," Chloe says, wiggling her eyebrows.

"I'm not hearing this," Nick says from behind the counter, turning on the espresso machine.

"Nick," Chloe says with a sugary-sweet smile as soon as the machine shuts off. "Have you given any more thought to my suggestion?"

"You mean your suggestion that I change the name of my place?" Nick asks, rubbing one hand over the brown scruff on his chin. Nick's in his early thirties, lanky, and one of those guys whose face is covered in a perpetual five-o'clock shadow, even at ten in the morning. "Nick's my name. I own the shop. It makes sense."

Chloe sighs in exasperation, pursing her pink-glossed lips. "Haven't you ever heard of puns, Nick?"

"I hate puns," Nick says, handing the espresso to a regular customer named Gary, an older guy who always wears a beat-up Ohio State baseball cap.

"The Daily Grind! Thanks a Latte!" Chloe shouts.

"Brewed Awakening," says Tobin. Nick shoots him a dirty look.

"Pizza My Heart," Gary says as he takes a seat, and we all turn to look at him.

"I mean, you'd have to become a pizza place for that one to work," he says, taking a sip.

Nick shakes his head. "I trusted you, Gary."

"I think it's a great suggestion," Chloe says, beaming at Gary. With her cute blond milkmaid braid and her flowered apron, she looks like some sort of adorable coffee angel.

"Why are you sitting down, again?" Nick asks. "Instead of, I don't know, working?"

"I'm on my break!" Chloe says, pulling out her phone. "And hold on, I'm trying to help Annie Cassidy find true love."

Chloe doesn't only work at Nick's, although dealing with Nick's endearing grumpiness could be considered a full-time job. She also goes to business school, where she's been taking classes super slowly at night since most of her time and money goes toward her dad and the payments for his memory-care facility. Because I know she's busy, I try to discourage her from making my quest for love her side hustle, but so far I haven't had any luck.

"Thank you for your efforts," I say, "but that isn't how this works. I'm not going to find my Tom Hanks by actively looking for him, which is why all the dates you've set me up on or that I've found through whatever app you made me download that week have been miserable failures. I just have to find him, through fate or luck or—"

"Oh, my God." Chloe slams a hand down on the table, making coffee slosh over the edge of my mug. "Have you read the *Dispatch* today?"

"Why?" Nick asks, uninterested. "Does it have a headline about Annie's love life?"

"There's going to be a movie filming here, in German Village!" Chloe says.

Nick wipes down a counter. "Big deal. Remember when Bradley Cooper filmed a movie here? All that happened was his bodyguards camped out all day to use the Wi-Fi and they never ordered anything. Also they peed on the toilet seat."

"They were so cool," Tobin says wistfully.

"Oh, my God, it's a romantic comedy from Tommy Crisante, and filming starts next week," Chloe continues, her eyes scanning the article on her phone.

"Was he the guy who directed all those cheesy movies in the '90s?" Nick asks, because Tommy Crisante is Steven Spielberg–level famous. Everyone knows his name.

"Yeah, that's him," I say, my mouth going dry. A romantic comedy filming *here*, blocks from my house?

"We have to get you onto that set," Chloe says, and hearing her say the thought I hadn't yet formed makes me realize how ridiculous it is.

"Why?" I ask, shutting my computer. "I don't want to be *in* a movie. I want to *write* one."

"Yeah, but," Chloe continues, "if you could weasel your way onto set, wouldn't this be such a great learning experience? If you won't move out of Ohio—not that I want you to leave my side literally ever, but come on, you know this isn't exactly the cinematic hub of the country—then this could be your chance to actually be involved in a movie!"

I nod, but I'm thinking *Sure, Chloe.* Because what am I supposed to do? Send a letter to the director that reads, "Rom-com fanatic with zero experience and an unused, dusty film-studies degree seeks literally any job on your film"? That's, like, the world's worst personal ad.

Then Chloe lets out a low whistle. "And—whoa, okay, apparently the lead is Drew Danforth, that hot guy from that sitcom. Have you even seen what he's looking like these days?" She turns her phone so I can see the screen, which is showcasing a picture of a very shirtless, very muscled man.

But I already know who he is. Everyone does.

If there was ever a man who was the complete and polar opposite of Tom Hanks, it would be Drew Danforth. Where Tom Hanks is known for being humble and respectful, Drew Danforth is known for acting like none of his acting success matters and like he's way too good for Hollywood traditions. He's always showing up in gossip columns for doing ridiculous things like pratfalling whenever he sees the paparazzi taking his photo. Once, he went on *Late Night with Seth Meyers* wearing sweatpants and with uncombed hair, as if he couldn't even be bothered to look presentable. And then there was the time he did an entire day of press while wearing a fake mustache, but never acknowledged it, or the time that he recited the Declaration of Independence on the red carpet instead of answering reporters' questions.

He's known for not taking anything seriously, and the last thing this all-too-rare studio rom-com needs is some jerk who probably thinks the entire genre is formulaic and beneath him.

I take another glance at the picture, staring at it a little longer than I need to. Sure, he looks good, but romantic comedy leads are usually more cute than sexy, and they definitely don't spend a lot of time showing off their abs (unless we're talking about a rom-com starring Chris Evans, in which case he *will* be shirtless 90 percent of the time).

"Okay, first of all, rom-com leads don't have to be muscular. And this guy doesn't take anything seriously—everything is a joke to him. There's no way he's going to treat a romantic comedy with respect."

Chloe turns her phone back toward her and reads. "Whatever. He could treat *me* with respect, if you know what I'm saying. I guess after he was in that sitcom, he was in some action movie so he got, like, super ripped." She looks up at me with wide eyes. "Oh, my God, Annie. What if your life isn't a Nora Ephron romantic comedy? What if it's *Notting Hill*, and you're supposed to end up with Drew Danforth?"

"That's not how this works. My Tom Hanks doesn't have to be a celebrity."

"But it couldn't hurt!" Chloe says. "Just think about it . . . Annie and Drew. Your celebrity name would be Andrew."

"I'm not a celebrity . . . and I'm pretty sure his full name is already Andrew." I open up my laptop and find the *Dispatch*'s website.

Gary drains his cup, then stands up and puts on his coat. "You'll find your Tom Hanks, Annie, just like I found mine. Her name is Martha."

"How did you meet?" Chloe asks, turning around and leaning over the back of her chair. She may not believe in fairy-tale love for herself, but don't think I haven't noticed she loves hearing other people's stories.

Gary wraps his scarf around his neck. "She was married to my brother, but she decided she liked me better."

Chloe slumps back in her chair. "Oh. Geez, Gary."

"Love's weird," he says, and with a wave he leaves.

I focus on the article, which runs through all the Drew Danforth facts we already know. He got famous when he was on a long-running sitcom about a restaurant called, creatively, *Mike's Restaurant*. Everyone called it the next *Cheers*, and it was just as popular. He played the sweet restaurant owner who pined after a beautiful waitress for four seasons before they finally got together. He even won an Emmy for it (although, surprise, he didn't attend the ceremony and had his then-seven-year-old brother accept the award for him via satellite). After that, he bulked up and tried to become an action star in some movie called *The Last Apocalypse*, which featured a lot of helicopter explosions. It was a huge bomb (the box-office-disaster kind, not the kind that blew up that helicopter), and I guess now he's trying his hand at rom-coms.

The article, of course, repeatedly refers to him as a "funnyman" and a "prankster," because I guess that's another way to say "an overgrown man-child who doesn't appreciate his enormous privilege."

"Well, whether or not you go after Drew Danforth, I still think you should try to get on the set of this movie," Chloe says. "You never know what could happen."

"Do you ever intend to get back to work?" Nick asks, leaning against the counter with his arms crossed and a small smile playing across his lips. I've long suspected that he and Chloe secretly have a thing for each other, which, in true rom-com fashion, is apparent in their constant bickering. In fact, although I would never tell either of them this, my screenplay is based on their relationship. He's the gruff, rough-around-the-edges tough guy, and she's the quirky, fun girl who teaches him to look on the bright side . . .

I stop daydreaming long enough to notice that they're both staring at me. "She's doing the thing," Chloe says, glancing at Nick. Then, one eyebrow raised, she asks me, "Were you imagining your life as a rom-com again?"

"No," I say smugly. I don't bother to tell her that I was actually imagining *her* life as a rom-com.

Then Tobin drops several mugs and, in the ensuing chaos, everyone forgets about me, and I'm able to get back to writing about easy ways to freshen your diaper pail.

But I can't stop thinking about Chloe's insistence that I get a job on set. I have no idea how that would even be possible, but I don't get my hopes up, because at this point, dating Drew Danforth seems more likely.

Chapter Three

Have you ever felt like you're not the main character in your own story?

I look at Chloe and I think, now *there's* someone who could carry a movie. I mean, I *am* writing a movie about her, not that she knows that. She's the one who's cute and quirky, with those adorable braids and her vintage clothing and the various schemes she's constantly getting herself into. Not that Chloe even believes in true love for herself, but she meets people everywhere.

Of course, I don't know if they count as meet-cutes if they're only ever around for a week or two of sex, but that's one of the many ways Chloe and I are different. I believe in long-term relationships, and she's the proud queen of the one-night stand.

Chloe and I walk home together after her shift. She lives in our carriage house, which is a pretentious way to say she lives in the small apartment over the detached garage. She's been living there since we were undergrads, when she claimed that the nominal rent Uncle Don was charging her was way less expensive than the dorms, but I know the truth. She moved in there because she wanted to be able to watch over Uncle Don and me and occasionally make us her special Knock You Naked Cheesecake (it's just a name and has never actually knocked anyone's clothing off, although I certainly wouldn't put it past Chloe to seduce someone with cheesecake).

The truth is, Uncle Don and I could never afford to live here—in this exorbitantly high-priced neighborhood, in this giant brick house with its million rooms and cozy front porch and lovely landscaped lawn—if my mom hadn't owned it outright when she died. I don't exactly make a ton of money from writing, and Don only works part-time, but since we don't have a mortgage, it works. Uncle Don and I quickly fell into a comfortable rhythm after he moved in. And then we both just . . . stayed.

Which is yet another reason I couldn't possibly fathom ever leaving Columbus. Not only do I have a giant house I don't have to pay for, but Uncle Don and I are all we've got.

I mean, besides Dungeon Master Rick.

Chloe pokes me in the side with her elbow, which is surprisingly bony for someone who's wearing a huge down coat. "You're being a terrible conversationalist."

"Sorry," I say, opening the wrought iron gate that leads to our small front yard. "Do you want to have dinner with us? Uncle Don's cooking tonight."

"It is literally impossible for me to say no," Chloe says. "My apartment is full of nothing but snickerdoodles, and I think I might barf if I don't eat a real dinner soon."

The smell of garlic and onion greets me as soon as we walk in the door. "I'm home! Chloe's here!" I call.

"Great!" Uncle Don says as we walk into the kitchen. As usual, he's wearing a novelty *Star Wars* T-shirt, because I'm pretty sure he doesn't own any other kind of shirt. Sometimes Don feels less like my fifty-something uncle and more like a twelve-year-old boy who got a gift card to Hot Topic and went wild. "I made enough Cajun chicken pasta to feed an army of Orcs!"

"I don't know what that means," Chloe says, taking a seat at the island. "But I'll gladly partake."

Uncle Don heaps generous portions onto our plates, and we dig in.

"So how was your day?" Uncle Don says, standing across the island from us and chewing with his mouth open. It's a habit I hate, but he spends most of his time with other men, and all of my attempts to make him more marriageable have failed. "You write about unclogging toilets?"

"Freshening diaper pails," I say, pointing my fork at him.

"Forget diaper pails! God, now there's a sentence I never thought I'd say, but I mean it!" Chloe says. "Did you hear about the movie that's filming here next week?"

"In my house?" Uncle Don asks.

I stifle a laugh. Again, perhaps the result of most of his socialization occurring with other fifty-something men, Uncle Don takes everything very literally.

"No, here in German Village!" Chloe says. She whips out her phone and reads from the *Dispatch* article for the second time today. "Directed by Tommy Crisante, the romantic comedy stars—"

Uncle Don stops with his fork in midair. "Tommy Crisante's the director?"

"Yeah, why?" I ask. "Do you like his movies or something?"

"He was my college roommate!" Uncle Don says, throwing his hands in the air. "Freshman year at OSU! He had the top bunk! And then he transferred out to go to NYU."

Chloe slams her hands on the island, making both Don and me jump. "You guys. Don. Knows. Tommy. Crisante."

Don nods and takes another bite. "I do."

She turns to me, a far-too-enthusiastic look in her eyes. "This is it, Annie. This is fate. This is a sign from a loving universe that you are supposed to work on this movie and/or fall in love with a movie star."

"Chloe, how does that—" I start, but she's not listening to me.

"Don, can you get Annie a job on set?" Chloe asks, turning to him.

"Right," I say. "Because that's how this works."

Uncle Don shrugs. "Tommy and I haven't talked in a few years, but I can try."

"Uncle Don," I say cautiously. "Seriously, I don't have any experience, and I don't expect—"

But he has his phone out, and he's scrolling through his contacts, muttering, "Crisante, Crisante, Crisante . . . there he is."

"Uncle Don, please!" I yelp as Chloe whispers, "Yessssss!"

"Tommy?" Uncle Don asks, putting his hand over his ear to block us out. "Yeah, it's Don! I know, long time no talk!"

And with that, he walks into the pantry and shuts the door.

"What the hell?" I turn to Chloe and smack her arm.

She rubs her hands together, as if she's a cartoon villain executing an evil plan. "You're welcome."

"For what? For embarrassing me in front of Tommy Crisante? For forever making my name synonymous with 'girl who makes her uncle beg for a job for her'?"

"Don't be so dramatic," Chloe says, taking another bite of pasta.

"You're calling *me* dramatic? You literally just rubbed your hands together like you're a bad guy in *Scooby-Doo*. And how have I never known that Uncle Don is besties with a major American film director?" I ask, even though I know it's because Uncle Don pretty much watches *Lord of the Rings* and *Star Wars* over and over. Maybe I should ask him if he knows Peter Jackson or George Lucas.

The door clicks open, and Uncle Don emerges from the pantry, then heads straight for his plate. He takes another bite as we stare at him. "What?" he asks when he looks up.

"Well?" Chloe prods. "How did it go?"

"Oh!" He brightens. "You got the job!"

My heart stops. "*What* job?"

"As Tommy's assistant. His last one quit to go work for an underwear model. So, perfect timing, I guess."

Chloe raises her arms in the air and starts humming the theme song for *Rocky*, which is an annoying thing she does whenever she has a perceived victory, major or minor, in any area of her life. "This is it!" she squeals. "Annie, you're getting a job on a movie! You can show Tommy your screenplay and meet your Tom Hanks!"

"Tom Hanks is in this movie?" Uncle Don asks, putting down his fork. "I love that guy."

I shake my head and put my hands over my face, then decide that isn't enough and slump over the island, talking into the counter. "Everybody loves him. That's the entire point of Tom Hanks. But no, he's not in this movie. Just . . . never mind."

Chloe and Don are silent, and then I feel a hand on my shoulder. Don's. "Sweetheart," he says. "Your mom would be so proud of you."

I lift my head a little and peer up at him. "Yeah?"

He nods. "Yeah."

And I know he isn't going to say anything else—isn't going to give me an emotional speech about what romantic comedies meant to my mom or a pep talk about how I can do it. Neither of those are things Uncle Don would ever do, or may even be capable of doing. But in those few words, and in the look on his face, I get what he's trying to tell me. That he misses his sister just like I miss my mom. That she wouldn't have wanted me to be here, still, static, instead of pursuing something I've always loved. That she would be so happy to know I was going to be on an actual movie set, even if it's only in German Village, even if it's only for a few days, even if I'm only an assistant.

"Thanks, Uncle Don," I say, sitting up as tears start to tingle the edges of my eyes. And although I'm still nervous (that's putting it mildly), maybe what Chloe said is true. That this is meant to be, and maybe my mom had some hand in making it happen. I just wish I could tell her about it.

Chapter Four

FILMING DOESN'T START UNTIL MONDAY, SO I'M NOT EMPLOYED YET, but crewmembers are already closing down the street, putting up signs, and moving cars.

"This is ridiculous," Nick says, handing a coffee to a customer. "You can't shut down an entire neighborhood because some Hollywood big shots want to make a movie."

"They took over an empty storefront and closed down one block," I point out. "And it's not even this one."

"Still," Nick grumbles.

"You're such a negative Nancy," Chloe says, squirting whipped cream onto a drink. "It's like if you don't have something to complain about, you'll shrivel up and float away on a breeze."

"What are you doing?" Nick grabs her arm, looking at the cup.

"Adding some sprinkles," she says with wide eyes.

"Does this look like a sprinkle smiley face to you?" Nick asks the customer, a middle-aged man in a puffer coat and a knit hat.

"It does indeed," he says.

"And how does it make you feel?" Chloe asks with a smile.

The man appears to think about it. "Pretty good," he says finally, taking his cup and walking out.

"See?" Chloe asks. "Customers like a personal touch!"

"Just serve the coffee, okay?" Nick asks as "What a Fool Believes" starts playing. "Chloe."

"What's that?" Chloe asks, suddenly very interested in the espresso machine.

"Did you mess with my playlist again?"

"Hmm?"

I stifle a smile as I watch the scene that plays out almost every day.

"Is this or is this not the Doobie Brothers?" Nick asks, crossing his arms.

Chloe turns around and throws her hands up in frustration. "Fine, it is! Do you know how upsetting your sad music is? I'm so tired of listening to Sufjan Stevens!"

"'Carrie and Lowell' is a masterpiece," Nick grumbles.

"And it makes our customers cry," Chloe says.

"She has a point," I say.

Nick points at me. "You stay out of this."

"Totally unfair that Chloe gets to play what she wants all the time, and you wouldn't even let me play what I wanted *once*," Tobin whines from behind the espresso machine.

Nick runs a hand over his face. "That's because I'm not going to play a five-hour loop of ambient whale sounds, Tobin."

"But it's *so* chill," Tobin says, handing a latte to a customer.

I smirk and turn back to my computer, but Chloe whips off her apron. "Okay, it's my break, so feel free to change it back to your Crying Alone playlist."

"No more yacht rock!" Nick shouts.

"Come on," Chloe says, grabbing my arm. "We're gonna go get a closer look at your new workplace."

"I'm in the middle of typing this sentence—" I say as Chloe pulls me out of my chair. I manage to bring my coffee along because I have a feeling I'll need caffeine to fortify me for this.

"I'm nervous to get too close," I whisper to Chloe as we walk, my breath puffing in the air.

"Why are you whispering?" she asks.

"I don't want anyone to hear me and know how nervous I am!" I hiss. But she has a point—it's ten A.M., and there aren't even that many people on the brick sidewalk. Almost everyone is at work, although there are definitely some people standing right at the edge of the caution tape, looking at what appears to be nothing more than a few guys in winter coats milling around.

Chloe sighs. "This is way more boring than I expected. I guess I thought, like, Drew Danforth would be right there, and we could shamelessly ogle him for the remainder of my break."

"The chances of him being shirtless in this weather are slim, you know."

She looks wistfully out into the street. "A girl can dream, Annie."

Staring at my future place of employment is making me feel kind of shaky, so I link my arm in hers. "Come on. Let's go make fun of Nick for the next fifteen minutes."

I spin us around and immediately collide with a wool-coat-clad chest. My coffee flies out of my hand and drenches the person in front of us.

"Whoa!" he shouts, and when I look up I topple backward.

It's Drew Danforth.

Chapter Five

"Are you okay?" he asks, grabbing my arm and pulling me off the ground.

I wouldn't describe myself as someone who is normally at a loss for words. I mean, I write for a living and as a passion. I have no problem making small talk with strangers, and I can handle myself at parties. But right now, the only words running through my mind on a loop are *Holy shit.*

I blink a few times, staring straight into Drew Danforth's face. It's like when you're a kid and there's a solar eclipse, and all the teachers are like, "Don't look directly into the sun! You'll destroy your retinas!" but there's always that one kid (Johnny Berger, in our class) who can't stop staring.

In this situation, I'm Johnny Berger. And I guess Drew Danforth is the sun.

"Are you okay?" he asks again, enunciating his words even more, as if my understanding him is the problem. His brown eyes, I notice, are flecked with tiny bits of gold, which is something you can't see when you watch him on TV. His hair is just as voluminous as it seems in pictures, but in person, I have the almost overwhelming urge to touch it, to reach out and pull on that one lock of hair that hangs over his forehead.

"She's not responding." He turns to Chloe. "Is something wrong?"

"She's French," Chloe says without missing a beat. "She only speaks French."

"I'm not French," I say, breaking my silence. Chloe's and Drew's heads swivel to look at me.

"I'm sorry about your coat," I whisper, then I run toward Nick's.

Chloe bursts in the door behind me, the bell jingling in her wake. "*I'm not French*?" she screeches. "Those are the first words you spoke to Drew Danforth? Really?"

"Well then, why did you tell him I was French?" I shout, ignoring the curious stares of everyone working on their laptops and the calming melody of whatever Nick put on to replace the Doobies.

"I don't know!" She throws her hands in the air. "You weren't talking, so I thought I'd give you an interesting backstory!"

I put my hands over my face. "This is ridiculous."

"No," Chloe says, grabbing me by the shoulders. "This is your meet-cute, and now you need to go back out there and find him and say something that isn't a negation of your Frenchness or an apology for destroying his probably very expensive coat."

"Meet what?"

Nick stares at us from behind the counter, a dish towel in his hand.

"A meet-cute"—Chloe stands up straight, shoulders back, as if she's delivering a Romantic Comedy 101 lecture to Nick and his patrons—"is the quirky, adorable, *cute* way the hero and heroine of a romantic comedy meet."

Everyone stares at her blankly.

"Or hero and hero. Or heroine and heroine. Not to be heteronormative," she clarifies.

"Like how me and Martha met at her wedding," Gary says.

Chloe thinks about it. "I don't know that I would necessarily call that one a meet-*cute*, but sure, Gary."

"Did you just make that up?" Nick asks, arms crossed.

I shake my head. "No. It's a thing."

"Watch a romantic comedy, dude," Tobin says.

Nick rolls his eyes.

"Anyway," Chloe continues, "Annie straight up ran into Drew Danforth and spilled a cup of coffee all over his coat, which is, like, the cutest of meets."

"That doesn't sound very cute," Nick says skeptically, rubbing the scruff on his chin. "Was it still hot?"

"Scalding," I say, sinking into my chair and resting my head on the table.

"Sounds like a meet-painful," says Gary, and a few people laugh.

"Thanks," I mutter. "I'm so glad you all find my embarrassment entertaining."

"Annie!" Chloe sits down across from me as a customer walks in and the rest of the shop stops paying attention to us. "This isn't embarrassing. This is merely a story I'll tell in my toast at your wedding to Drew."

I lift my head to look at her. "I hate to break this to you, but I don't think he's my Tom Hanks. I think he's just a famous guy with a possible third-degree burn on his chest. And now my first day on set is going to be super awkward because I accidentally assaulted the lead actor with a beverage."

Chloe's about to say something, but then a song starts and she closes her mouth, looking up toward the speakers. "I swear to God, I told Nick not to play any more Bon Iver. It makes people look up their exes on Instagram, not buy coffee. I'm gonna go put on some Hall and Oates."

As she walks away, I rest my head on the table again. As if it wasn't embarrassing enough to have my uncle get me a job on set, now I have to deal with this.

But maybe the most embarrassing thing—more embarrassing than having an uncle who pulled strings to get me a job and more embarrassing than spilling coffee on a famous person—is how I felt when I looked into Drew Danforth's eyes. Frozen. Tongue-tied. Starstruck. Like the world slowed down and all of a sudden it was just the two of us there on that sidewalk, like nothing and no one else mattered.

Snap out of it, Annie, I think. *He's a movie star . . . a dude who gets paid to make millions of women feel like that all the time. Just because he's very good at his job, at making you think he's the (extremely hot) guy next door and he would totally love you if only he knew you, doesn't mean that he's your Tom Hanks.* I mean, I've also thought on numerous occasions that Drake and I would be great friends if we hung out because we like the same things (cozy sweaters, hometown pride, Rihanna), but that doesn't mean I *actually* think we're going to become BFFs. Also, Drew is known for *pranks*, and while some people may find that kind of stuff funny, I definitely don't.

Drew Danforth isn't a sad widower or a seemingly callous chain bookstore owner, I remind myself. He's a literal movie star, and

Tom Hanks didn't play a movie star in any of his rom-coms. That would be more like *Notting Hill*, and honestly, Julia Roberts was kind of a jerk in *Notting Hill*. A *beautiful* jerk, but still a jerk.

Maybe Drew will forget all about me by the time we start filming. He probably meets a lot of people every day, and although most of them don't spill coffee on him, I'm not under the assumption that I'm all that memorable. Maybe frizzy-haired, klutzy women who barely speak are normal for him. Maybe this sort of thing happens all the time.

Chapter Six

Since formally accepting Tommy's offer to be his assistant, I've e-mailed back and forth with him a few times about details. He sent me the script for the movie, which is currently untitled, but which might as well be called *Modernized, Gender-Swapped Runaway Bride*. And that's not a complaint, because, hello, I love *Runaway Bride*. Basically, it's about a journalist who's writing a story on a guy who left his fiancée at the altar. One of the wedding guests filmed the whole messy thing and uploaded it to YouTube, and now he's famous for being an asshole. Of course, because this is a rom-com and journalistic ethics don't exist, the journalist ends up falling in love with him, and then there's a big *"wait, this was all for a story?"* scene, aka one of my all-time favorite romantic comedy clichés.

In other words, it's great. A little cheesy, a little unbelievable, but still full of heart. I know that Tarah Thomas, the lead actress who found fame on teen dramedies, will do a fantastic job, but I wonder if Drew Danforth can pull it off. Although, since it does involve him playing a jerk, I think he might be able to handle it.

The night before my first day on set, I rewatch *While You Were*

Sleeping. It was another one that Mom and I used to watch over and over (and unlike some of the other rom-coms she showed me, it was relatively appropriate for a small child). It confirmed that this "search for love" thing isn't for the faint of heart. I mean, Sandra Bullock had to rescue a man from an oncoming train, and even once that was done, she had to keep up an elaborate ruse to his entire family and pretend she was in love with him while he was in a coma. And that wasn't even the man she eventually fell in love with!

Love is complicated is what I'm saying. It relies on fate and Peter Gallagher falling onto a train track and, more often than you would find plausible, comas. I can't engineer that; I just have to let it happen, and if that means waiting, then I'm okay with that. Chloe may think that I'm not "trying" or "putting myself out there" or "actually using the apps she put on my phone before deleting them," but she doesn't get it. You can't methodically stalk your way into true love (although I guess Meg Ryan did kind of do that in *Sleepless in Seattle*, and it worked out pretty well for her). And no one would ever make a romantic comedy about aimlessly scrolling through Bumble, because that would be one hell of a boring movie.

As I walk to work on Monday morning I wonder, for what must be the five millionth time, if I'm being unrealistic or ridiculous for wanting what my parents had. If looking for that person to grow old with, to run through the airport to find in a time before strict TSA regulations, to confess their love for you via a grand gesture that involves a boombox or a field of daffodils, is just ridiculous. I wonder if Chloe is right, that I should settle for someone perfectly fine in the right now.

But that's not what I want, I remind myself, my breath puffing in the cold air as my boots crunch through the dead leaves on the

brick sidewalks. I want real love. *While You Were Sleeping* love. Tom
Hanks and Meg Ryan love.

The walk to set is a short one, because German Village is a
small neighborhood. It may be part of Columbus, which is actually
the fourteenth most populous city in the United States (thanks,
Wikipedia), but it has its own small-town feel. Like any small town,
it has its cute, quirky shops and its cute, quirky residents. Like the
Coatless Wonder, a guy who always, always wears a T-shirt even in
below-freezing temperatures. Once Chloe chased him down and
tried to give him a coat from Nick's lost and found, in case he didn't
have one, but he said he just liked to keep his arms unencumbered.

As I walk through Schiller Park, I think about how much I love
living here. The old and beautiful homes, the history, Katzinger's
Deli with its barrels full of pickles, the dogs that run through the
park most days—it's home, and I can see why a movie would want
to film in a neighborhood so lovely. Sure, it's not Central Park,
where so many iconic rom-com scenes have been set, but love does
occasionally occur in places that are not New York City.

As I cross a bridge over a small, frozen pond, the nervousness
I've been avoiding starts to catch up with me. I mean, who am I to
think I can do this? Be an assistant to one of the most famous and
successful film directors in America? The man who directed *Tangled Leashes*, the ensemble comedy about a bunch of couples who
meet at a dog park? I even overheard Dungeon Master Rick talking
about how that one made him cry, and the only other time I've
heard of him crying was when his black Lab ate the D&D miniatures he had spent weeks painting.

Sure, I've seen every single one of Tommy's movies, but what
if he needs me to do something I can't do? Or what if he asks a

question I don't know the answer to? What if I look incompetent in front of one of the most famous directors in the country?

What would Nora Ephron do? I ask myself silently. Although I love her sweet and sad romantic comedies, I also love her indomitable spirit. Once I saw an interview with Meryl Streep where she talked about how when Nora was a young writer, she tried to get a job at a magazine and was told she couldn't be a reporter because reporters were men. And did she turn around, go back home, get into bed, and drown her sorrows in whatever the time-period-appropriate version of Netflix was? Hell, no. She became an incredibly important and celebrated writer and showed those assholes what was what. If Nora Ephron was here, she would march onto that set and she would *get shit done.*

And just in case thinking about the ever-present spirit of Nora Ephron isn't enough, I think about my mom. Because she would love this. She would want to know everything about what it was like to be on the set of a romantic comedy, and she'd have a million questions for Tommy about *Tangled Leashes*, and what it was like to work with Julia Roberts, and if Billy Crystal was as nice as he seemed.

For a moment, I allow myself to imagine what that would be like. To come home at the end of the day to her, to curl up on the couch and talk about everything that had happened. A bloom of sadness unfurls so quickly in my chest that I almost gasp.

Because she's not here, and she'll never know. And I have to do this, because she'd want me to. And also because, in the five years since I graduated from college, I've done exactly nothing to get closer to my dream of working in movies. To do that, I'd have to move somewhere, which means I couldn't stay here and be with Uncle Don, and there's no way I'd ever leave him all alone. A movie that's filming right in my own neighborhood? It's fate, like a gift Mom sent me from the afterlife.

I was worried about finding Tommy Crisante on set, but it turns out it's pretty easy. For one thing, he's standing in the middle of the blocked-off street. And for another thing, he's incredibly loud.

"Hi, Tommy? I'm Annie," I say, approaching him as he talks to a young guy in a headset and a black jacket.

He cups a hand over his ear. "You'll have to speak up, sweetheart. I can't hear for shit. My ears got blown out when I did all those action movies with explosions in the '90s."

"Um." I push back my shoulders, brush my hair out of my face, and force myself to be louder. "I'm Annie. Don's niece?"

Tommy's eyes light up and before I even know what's happening, he's hugging me. "Donny's niece? Am I ever glad to see you!"

His hug squeezes the air out of me, and I barely manage to choke out, "I'm, uh, happy to be here!"

"How's Don? Aw, you look just like him!" Tommy says, holding me at a distance.

I hope I don't look like Uncle Don, since he has a gray ponytail and a slight potbelly, but I don't contradict Tommy. "He's great. We live a few blocks away."

"When he called me, I thought, 'This! This is a sign!' My assistant quit last week to work for an underwear model. What's he got that I don't?"

I'm not sure if he really wants an answer to this, so I open and close my mouth a few times, but he keeps talking.

"Come on," he says, guiding me toward a crowd of people. "Let me introduce you to the cast."

Oh, no. *Oh, no.* I knew I'd have to see Drew eventually, but I was hoping it wouldn't be today. Now I'm wishing I thought to wear a disguise, like some glasses or a wig or maybe the giant Predator costume Uncle Don has from the last time he and his friends went to a convention. Anything to stop Drew Danforth from recognizing me from my classic role as Woman Who Spilled Coffee All Over His Coat and Refused to Speak.

But Tommy's already walking across the street, and people are moving out of our way, and it's impossible to stop this momentum. Suddenly, there are just three people in front of us; three people who stop talking and look at us expectantly when they see Tommy.

"Annie," Tommy says, gesturing to several people, "I'd like you to meet our stars. This is Tarah Thomas, our lead actress."

She smiles, and I'm immediately struck by the thought that she's the most beautiful woman I've ever seen. Obviously, I've seen her before—I haven't been living under a rock that doesn't have cable access—but in person it's a whole different level. Her dark brown skin glows so much it practically radiates, her curls are artfully styled, her teeth are straight and white. I smile back weakly.

"This is Brody Johnson," Tommy continues, pointing to a pale guy in a slouchy knit hat and puffy coat.

He lifts a hand in greeting. "I'm the comic relief," he says with a straight face.

I smile, instantly comfortable around him. He doesn't even look like a movie star—he looks like a guy you would see in line at the grocery store, which I guess is sort of his appeal. Maybe this won't be so bad . . .

"And, of course, this is Drew Danforth."

My smile instantly fades. Here he is, right in front of me, this man with the gold-flecked brown eyes and that voluminous hair. Unlike Brody, Drew does *not* look like someone you'd see in line at the grocery store. If he was in a grocery store, people would be staring at him and thinking, "Who *is* that guy?" even if they'd never seen one of his movies.

But I guess he does look like a guy you'd run into on the street, because I literally did.

"Bonjour," he says with a small smile, before taking a sip of coffee.

I narrow my eyes. "Bonjour," I mutter back.

"Oh, do you speak French?" Tarah asks.

"N-no," I stammer, stealing a glance at Drew. He tries to hide his smile behind his cup, but it reaches his eyes. "I mean, I took French in high school but I don't remember anything. *Ouvre la porte.* Open the door. I remember that."

I clamp my mouth shut to stop myself from rambling. I avoid looking at Drew, but from the way his shoulders are shaking, I can tell he's laughing at me. My embarrassment turns to rage—this guy is famous and rich, and he's getting his kicks making fun of me, a pathetic assistant/freelance writer?

Tommy claps me on the back. "Well, that might come in handy if you ever get stuck in a bathroom in France. Let me introduce you to our prop department . . ."

With that, he whisks me away from the cast, and I take a deep breath of relief. I refuse to look over my shoulder, but I can feel Drew's eyes on my back, and I know that if I turned around, I'd find him still watching me.

Tommy isn't big on please and thank you, but he's always clear about his demands, and he never gets upset when people don't get things right the first time. He just asks for what he wants again and again and again.

And as for me, he mostly wants me to bring him coffee. Like, a lot of coffee. He decides pretty quickly that he doesn't like whatever the craft services department is serving and asks me to get him some from Nick's, and on my fifth trip in there, Nick says, impressed, "This guy really puts it away."

"Tell me about it," I say, out of breath from running up and down the street. "I think he's ninety-five percent caffeine at this point."

"So how's it going?" Chloe asks, leaning over the counter. "Have you talked to Drew yet?"

"Have you showed Tommy your screenplay?" Nick asks at the same time.

I ignore Chloe's question and give Nick an exasperated glance. "No, it didn't exactly come up in between my coffee runs. 'Here's your fifth cup, and by the way, here's a screenplay I wrote that you didn't ask for or want.'"

Nick hands me another black coffee. "Couldn't hurt."

I shake my head as Nick smirks at me and I find myself wondering, for the hundredth time, why Chloe can't see that he's perfect for her. They have the perfect romantic comedy flirty-bickering chemistry, and I see the way he looks at her when she isn't paying attention. The thing is, Nick is cute—he's tall and skinny, with light brown skin and that perpetual five-o'clock shadow. Chloe could do a lot worse, and as I know all too well, she *has* done a lot worse.

"Escape (The Piña Colada Song)" starts to play, and Chloe sways back and forth. "This is my jam," she says, pouring syrup into a cup.

"*This* song?" Nick asks. "Seriously? It's all about a guy and his wife who are trying to cheat on each other."

Chloe hands the cup to a customer with a smile, then turns to

Nick and immediately becomes indignant. "Um, did you miss the end of the song? They end up together! It's romantic!"

Nick throws his hands in the air. "They hated each other! She wrote a personal ad, looking for some other dude, and he responded because he was trying to leave her. How is that romantic?"

"Oh, my God," Chloe says, looking at me as if I can help her. "Do you have to ruin every little thing, Nick?"

I bite my lip to keep from cracking up at the rom-com playing out in front of my eyes.

I raise my cup. "Gotta get this to Tommy before it gets cold."

Nick raises a hand. "See you in half an hour."

As I scoot out the door, I can hear Chloe groan as Nick says, "And don't even get me started on that personal ad. 'Getting caught in the rain'? Seriously? These people are walking clichés and they deserve each other."

When I find Tommy, he's deep in conversation with some crewmembers, so I stand off to the side, holding his coffee. As I wait, I look around and take it all in. I'm here. On a movie set. And, sure, it's not quite as glamorous as I thought it might be—after all, it's practically in my backyard, not on the New York City streets or an LA backlot—but it's a real, big-budget movie. One with fancy lighting and sound machines and a costume department and . . .

Actors.

"Be careful around this one," Drew says to Brody as they appear in front of me. "She once spilled an entire cup of coffee on me."

Brody raises his eyebrows, and I can feel my cheeks redden. I mean, yes, technically this is a statement of fact, but I know he's making fun of me. "Sorry about that," I mumble.

"Looking for someone to throw that one at?" Drew asks, pointing to the cup in my hand. "Because I'll move out of the way. I don't really want to take another coat to the dry cleaners."

Brody takes a bite of the candy bar he's holding and keeps silent. Even though his character is Drew's fast-talking, goofy best friend, in real life he's apparently more taciturn.

"I can pay for your dry cleaning," I say, because really, it's the least I can do, but Drew just chuckles.

"I'm not going to make you pay for my dry cleaning." And then he leans in—surprisingly close—and says, "See you around, Coffee Girl."

Brody lifts his candy bar to me like a toast. "Coffee Girl."

And then they walk away, and I'm left thinking about what I should have said back. *Coffee Girl?* Okay, so Tommy's troubling caffeine dependence does mean that I spend a large part of my job getting him coffee, but seriously? That's not my job title, and it's a little—or a lot—condescending to reduce me to Coffee Girl. I'm an assistant. I'm a writer. I have a *name*.

"Thanks, Annie," Tommy says from behind me, and I turn to hand him his coffee.

"Yes," I say forcefully. "Annie. That's my name."

"Sure is!" Tommy says cheerfully, looking at the clipboard he's holding.

I let out a frustrated sigh and look across the street. Drew's standing there, talking to Tarah and Brody, his annoying profile directly in my line of vision. Try as I might to look away, my eyes snag on him. I mean, I get it—I get why he's famous. He's cute, yes, but there's more to it than that—there's something about him, some sort of charm that he radiates, some ineffable quality that the rest of us mere mortals don't have. Although if Chloe were here, I'm sure she'd remind me that he's *very* effable.

But even Chloe's imagined double entendre isn't enough to make me not mad at him right now. White-hot indignation floods my system as I think about what he just said. Coffee Girl. Ugh. There's no way this guy can give the romantic comedy genre the respect it deserves.

Chapter Seven

I MANAGE TO MORE OR LESS AVOID DREW ON SET THE NEXT DAY, SINCE he's actually focused on his job instead of putting me in my place. Whenever I'm not on set, though, I have to write articles, because internet content doesn't make itself. Tommy has some phone call with an executive scheduled for Thursday evening, so we wrap up in the afternoon, and I'm free to spend the rest of the day in bed, writing.

Well, writing and researching Drew.

It's not that I feel *good* about typing his name into the search bar on my laptop. In fact, I feel pretty creepy about it, like Meg Ryan does at the beginning of *You've Got Mail* when she's trying to se-cretly e-mail Tom Hanks without arousing Greg Kinnear's sus-picions.

But I don't have a bland, clearly-not-right-for-me boyfriend to observe my actions. I only have my own secret shame as I ignore the article I'm supposed to be writing on at-home hemorrhoid relief.

It's just that the last time Chloe was trying to convince me that I should be actively pursuing Drew because he's my Tom Hanks, she was trying to describe his specific brand of hotness. She claimed that he was sexy in a John Krasinski way, then *I* said that John Krasinski is more cute than sexy, and then *she* was like, "Oh, so you admit you find Drew sexy, which, FYI, means you totally want to have sex with him," and then stared at me like she was a detective on *Law & Order* and she'd cornered me into a confession, which was very annoying.

So here I am googling Drew, trying to convince myself . . . what, exactly? This is like when I look up the Facebook profile of some girl I hated in college—like I'm hoping to find something that confirms my feelings and makes me say, "Yep, still hate her, I was right all along." I already know plenty of annoying things about Drew, and from the safety of my blanket cocoon, I intend to find out about any scandals or embarrassments.

At first, I don't come across anything juicy; just his IMDb page and a Wikipedia article that tells me where he went to high school and that he was the football team's mascot.

On the second page of results, I see a post on a blog called Hollywood Gossip. In glaring capital letters, the headline screams, "HOLLYWOOD HUNK DREW DANFORTH VISITS DYING GRANDFATHER," right above a picture of Drew next to an ailing elderly man. A fake smile is pasted on Drew's face, but it can't hide the exhaustion and anguish he's obviously feeling. It's so raw that I'm uncomfortable looking at it, and I wonder how the hell this picture even ended up on this terrible website.

I click away and onto an article about Drew's most famous relationship: the years-long one between him and Gillian Roberts, his costar on *Mike's Restaurant.* They slowly fell in love on the show, but apparently in real life they got together a lot more quickly. Gillian played this supposedly mousy waitress on the show, someone who didn't wear a lot of makeup and had messy hair and never really dressed up (so . . . someone a lot of us, myself included, related to). But in real life? I scroll through pictures of her on the red carpet, her hair sculpted into waves and some designer dress hugging her perfectly toned body. She's beautiful. I remind myself that she has trainers and nutritionists and professional hair and makeup artists, but I can't help comparing myself and my hair (abysmal) and wardrobe (leggings-based) to the glamour on my screen.

I click away from that article, too, and keep reading results. Aside from the time he was photographed making out with a Victoria's Secret model at a party, most of the articles have headlines that refer to Drew as a "Hollywood prankster" or "funnyman" and are about all the weird things I already know he did.

Does this guy take anything seriously? Or does he think his entire life is a joke, when most people would literally chop off a body part to have the career and lifestyle he has? *Coffee Girl*, I think.

Annoyed, I slam my laptop shut. I need to be reading about hemorrhoids, not movie stars, so I decide to go to Nick's, where at least I'll be too embarrassed to openly research Drew Danforth.

I step into the coffee shop and wave to Chloe and Nick behind the counter, then grab the one open table by the window—Thursday is board game–night, and Monopoly aficionados have every other table pushed together. Nick loves it because they have to order seriously massive amounts of coffee to stay awake for such a boring game. I settle down and open up my Word doc, ready to write the guide to at-home hemorrhoid relief that will take the internet by storm. I type a few words and take in the comforting sounds of the coffee shop: Chloe berating Nick for putting on his Elliott Smith playlist ("It's like a real bummer of a Wes Anderson movie scene in here, and that doesn't make anyone buy lattes!"), the comforting hiss of the espresso machine, the chuckles of the Monopoly players. As much as I sometimes wish my life would change, or that something would happen, I have to admit that I do love these comforting sounds. I inhale the warm, rich coffee scent and think that if I could wrap up in this evening like a blanket, I would.

Since Chloe and Nick are distracted by yet another one of their sexual-tension-filled arguments, I take a moment to open up my screenplay. But when the bell above the door jingles, I quickly close the document and decide to return to a little guilty Drew Danforth research. Sure, reading about a celebrity is kinda pathetic, but at least it's not vulnerable in the same way my writing is. Not that I think some random coffee drinker is going to care about my screenplay, but it still makes me feel naked and exposed to work on it here. Maybe if I was writing a blockbuster action film or a slick mystery, I wouldn't feel like this, but this is a romance. This is a document full of my deepest desires and dreams, my beating heart contained behind the glare of a computer screen.

Drew Danforth's face smiles at me from an article I just opened, and I grimace, then look up to see . . . Drew Danforth.

I do a double take as I watch him walk past my table and toward the counter.

"Hey, man," Nick says, clearly not recognizing him. "What can I get you?"

"A small black coffee, please," Drew says, then glances into the bakery case beside the counter. "And, uh . . . one of those, I guess?"

"Oh! Those are my cherry-almond bars, and—" Chloe's friendly, customer-pleasing smile melts off her face, replaced by sheer amazement. "Wait . . . you're . . ."

Drew pulls off his beanie, sending droplets of water flying. "Nope. Not me. I just look a lot like him."

Chloe ignores his words and grabs Nick's arm. "Drew Danforth!" she squeals. Even the Monopoly players look up.

Nick looks at me and says, exasperated, "What's going on?"

At this, Drew turns and sees me. His eyes light up with recognition, and his mouth quirks into that infuriating little smirk. I self-consciously pat at my hair, which the misty snow-rain outside has turned into even more of a frizz ball than usual.

He walks toward me, the coffee shop floorboards creaking. "Coffee Girl!" he says easily. "In your natural habitat, I see."

"Hello," I say, lifting my chin and trying to appear confident. "Guy Who Just Looks Like Drew Danforth."

He bites his lower lip. "Yeah. It's me."

Then he takes a glance at my laptop screen. I follow his eyes.

"Oh. No. Oh, no," I say, hurriedly closing the gossip site about Drew.

"Were you . . ." he says slowly.

"No."

"Were you googling me?" He looks at me again, eyebrows raised.

"I wasn't. I was . . ." I angrily click out of two more tabs with pictures of Drew. "I was . . ."

I stare at my screen in disbelief. How can this be happening?

"At-Home Hemorrhoid Relief," Drew reads, leaning in as if to get a closer look at my screen.

"This is for work," I say, snapping the laptop shut. "Not that it's any of your business."

"I don't know." Drew shrugs. "It seems pretty informative."

"Black coffee," Nick calls, and Drew turns around to grab his cup. Chloe hands him a paper bag containing his cherry-almond bar and smiles so sweetly that I start to think she's going to curtsy.

"Have a good night," Drew says to Nick and Chloe as he heads toward the door. Right before he opens it, he meets my eyes and says, "Good luck with your work. I think it's gonna help a lot of people."

I don't say anything as the door jingles shut. For a moment, the coffee shop is mostly silent, save the murmurs of the Monopoly players.

"What. The hell. Was that?" Chloe asks, ripping off her apron and walking out from behind the counter.

"I don't know!" I say. "He came in here, made fun of my work—"

"No," she says, sitting down across from me. "I mean what the hell did you just do?"

I raise my eyebrows.

"You have a chance to star in your very own rom-com," she says, pointing at me like she's a mother lecturing a child, "and instead you decide to be combative?"

"Chloe!" I say. "This isn't a rom-com. He was being a jerk. He was mocking me. Like, sorry, I don't make a million billion dollars, and instead I have to write ridiculous internet content and bring coffee to directors."

She waves a hand. "It was playful banter."

I shake my head. "I don't like that guy. Tom Hanks would never do this."

"Wasn't he kind of a jerk to Meg Ryan in *You've Got Mail*?" Chloe asks.

"Outwardly. But he had a heart of gold and he cared about his family and—"

"Did he have a dog?" Chloe asks flatly. "A big, fluffy dog to show that he truly cared about someone other than himself?"

"Yes," I say icily. "He had a lovely golden retriever."

"Well, maybe Drew Danforth also has a heart of gold," Chloe says. "You don't know."

I think about what I read about him online, all that stuff I already know about him making everything a joke. And about him making out with a literal model. But then there was that picture of him and his sick grandfather, so out of place among everything else.

"I kind of doubt it. Anyway, he saw me writing about at-home hemorrhoid relief, and I'm pretty sure no romantic comedy has ever mentioned hemorrhoids."

"I don't know." Chloe tilts her head, walking slowly back to the counter. "Maybe something by Judd Apatow."

"Hemorrhoids aren't anything to be embarrassed about," Gary says from the Monopoly table. "Half of people over the age of fifty have them."

"Thanks, Gary," I mutter, and I'm kind of being sarcastic but not really because I can use that in my article.

"Listen, I'm happy that you had your sweet meet or whatever," Nick says.

"Meet-cute," Chloe corrects him.

"Sure. But I'm not jazzed that Drew Danforth is waltzing in here. Remember when Bradley Cooper was here? We had people walking in for weeks, camping out at the tables and waiting for him to show up. They didn't order anything."

Chloe waves a hand dismissively. "Don't worry about it. It's like that time Taylor Swift and Jake Gyllenhaal visited a coffee shop and people were really into maple lattes for a while, but everyone soon forgot about it. Except for Taylor. She wrote, like, an entire album about it."

Nick stares at her. "Sometimes it's like you're speaking a foreign language."

I zone out as Nick and Chloe keep talking. On paper, maybe Chloe's right; maybe this would be a great romantic comedy. But Drew Danforth is a movie star, and I'm very much not, and he's determined to repeatedly put me in my place. What kind of guy does that? Makes fun of a woman who makes possibly millions of dollars less than he does? Thinking about him makes me queasy and mad and nervous, and I don't want to feel that way.

"Chloe," I say suddenly and with force. She stops arguing with Nick long enough to look at me. "Set me up again, okay? Didn't you say there's a guy in your class I would love?"

She gasps, then claps. "His name's Barry."

"Great," I say, getting back to work on my article. "Give me his number."

I'll text this Barry guy and talk to him about . . . whatever. It's not romantic and it sure doesn't feel like fate, but look at me! I can get dates, too. I might not be making bajillions of dollars on movies or dating models, but I can do this. Drew Danforth can suck it.

Chapter Eight

THE ONLY WRENCH IN MY "TRYING TO FORGET ABOUT DREW DAN-forth and how much I hate him" plan is that I'm on the set of a movie he's starring in, meaning I have to hear about him, oh, pretty much constantly.

"Where's Drew?" Tommy asks, his voice booming so loudly that he doesn't need a megaphone.

"His trailer," Brody says, his mouth full of a burrito.

"Are you ever not eating?" Tarah asks.

Brody gestures to his body, ensconced in a puffy winter coat. "This takes work, okay? I've gotta maintain it with daily burritos."

Despite my general annoyance with Drew, I've developed a nice, casual relationship with both Brody and Tarah. Both of them are polite, genuine people, unlike some movie stars whose names rhyme with Schmew Schmanforth. Both of them seem to like Drew, though, and Brody is even one of his friends, which does make me question their judgment.

"What's he doing in his trailer?" Tommy ask-shouts.

Brody shrugs, and Tommy turns to me. I certainly don't know, or care, what Drew is doing, so I shrug, too.

"Go check on him," Tommy says, jerking his head in the direction of Drew's trailer as he looks at his phone.

My mouth twists into a frown, but as Tommy's assistant I must assist him with anything he needs, which in this case apparently involves corralling diva actors.

"You want a bite?" Brody asks, holding his burrito toward me.

"Uh, no thanks," I say before I stomp off toward Drew's trailer.

I hesitate outside the trailer door, hearing a voice on the other side. Should I knock? Should I barge in? What if he's naked? The thought of Drew naked is not an altogether unpleasant one, because although I'm not impressed by muscles, I did see that shirtless picture Chloe sent me plus a few more when I googled him and it wasn't like he was hard to look at . . .

I shake my head. What the hell? Why would he be naked, Annie? Focus.

I knock quietly. No response. I knock a little louder, and all I hear is a laugh. Frustrated, I push open the door.

Drew is facing away from me, pacing the short length of his trailer, and he's on the phone.

"If anyone's a turd burglar here, it's definitely you, bud," he's saying with a laugh. "Yeah, I went there."

He turns around to pace back and his eyes widen when he sees me. "Good God!" he shouts as he drops his phone.

"I knocked!" I yell. "Twice!"

"I'm on the phone," he says, exasperated, as he picks it up. Then, to whomever he's talking to, he says, "Listen, I dropped the phone. Yeah, okay. Uh-huh. Tell Mom and Dad I love them. Later, loser."

He hangs up and looks at me expectantly.

"Tommy needs you," I say, then turn to leave.

But before I step away from the door, he says, "I was talking to my brother. Not avoiding everyone."

I stop and look at him. "I didn't ask."

"Yeah, but." He pulls on his gloves. "I can tell you're thinking that I'm some asshole hiding in his trailer and slowing down production. But my brother's ten, and he's dealing with some little shits bullying him because he has a speech impediment and he can't pronounce his Rs, and I wanted to make him feel a bit better."

I raise my eyebrows. "By calling him a turd burglar and a loser?"

Drew smirks. "Terms of endearment in the Danforth family."

It *is* actually kind of sweet that he cares so much about his family. Tom Hanks, after all, is usually very good with children, whether they're his own or his dad's or grandfather's much younger kids. I open my mouth to ask him more about his family, but then I hear someone burp outside through the thin walls of the trailer, and I remember that this isn't a movie. This moment is not sound tracked by Harry Connick Jr. or Harry Nilsson or any other Harry who sings in a Nora Ephron film. This is depressingly real life, and Drew Danforth will be gone the second this movie is done filming.

"You'd better hurry," I say before I make my way down the stairs. The cold air hitting my cheeks helps bring me back to reality.

By the time we're done with the day's scenes, I've made about a million phone calls, fetched about a hundred cups of coffee, and even (thrillingly!) helped Tommy make some minor script changes when he asked me which word was funnier, *bozo* or *jackass*. (Bozo, obviously. Duh.) Everyone's exhausted, and I hear Brody and Tarah talking about going out to dinner somewhere. They bring up the names of a few places I know are good and decide on an Italian place before asking Drew to go with them.

"Thanks, but I gotta pass," he says, heading off toward his trailer.

"He needs to have some fun," Tarah says as he walks away, rubbing her hands together to keep them warm.

"He needs to have some food," Brody says, his hand in a bag of Fritos.

"Annie, listen," Tommy says, grabbing my arm and pulling me gently to the side. "Are you busy tonight? I need something."

"I'm not busy," I say, shaking my head, because sure, I should be writing some internet content about how to properly use painter's tape, but it can wait if Tommy needs me.

He points a thumb toward Drew's trailer, where the door has just swung shut. "I need you to take Drew out."

My mouth opens. Once I've regained the power of speech, I say, "I'm sorry, what?"

Tommy waves his hand dismissively. "He's spending too much time by himself, and I think he needs some human interaction."

I shake my head quickly. "I don't think I can—"

"Annie," Tommy says, placing his hands lightly on my shoulders. "Are you my assistant?"

I nod.

"I need some assistance, please," he says. "If you really can't, then okay. But Drew's performance is gonna be better if he doesn't just head back to his hotel and spend his evening staring at a television, and if his performance is better, the movie is better. You care about the movie, right?"

Well, he has me there, because I *do* care about this movie. My name will be in the credits . . . I mean, probably five minutes into the credits and so tiny that no one will ever see it, but still. I need the first movie my name is on to be as good as it can possibly be.

"I don't think he likes me," I say.

"He needs to be around someone who's gonna take the piss out of him," Tommy says. "And I have a feeling that's you."

I frown. Going out to dinner with Drew Danforth? The guy who caught me googling him, made fun of my job, and seems amused by my general presence on this earth? I guess if we run out of conversational topics, I can always trot out some mortifying memories from my childhood. How about the time I puked on a field trip to the art museum? I'm sure he'd love that one.

Tommy must be able to read the hesitation written on my face, because he claps me on the back like he's a coach for a youth soccer team. "Live a little, okay? Go have some fun."

Chloe was excited when I texted her about this dinner—in fact, she called it a date, a designation I quickly denied. This is a work obligation. This is a cocky movie star who's too good to even spend time with his castmates being stuck going to dinner with a lowly assistant. This isn't anyone's idea of a good time, and it certainly isn't "straight out of a rom-com," as Chloe insisted.

"You don't even believe in love," I texted.

"Not for me," Chloe texted back. "But *you're* a hopeless romantic. Love exists for people like you. At least you'll get to eat somewhere good."

She has a point there, I think as I slide into the passenger seat of Drew's car. I don't know the first thing about cars, but even I can tell that this is a lot nicer than Uncle Don's Prius. If cars had names,

Uncle Don's would be Brenda, and she would be a sassy, no-nonsense HR manager. This car, whatever it is, would be named Cristal, and she would probably be an Instagram influencer.

"You drive yourself, then?" I ask, clicking my seat belt into place. "No drivers or limos?"

I don't look right at Drew, but I can tell he's looking at me with that infuriating smirk on his face. "I think you might have a slightly inflated sense of my net worth."

And you definitely don't understand how little I get paid for writing articles about DIY bathroom renovations, I think.

He insisted on driving, even though I offered—it's not like he knows his way around, but perhaps he was feeling chivalrous or, more accurately, thought I was incapable of operating a motor vehicle or doing anything other than fetching coffee. As his phone calls out lefts and rights, I finally ask him where we're going.

"Oh," he says, his voice sounding both teasing and ominous, "you'll see."

It's McDonald's. Drew Danforth, star of screens both large and small, takes me to the home of the McNugget.

"This is a joke, right?" I ask as I stare up at the golden arches, but he's out of the car before he even hears me. Of course, when Drew has a chance to go somewhere good—to take me, someone who rarely goes to fancy restaurants, to a nice place—he decides it would be oh-so-funny to visit a fast-food joint.

"Oh, my God," I mutter, and I'm about to swing my door open when he opens it for me.

"You don't have to do that," I snap, about to tell him not to make fun of me by opening the door as if I'm the famous person and he's my driver. Then I remember that I promised Tommy I would keep Drew company. I can do this, for the good of the movie, because it's part of my job.

"I'm fully capable of opening my own doors," I say in a more measured tone.

"What can I say?" Drew says, smiling. "It's these Southern manners. My mom drilled them into me, and now I can't ditch them, even if I try."

We walk inside, and I remember, from my ill-fated research, that Drew is from Louisiana. Apparently he managed to drop his accent much easier than the manners.

As McDonald's go, this is one of the better ones. It's clean and bright and appears to be both staffed and patronized largely by teenagers. Drew strolls up to the counter and orders, unaware of stares from the employees, then motions for me to do the same.

After we get our food and sit down, Drew immediately takes a huge bite of his Big Mac. "Oh, God," he groans, and it sounds so inappropriate that I have to look away from his face. "This is the best thing I've ever eaten."

The Big Mac isn't the only thing he ordered. His plastic tray also contains a ten-piece order of Chicken McNuggets, the biggest order of fries I've ever seen, two apple pies, and a hot fudge sundae. The cashier, a cute girl in her early twenties, claimed the ice-cream machine was broken, but one smile from Drew and it magically worked.

"So you . . . like fast food?" I ask, dipping a Chicken McNugget in honey.

"I don't like it." He shakes his head. "I love it. But this is the first time I've had it in . . . two years, maybe? I was on this intense high-protein diet when I was filming *The Last Apocalypse*, and I had to eat, like, fifteen chicken breasts a day. No carbs."

"That sounds disgusting," I say, feeling sympathy for Drew for the first time ever. "No fast food?"

"No sugar." He holds up a hand, ticking things off with his fingers. "No pasta, no bread, no beans, no oats, no potatoes."

"Just chicken breasts?"

"Chicken breasts and broccoli. It was harrowing. And then even when we were done filming, I had to promote the movie so I still had to eat pretty healthy," he says, dipping a fry into his sundae. "I mean, sure, I was a hundred percent muscle, but now that I'm not working out three times a day, my soft, doughy middle is going to return."

I try to stifle a laugh and it comes out as an unappealing snort, which makes Drew smile. Not that I noticed or cared.

I think back to the pages of Drew pictures I scrolled through online. Honestly, he looked better when he was in *Mike's Restaurant,* back when his face was rounder and he was surrounded in appealing baby fat. He looked . . . sweet.

"You looked fine before," I say.

He raises his eyebrows. "You think I looked fine?"

"Fine like okay. Not *fine* like a '90s R&B song."

He clutches his chest. "Wow. Be still, my beating heart, the great Annie Cassidy deigns to pay me a compliment."

I can feel my face getting red, and I'm pretty sure Drew is making fun of me. I'm not sure how he even knows my last name—I thought I was just Coffee Girl to him. Is he learning personal details about me for the purpose of being kind of condescending? God, what in-depth jerkery this is.

He gestures toward his apple pies, not noticing my silent seething. "You want one of these? I only ordered one, but the girl at the register gave me two for some reason."

I snort. "I wonder why?"

He looks at me, genuinely confused.

"Because that cashier wants to marry you and have, like, ten of your babies," I say.

He turns and looks toward the counter, where the cashier is staring at him. She quickly looks away.

"And that table over there is definitely filming you on their phones," I say, gesturing toward a table of teenagers who aren't even bothering to hide their interest.

"Hey," Drew says, waving at them, then turns back to me.

"You must love this, right?" I ask. "All the attention. The pictures. The extra apple pies."

He gestures toward me with his. "Who among us could resist this deep-fried perk?"

Just like he does on the red carpet, he's deflecting questions, not taking anything seriously. It's more than a little infuriating. "Why are you even in this movie?" I ask, irritation dripping from my voice.

Drew raises his eyebrows. "What?"

I shrug. "I mean, you don't want to talk to any of your coworkers, you hide in your trailer all the time—"

"Who said I hide in my trailer all the time?"

"Uh, anyone on set?"

"I talk to people!" he says, indignant. "I'm talking to you, aren't I?"

"Under duress."

"Oh yes, poor me," he says. "Forced to eat Chicken McNuggets with a beautiful woman. My life is so rough."

I ignore the sarcastic comment about my appearance. "Do you even *like* romantic comedies?" I ask.

"What?"

I cross my arms and lean back in the booth. "What's your favorite rom-com?"

"What kind of question is—"

I lean forward. "Answer me!"

Drew sighs. "*Her*, I guess."

"The movie where Joaquin Phoenix falls in love with Siri?" I ask flatly.

He nods. "Yeah. Why?"

I shake my head quickly. "That's not a— Wow, that's not even remotely a romantic comedy. I mean, I guess it's romantic, sort of, and I *did* laugh a couple of times. But it's not a rom-com."

His mouth quirks up at the side, and he folds his hands on the table in front of him. "What, are you some kind of rom-com expert or something?"

I raise my eyebrows and find myself mirroring his posture. "Kind of."

He smacks the table. "Qualifications. Go!"

I hold up my fingers as I count. "One. I have seen the classic film *You've Got Mail* approximately one hundred times and can quote it on command."

Drew shakes his head. "That shows a depth of knowledge, not a breadth."

"Two," I say, my voice more forceful. "I've seen every film on AFI's list of the best romantic movies, even though some of them are more rom-drams than rom-coms. Three, I have a framed photo of Nora Ephron on my desk, because she's my hero and I want to be her."

Drew nods.

"And four," I say, even though I wasn't planning on sharing this with Drew, but somehow it slips out, "I've been working on my own rom-com screenplay for years, because I'm a writer."

"You're writing a—" he starts, but I cut him off, already embarrassed that I mentioned something so personal to someone who will probably use it as ammunition to make fun of me later.

"Moral of the story, I have serious doubts about your ability to do justice to the genre," I say.

He snort-laughs. "Okay then, wise one, tell me three movies I have to see, and I'll watch them right away."

I exhale. "I mean, there are a million. But if we're going for classics, you can't get better than the Nora Ephron/Meg Ryan holy trinity. *When Harry Met Sally . . .* , *Sleepless in Seattle*, and *You've Got Mail*."

"All right," he says, tapping them into his phone. "I will watch them and report back."

An electric thrill runs through my body at this, because it feels slightly like flirting. But it's not, I remind myself. For starters, this guy is literally starring in a movie where he has to act like he's falling in love with someone, so I can't trust anything he says. And also because Drew has made it abundantly clear that he thinks I'm mostly mockable, certainly not someone to flirt with.

"You never answered my question. Why are you even in this movie?" I ask, sounding like a pouty child.

"Well, in case you didn't notice," Drew says, slipping his phone back into his coat pocket, "*The Last Apocalypse* was an embarrassing dud, and it's been a couple of years since *Mike's Restaurant* ended."

I roll my eyes. "So even though you think rom-coms are beneath you, they're all you could get."

"Let me finish, okay? And because I like Tommy, and I know

he's a great director, and I know that this movie will make people happy. Did you know that there are almost no big-budget romantic comedies with interracial couples?"

I mean, yes, of course, I know that. Anyone who likes romantic comedies know that there are plenty of criticisms lobbed at the genre, like that the films are vapid or sexist, or that they create unrealistic relationship expectations or encourage abusive behavior. None of those criticisms mean anything to me because I don't think they're true. But it stings when people complain about the genre's lack of diversity because they're obviously correct. There *are* romantic comedies about people who aren't white and straight—lots of amazing ones—but they typically have small budgets and even smaller marketing campaigns, so people often don't know they exist. It's awesome that successful rom-coms like *Crazy Rich Asians* and *To All the Boys I've Loved Before* are changing things, but there's no denying that the rom-com classics of my youth are pathetically homogenous.

But Drew Danforth probably doesn't care about my thoughts on this, so I just nod.

"Tommy's wife is black, and he wanted to make a movie that reflected their relationship, so that's why he was drawn to this movie even though he hasn't done a rom-com since the '90s."

"Oh," I say, impressed that Drew knows all this.

"Plus," he says around his straw, "who could miss the chance to hang out in beautiful Columbus, Ohio?"

"Need I remind you that going to McDonald's was your decision?" I ask. "Columbus has plenty of fine dining. And museums! And parks! And an award-winning zoo! And—"

He holds up a hand, annoying smile back on his face. "I was kidding, Annie."

Blood rushes to my cheeks. Something about the way my name rolls off his tongue, so familiar, makes me feel like I've already heard him say it a thousand times before, instead of just once during this conversation.

I shake my head. "I hate city snobs like you. The ones who act like everyone who isn't from New York or LA is some kind of hick. You probably use the phrase 'fly-over country,' don't you?"

"I don't . . . no! For God's sake, I'm from Shreveport, Louisi-ana!" Drew says, eyes wide. "For the record, Columbus is now my favorite city in the world."

I narrow my eyes. "Don't overdo it."

"I love it here. I'm going to move here," he says. "I want to be buried here."

"In this McDonald's? If you keep eating like that, it might be a possibility."

He rolls his eyes. "Let's get out of here. Early call time tomorrow."

He grabs my tray before I can make a move for it. On our way out, he stops to shake hands with the table of teenagers.

"I can see how much you hate the attention," I say as we go out the door.

"I'm being nice," he says, giving me a wry look.

"Right," I mutter as I get back into his absurdly fancy car.

Chapter Nine

I PREGAME FOR MY DATE WITH BARRY BY WATCHING *THE SHOP Around the Corner*. It might seem like a bad idea to watch a romantic comedy before a date, and it's certainly setting a high bar to expect Barry to have the charm of an in-his-prime James Stewart, but it's one of my favorites. It's the original *You've Got Mail*, but with letters instead of dial-up internet.

Through a series of nondescript texts, Barry and I agree to meet at, where else, Nick's. Barry doesn't do anything egregious, like use that weird winking emoji or request nudes, but he also isn't exactly a master of the form. I know I shouldn't be expecting *The Shop Around the Corner* letters or *You've Got Mail* e-mails, but in a perfect world, I would like something a little more than "hey, waz up?"

Waz up. A truly baffling spelling in this, the age of the predictive text. I'll be wondering how and why he spelled it like that all night.

But I try my hardest not to judge. Although I fully believe that my Tom Hanks is out there somewhere, I have to live in the real world, like Chloe said. And maybe in the real world, most of the men are like Sandra Bullock's weird neighbor in *While You Were Sleeping*, not like Bill Pullman in *While You Were Sleeping*. Maybe all the cute guys are actually big jerks who make fun of your job and your city and your totally normal romantic comedy obsession.

As the movie ends, I have to fight the urge to stay home all evening. It's just that the couch in our living room is truly one of my favorite places on this Earth. It's big and so soft that you sink into it when you sit down, which means it's easy to convince yourself you should stay put. It's been here since I was a tiny kid, and even though it's covered with a dingy rose print that looks like it's straight out of the '90s, neither Uncle Don nor I can bear to replace it.

This is where I watched all these movies with my mom. This is where she told me, while we were watching *Sleepless in Seattle*, to always keep hoping for a brighter tomorrow. At the time I was upset because I'd failed a spelling test (my spelling has since improved, thanks), and she, as usual, had found a way to compare everything to a romantic comedy.

"Tom Hanks is facing his darkest day here," she said, staring at the screen. "But he doesn't give up. And maybe not everything gets fixed—his wife doesn't come back to life—but he's happy again, eventually."

Of course, that was just something to say to a small child who was upset about flunking a test—something that, ultimately, didn't end up mattering all that much. What I wouldn't give to hear what she had to say about this date.

But I do have Uncle Don, I remind myself as I get up and walk into the kitchen, where he's banging a bunch of pots and pans around. Our kitchen probably wouldn't be very impressive if it was on one of those house-selling shows where people always want "open floorplans" and "chef's kitchens" even though they probably only cook dinner, like, once every two weeks. I mean, if this kitchen was on *House Hunters*, a disapproving wife would definitely tell her husband, "This entire thing needs to be gutted," while a hopeful Realtor lies to them about how easy that would be.

But I love this kitchen as much as I love the rest of this house, because it's suffused in memory and drenched in comfort. Sure, it doesn't look like a kitchen Meryl Streep would use in a Nancy Meyers movie, and the cabinets are a deep green color instead of a trendy white, but it's still where so many conversations and meals have happened. It's home.

"Headed out?" Don asks, dumping chopped carrots and onions into a pot.

"I have a date," I say, wrinkling my nose.

"Good for you!" Uncle Don says.

"Uncle Don," I say, leaning against the island. "Blind dates are the worst. This is someone Chloe set me up with, and I don't even know anything about him."

"But you're putting yourself out there," he says. "And that's what's important."

Right. Like Uncle Don knows anything about putting himself out there. He's been just as frozen in time as I have.

"Oh," he says, "I wanted to let you know that I'm gonna be gone next weekend. The guys and I are going to meet up with our friend Tyler at a con in Chicago."

"Thanks for letting me know—now I can plan a huge rager," I say.

"So how's the job going?" Don asks, changing the subject.

I shrug. "Pretty good. Tommy's not a bad boss. He's demanding but not mean."

Don nods. "He snores, you know."

"I'm sure that information will come in useful on set."

"I invited him to the next D&D night, but he's pretty busy with the movie and everything," Don says, stroking his chin. "Did you know he was a huge gamer in college?"

"Uh, no," I say, because Tommy and I have mostly been discussing work, not his youthful enthusiasm for tabletop gaming.

"How's everything else going?" Don asks. "Do you like the movie?"

"It's hard to think about it like a movie when I see them filming bits and pieces out of order," I say. "But yeah. Everyone seems to know what they're doing, and . . ."

I think about Drew, and how he actually doesn't know the first thing about rom-coms. Okay, so maybe not *everyone* knows what they're doing.

"Whoa," Uncle Don says.

"What?"

"You look like you just saw an abominable yeti," Don says, and I'm assuming that means the look on my face when I thought about Drew wasn't exactly a happy one.

I shake my head. "I have to get going or I'm going to be late," I say.

But it turns out I shouldn't have bothered, because Barry is twenty minutes late.

Five minutes late is basically on time. Ten minutes is fine. Fifteen minutes is really pushing it. But twenty? That's almost half an hour, almost the length of a sitcom episode, and it's getting into "definitely send a text, possibly even reschedule" territory. From my usual table, I watch customers walk in and out. Out the window, I see the Coatless Wonder stroll by, oblivious to the flurries swirling down from the sky.

"Nick," I say when I'm at the counter to get my second mocha, "did this guy bail on me?"

Nick hands me my drink, unconcerned. "Maybe he's caught in traffic."

I sit back down and consider this. If this was a rom-com, Barry's bad first impression would only be a setup for our eventual love affair. It's like *When Harry Met Sally* . . . I mean, even their names rhyme! Barry, Harry, it's all pretty much the same, right?

The bell above the door jingles and a man walks in. I immediately recognize him from the picture Chloe showed me.

I wave as he crosses the room. "Hi, I'm—" I start, standing up and holding out my hand, but he pulls me into a hug.

"Ooof," I exhale into his puffy jacket.

"Sorry, I'm kind of sweaty," he apologizes, taking off his coat to reveal that he's wearing extremely tight leggings and a sweat-soaked T-shirt. "I ran here."

"Oh, you . . . you run?" I ask, sitting down and trying not to focus on the sweat on his light-gray T-shirt.

"Big time," he says. "Do you?"

"Oh, certainly not," I say with a laugh. "Only if there's a particularly great-looking donut across the street and time is of the essence."

He waves a hand. "I used to be like you. Inactive, a few pounds overweight, but running changed everything. You should give it a try."

I blink a few times and attempt a polite smile. Surely he didn't mean to comment on my weight.

"Right. Um, well, did you want to order something?"

Barry squints toward the counter. "Do you think they have anything sugar-free?"

I think about the case full of Chloe's white chocolate macadamia-nut brownies. While I'm sure she'd be happy to bake something for someone with dietary restrictions, I know that her personal beliefs tend toward butter and sugar. "To be honest with you, I highly doubt it. But you can grab a black coffee . . . Nick's is the best."

Barry shakes his head. "I don't do caffeine."

I nod slowly, wondering why he agreed to meet me at a coffee shop. "I think he has some herbal tea . . ."

"I actually don't like any hot liquids," Barry says, leaning forward. "They slow down my metabolism."

"How about I grab you a water?" I ask, then bolt up to the counter before he can tell me anything more about his hydration preferences.

"Nick," I hiss. "This is a bust."

"Why?" Nick looks over at the table way too obviously, but luckily Barry isn't paying attention. "He looks fine . . . wait, is that sweat?"

"Yes. He ran here."

Nick looks at me in shock. "That's what that smell is? Thank God. I thought the sewage pipe backed up again."

"Nope. That's just the love of my life, stinking up the joint, telling me all about how he doesn't drink hot liquids."

"Wait, what?" Nick asks.

I shake my head. "Just . . . can I have a glass of water, please? Make it cold."

"Maybe you can toss it on him and wash off some of the stink," Nick mutters.

I sigh and glance down at my outfit. I dressed up for this. I'm wearing an adorable pair of booties and a comfortable-yet-cute sweater dress over thick tights. I was slightly inspired by Meg Ryan's giant, neutral wardrobe in *You've Got Mail,* but hopefully my look is a little less '90s and oversized. But it's looking like I shouldn't even have bothered; it's not like Barry has noticed anything about me, other than the fact that he apparently thinks I should lose a few pounds.

I sit down and hand Barry his glass of water, which he takes without a "thank you." "So what do you do?" I ask, hoping to change my initial impression of him.

"I wouldn't say I'm into traditional 'employment,' per se," he says, making air quotes. I hear the bell above the door jingle and Nick casually saying, "Hey, man."

The coffee shop is largely empty this evening—just Gary and a couple of other old guys silently reading the paper—so I'm the only one who notices who walks in.

It's Drew. What the hell is this guy's problem? This is a major American city and there are, like, twenty other coffee shops he could go to.

"Oh, no," I mutter.

"It's actually not that gross," Barry says. "I really inspect everything before I eat it."

"I'm sorry, what?" I ask, looking back at him, realizing he's been talking this entire time.

"The food I find in the dumpster," he says. "Most people only grab things that haven't been opened, but my belief is that a bagel with only one bite taken out of it is basically brand new."

I nod slowly, my eyes darting toward Drew. He's sitting at a table in the corner by the bathroom, and he's facing me. And staring right at me, that infuriating smirk on his face.

"Could you hold on a moment, Barry?" I ask. "I have to run to the restroom."

I stomp across the coffee shop, floorboards squeaking under my feet, and stand next to Drew's table. "What are you doing here?" I whisper-shout.

"You're on a date!" he says, his mouth open in amazement like he's a small child seeing a unicorn. He points at my shoes. "Those are date shoes. I can tell."

"These are just small boots and—you know what? Stop making fun of me. It's not like it's so shocking that someone would want to go on a date with me."

His brow furrows. "Why do you think I'm making fun of you?"

I cross my arms. "Ah, the old 'answer a question with a question.' Classic Danforth. So infuriating."

Drew peers around me to look at Barry, who's facing away from us. "Why is he wet?"

"He's a runner, okay?" I say. "He's very healthy. It's super hot."

My eyes snag on Drew's cup, maybe because I'm wishing my date also believed in hot liquids. Drew points at it. "Black coffee. I watched the movie . . . *You've Got Mail*. Gotta say, I agree with Tom Hanks's assessment of fancy coffee drinks. What did your date order, something complicated?"

"He doesn't like hot liquids," I mutter.

Drew raises his eyebrows. "No tea?"

"Presumably not."

"Hot chocolate? A hot toddy? Mulled wine?"

I stare at him, my face as blank as I can make it.

"What about soup?" Drew asks. "Does this man also not eat soup?"

"You know what?" I ask, incensed. "You shouldn't even be

here. You should be somewhere, like, publicly making out with a Victoria's Secret model."

"I did that *one time*," Drew says.

"Boo-hoo, Leonardo DiCaprio." I sneer. "The world isn't a playground for all of us, okay? Some of us are looking for real love, and who knows, maybe I'll find it with Barry."

Both of us turn to look at Barry, who's clipping his nails at the table.

"Did he bring nail clippers from home?" I whisper with disgust.

"I'm sure he's great," Drew says with a smile, crossing his arms in front of him on the table. "But here's my issue with *Sleepless in Seattle*—"

"You watched all three of them?" I ask, almost speechless.

"I haven't started *When Harry Met Sally* . . . yet," he says. "But listen. How does Tom Hanks afford to live on that houseboat? That thing is huge. It's gotta be expensive, and he's a single dad."

"He's an architect," I say.

"And why are there so many architects in romantic comedies?" Drew asks, clearly working up to something. "Are there even that many architects in the world? It's a hard job, right? Am I supposed to believe that—"

"That's not the point, okay?" I say, slamming myself down in the chair across from him. "It doesn't matter how someone in a romantic comedy affords their absurdly nice house, or whether or not their profession makes sense, or if technically they're sort of stalking someone they heard on a call-in radio show. What matters is that they have *hope*. Sure, they find love, but it's not even about love. It's the hope that you deserve happiness, and that you won't be sad forever, and that things will get better. It's hope that life doesn't always have to be a miserable slog, that you can find someone to love who understands you and accepts you just as you are."

I stop and take a breath.

Drew blinks, then leans back in his seat. "I'm sorry. I was being a dick."

After all that, his frank statement shocks me, and now it's my turn to apologize. "Wait, I'm sorry, you didn't ask for that weird rant about—"

He waves a hand at me. "Listen. Have a good time with Barry, okay? I'll give *When Harry Met Sally . . .* a shot."

He grabs his coffee, stands up, and meets my eyes for a second before he says, "You look nice tonight, by the way."

Then he walks out of the shop, giving Nick a wave but not looking back. I sit there in shocked silence.

"That was a really nice speech, Annie. Impassioned."

I turn to see Gary leaning back in his seat.

"Thanks," I say. "I should probably get back to my date."

"Is he the sweaty one?"

"That's Barry," I say with a sigh.

"Hey! Barry, Gary. Our names rhyme. Gotta be a good sign." Gary gives me a wink.

"Wow," Barry says when I finally sit back down. "You were in there for a while."

I think about explaining to Barry that remarking on the length of someone's bathroom visit isn't appropriate first-date small talk, but I decide against it.

"Do you, by chance, live in a houseboat?" I ask, hoping against hope that something can turn this around.

Barry shakes his head, unperturbed by this line of questioning.

"Actually, I'm a proponent of what I refer to as 'un-dwelling.' I have no permanent address."

"So where do you live?" I ask, then bite my lower lip.

He opens his arms in a gesture that takes in his surroundings. "Right here. I mean, not in this coffee shop. But everywhere . . . I'm a resident of this world."

I nod slowly, and he adds, "Specifically, right now I'm sleeping on my ex-girlfriend's couch."

I can't stop myself from grimacing. "Listen, Barry, I've really enjoyed getting to know you, but I don't think we have a connection."

He nods. "I get that a lot."

"I'm gonna get home, but . . ." I start to feel guilty about cutting this short and want to offer to get him another glass of water, but I notice his is still full. "Was there something wrong with your water?"

Barry shakes his head. "The thing about fluoride is—"

I cut him off. "Have a nice night." I give Nick a wave as I leave, the doorbell jingling. It's just dark, the January evenings getting lighter and lighter as we make our way slowly toward spring, and I can't help but replay my conversation with Drew. Mostly because I don't want to replay my conversation with Barry (what I wouldn't give to not think about him getting half-eaten bagels out of the dumpster), but also because I regret what I said—or at least how I said it. He seemed genuinely remorseful about his anti-romcom comments, which ultimately weren't that big of a deal—I mean, he's allowed to have whatever opinions he wants about romantic comedies! They're only movies!

But I know in my heart that they're not only movies to me. They're my family, memories of my mom, and comfort. And more than anything else, they're what I told Drew: hope. Hope that someone like me, someone who's lonely and searching, can find what she's looking for.

I can't expect Drew Danforth to understand that, I think as I walk in the front door. He's spent his life surrounded by beautiful women who stroke his ego and, presumably, other things. He wouldn't—couldn't—get it.

I text Chloe to ask her why the hell she thought Barry would be a good idea and turn on *Sleepless in Seattle*. Barry and all real-life men may be disappointments, but you know who has never (and, God willing, *will* never) let me down? Tom Hanks. And I'd rather watch him slowly fall in love for the five hundredth time than think about my own nonexistent love life right now.

Chapter Ten

CHLOE WALKS TO SET WITH ME THE NEXT MORNING. I HAVE TO GET TO work at the crack of dawn to help Tommy with whatever he needs, so for once we're on an almost identical schedule.

"I don't really know Barry that well," Chloe admits as we walk down the brick sidewalk. "He was in one of my business classes, and I had his number because we worked on a group project. He seemed nice!"

"Him being *nice* wasn't the problem," I say. "Lots of men are *nice,* and that doesn't mean I want to date them. Tobin, Gary, and Nick are all nice. Even Dungeon Master Rick is nice. That doesn't mean I should date any of them."

Chloe makes a face. "Gary's, like, sixty and Tobin's about twenty. And isn't Dungeon Master Rick kind of an asshole?"

I notice she doesn't say anything about why Nick is undateable, but I just shrug.

"Maybe you guys got off on the wrong foot," Chloe says. "Maybe you should give him another chance, and he'll smell better next time!"

"Chloe," I say, stopping outside Nick's. "If you even have to specify that someone *might* smell better *next time*, that's a pretty good indication that there shouldn't be a next time."

She sighs and shoves her hands into her coat pockets. "You're right. I just . . . if I say something, will you promise not to get mad?"

I cross my arms in front of my chest. "That depends on what it is."

She half-smiles. "I know you're all about Tom Hanks in '90s romantic comedies and all, but I want to make sure you're giving real, nonfictional guys a chance."

I bristle. "I am."

She raises her eyebrows. "Are you? Really? Did you ask Barry about the houseboat thing?"

I throw out my hands in exasperation. "What? Like it's so wrong that I would enjoy meeting a man who lives on a house-boat?"

"Annie!" Chloe practically shrieks. "We live in the middle of Ohio! We are landlocked as shit. Where is that houseboat gonna dock?"

"Maybe the Olentangy River," I mumble. "I don't know."

"Hon." Chloe reaches out to grab my shoulders. "Listen. All this 'soul mates, fate, till death do us part' stuff means nothing to me. You know that. But it's always meant something to you, and I don't want you to shut yourself off because you're waiting for some-thing perfect."

I sigh. "I'm not waiting for something perfect."

She purses her lips but nods. "Okay. Well, I can tell Nick's waiting for me to get in there and get things started."

I look over her shoulder and, through the window, I see Nick pointing to his wristwatch.

"But have a good day at work, okay?"

"Chloe," I say. "Barry doesn't eat sugar. Or hot liquids."

"What?"

I shrug. "I don't think it was meant to be."

She leans over to give me one more hug, then opens the door to Nick's. Before I walk away, I take a second to watch them through the window. Chloe pulls on her apron, yelling about something, and Nick yells something back, and it's so painfully obvious that they're living in their own rom-com. Of course, I can't tell Chloe this; much like a skittish animal, she'll run away if I make any sudden movements or try to convince her that the real love she doesn't believe in is right under her nose.

On my way back from the morning's first coffee run, I slow down on my walk back to the closed-off block that constitutes our set. Sure, all the lighting and equipment and people milling around in their puffy black coats may take away a little of the glamour, but not much. This is still a movie, aka my dream. Even though Tommy's coffee is rapidly cooling in this freezing air, I stop for a moment to take it all in. There's Tarah, a real-life famous actress, talking to someone and gesturing to something in a binder. There are the crewmembers, spilling out of the previously empty storefront that the movie took over. Before my eyes find him, I hear Tommy's voice booming, and then I see him, his arms waving and eyebrows raised, talking to Drew and a man who has a ponytail and—

Wait, what is Uncle Don doing on set?

I run-walk toward them, muttering curse words under my breath as the coffee sloshes out through the hole in the lid.

"Uncle Don! Hey! Why are you here?" I attempt to say casually, but it comes out as more of a breathless yelp. Three heads swivel toward me.

"Hey, Annie!" Uncle Don looks so happy to see me that I feel guilty for questioning his presence, but as usual, he doesn't seem offended. "Tommy invited me to check out the set! And meet the cast!"

Drew gives me a wide-eyed grin and wiggles his eyebrows a couple of times, like he's Groucho Marx or something. Even this bizarre gesture somehow looks good on him.

"How nice for you," I say, turning away from Drew and focusing on Uncle Don.

"Let me tell you something about your Uncle Donny," Tommy says, grabbing Don's arm and launching into a story I can barely pay attention to because of my growing discomfort that Drew Danforth is standing so close to my only living family member. Like, it isn't enough that he makes fun of me every day on set, in the coffee shop, and occasionally in a fast-food dining environment. Now he also has to learn personal details about my uncle's past that he can presumably use to mock me at a later date? No, thank you. It's all just too much.

"And anyway," Tommy says finishing his story, "in the end the chinchilla was a little startled but no worse for the wear."

"I wish I could say the same for myself," Don says with a laugh, and I'll admit, I'm at least a little curious about this story. But there's no time for that now.

I laugh as if I've been paying attention. "Okay, well, Uncle Don, you probably have to get going now, right?"

Don checks the Luke Skywalker watch I bought him for Christmas (the hands are tiny lightsabers) and shakes his head. "My shift at the Guardtower doesn't start for two hours."

"Great!" Tommy claps him on the back. "Then let me show you around!"

Before they walk away, Drew reaches out for a handshake, and Uncle Don turns to me. "Annie, can you believe that Drew has never read *The Wheel of Time*? Unbelievable, right?"

Truthfully, it's not unbelievable that Drew hasn't read a fourteen-volume high fantasy series, but I don't say that. "Shocking," I agree.

Once Don and Tommy are out of earshot, I point at Drew. "Stop talking to my uncle."

Drew shoves his hand into the pockets of that stupid flattering pea coat that looks like something Colin Firth would wear while playing an uptight barrister who's secretly a big softie. "I was being friendly. Maybe you should try it sometime."

I snort, resolutely promising to ignore that attractive pea coat and focus on the very annoying person inside it. "Oh, please. You're gathering intel so you can come up with more stuff to make fun of me for."

"Make fun of you?" Drew shakes his head. "Yeah, I'm assembling my Annie Cassidy dossier and that tidbit about the time your uncle inadvertently stole a sorority's pet chinchilla is the perfect addition. What *won't* I do with that information?"

"Don't act like you were so interested in what Don was saying."

Drew throws his hands in the air in an exaggerated shrug. "Like, yes? I was? I apologize that I enjoy talking about books with well-read people."

"Oh, are you going to start reading *The Wheel of Time* series now? Well, I've got news for you, buddy: each volume is like a thousand pages, so good luck."

Drew squints, his cheeks pink from the cold air. "I do know

how to read, you know. You may remember that I was perfectly capable of reading that McDonald's menu."

I blush at the mention of our fast-food quasi-date. "The Mc-Donald's menu is less challenging."

Drew shrugs again. "It's definitely shorter."

"And less gory," I say, subdued now that Drew doesn't seem interested in arguing with me. I mean, not that I enjoy arguing with him.

"I have to get back to work," Drew says. "I suggest you do the same, Coffee Girl."

Righteous indignation flows through my veins once more as Drew salutes me in a manner that can only be described as sarcastic, which wasn't even something I was aware salutes could be until this moment.

As he walks away, I say, "Don't give me that sarcastic salute," in a voice that is perhaps too loud, and one crewmember stops what he's doing to stare at me.

"Sorry," I mumble, then head off to find Tommy and Don.

Several hours later, long after Don has gone to work, Tommy hands me a big stack of papers and asks me to go put them in a binder in his trailer. Truthfully, I kind of love stuff like this—moments when all I have to do is competently use a hole-punch and feel great at my job. It's while I'm contemplating how capable I am that my foot catches on something, and then I'm falling, the papers in my arms flying skyward.

"Shit!" I say as my knees hit the ground, all delusions of competence gone. "Shit shit shit shit shit shit."

"Are you okay?" asks a deep voice.

All of Tommy's pages are now scattered on the pavement. I

keep muttering to myself, grabbing a sheet that fell into a puddle of brown Ohio winter slush. "Shit shit shit shit," I keep muttering, but this time much more quietly.

The deep voice laughs, and I finally look up. "Oh," I say, startled, as I look into the eyes of a surprisingly attractive man. I mean, it's not surprising that he's attractive, since I don't know him at all, but dropping a bunch of things and then being assisted by a handsome stranger is . . .

Well, it's something that happens in a rom-com.

The man keeps picking up papers, assembling them into a neat stack.

"Thanks for the help," I say, grabbing another one. "And, uh. Sorry for the shit tirade."

He laughs, a deep, throaty thing, and meets my eyes. His are blue and clear and, all of a sudden, I'm watching this interaction take place on a screen, while sitting in a plush movie theater seat and digging my hands into a large popcorn with extra butter and salt.

And then I do what I always do when I'm flustered. I keep talking.

"I'm not usually this clumsy. Really. But I was taking these papers to Tommy's trailer and I tripped over this wire and . . . seriously. What is this wire doing here? It's a hazard. There are, dare I say it, too many wires in the world generally, but specifically right here, in front of me. Who put this here, right in the path of everyone walking?"

The handsome blue-eyed stranger raises his hand. "That would be me."

"That would be you?" I say, my voice trailing off so that the last word is barely audible.

"Yep." He nods, then gestures around us. "I'm a gaffer. Responsible for many things, wires among them."

"Cool," I say. "Okay, well, I'm gonna go shut myself in Tommy's trailer and never return. Bye."

Before I can turn and flee, the handsome blue-eyed stranger with slightly curly hair reaches out to grab my arm. "Hey," he says, that throaty laugh appearing again. "It's okay. Really. I'm Carter Reid, by the way."

I push my hair behind my ear, then hold out my hand. "Annie Cassidy. Tommy's assistant."

He nods. "Yeah, I've . . . seen you around."

There's something about the way he says those few words, like he's been not only seeing me but liking what he's seeing, that makes my whole body flash hot and cold. It's nice to be seen by someone who likes what they're seeing, unlike some people who make it all too clear that they see you but want to simply make fun of what they're seeing and call you derogatory nicknames based on your job duties.

But there's a very attractive man in front of me, so I don't need to think about Drew Danforth right now.

Carter looks older than me—not by a lot, but maybe he's in his mid-thirties. There's just something about him that looks like he's been around the metaphorical block, like he's seen some stuff and lived to tell the tale. That makes him sound grizzled, which he emphatically is not, but I guess what I'm saying is that you know how some celebrities age really well? Like, how George Clooney looked so much better by the time he married Amal than he did when he was doing sitcom work in the '80s? It's kind of like that. This guy looks like he'll age well, like a wine or a cheese or a Clooney.

"Okay. Well," I say once I realize that I've been staring at his face for far too long. "Gotta get to Tommy's trailer."

"See you around, Annie," Carter says with a wave. I watch him walk away for just a second, long enough to really notice that he's wearing a thick and durable work jacket that looks, just a little, like something that Bill Pullman would wear in *While You Were Sleeping.*

I once read that Nora Ephron was obsessed with details. She knew her characters inside and out—how they dressed and spoke and decorated their homes.

And while I'm not saying Tommy is anything like Nora Ephron—for starters, I'm fairly certain she didn't sloppily eat Italian subs almost every day for lunch—he does share her attention to detail. In some regards, anyway.

Tommy's obsessed with some book, which he swears he needs in a scene, and his demand that I find it wipes my embarrassing wire-related incident with Carter Reid out of my mind. "It has a blue cover," he says.

"And what's the title?" I ask, getting out my phone so I can take notes.

"I don't know," Tommy says, rubbing his hands together as his breath puffs into the cold air. "I think I saw it on the *Today* show. Or maybe *Good Morning America.* But it had a blue cover."

"Do you know who wrote it?" I ask.

He shakes his head. "A man, I think. Or maybe it was a woman."

Well. That certainly narrows it down.

"Oh!" he says, eyes wide. "There was a wolf on the cover."

He smiles, like this should give me enough to go on.

"So," I say slowly. "You want me to go find a book with a blue cover that has a wolf on it, that's by a man or a woman and was featured on *Today* or *Good Morning America*."

He nods and claps me on the back. "Thanks, Annie."

And then he turns around, barking at some crewmember about something. I sigh and head toward the bookstore.

One of the most charming parts of living in Columbus in general, and German Village specifically, is our bookstore, the Book Loft. It has thirty-two book-filled rooms—some tiny, some large— that snake up and down like a maze. To get to the children's section, you have to go up one set of stairs and then down another. I've often thought it would be a great setting for a murder mystery— you could hide a body in the Civil War room and be fairly certain no one would find it for hours.

The Book Loft is almost as comforting to me as Nick's. The courtyard that leads to the door is charming and beautiful, even covered in slushy snow. And the light that glows from the front windows looks especially inviting on this dim, gloomy January day.

I walk into the main room and tell an employee what I'm looking for, not that I expect her to be much help. Even a seasoned bookseller would have a difficult time with the description Tommy gave me (seriously, "it has a wolf on it" isn't giving her a lot to work with). Still, she promises to do her best while I set off to look for it myself. I climb the stairs into the new-release room and almost bump into a broad-shouldered man in a pea coat.

"'Scuse me," I mumble, but he's too engrossed in the hardcover he's flipping through to notice me. I scoot around him—doesn't he know these rooms are tiny and difficult to maneuver in?—and scan my eyes over the shelf of new releases.

Then I hear him say, "Coffee Girl?"

I turn and find myself face-to-face with Drew.

"Oh, for God's sake," I say. "Are you following me?"

I'll admit, at least part of my prickliness is because I'm a little embarrassed about how I *may* have been a *little bit* rude to him when he was just talking to my uncle. And I guess I'm the *tiniest* amount ashamed that I *kind of* went on a romantic comedy tirade in his general direction on the night of the Great Barry Debacle. Drew snaps his book shut and gives me his crooked smile, the one that spawned a billion Tumblr gifsets when he flashed it in *Mike's Restaurant*. In person, it looks a lot more annoying . . . but okay, still cute. If it didn't belong to the man who insisted on following me around, giving me a rude nickname and stomping all over my most cherished form of entertainment, maybe I would find it endearing.

"Actually, I was here first," he says, placing the book back on the shelf. "Which means you're the one who's following me. I didn't get a chance to ask earlier, but how's Barry?"

We're so close to each other in this crowded room that I can see the gold flecks in his eyes. "It, uh, didn't work out," I say, turning around to get back to my job. "We were too different. I like hot liquids; he likes half-eaten garbage bagels."

Drew laughs out loud, the sound shockingly large in the small room. "I'll fill in the blanks myself, I guess."

I focus on the book covers in front of me. Purple, red, black . . . blue, but definitely no wolf. This is going to be impossible.

"Looking for something to read?" Drew asks, moving to stand beside me.

I turn my head to look up at him. He's a few inches taller than me, so my eyes are basically at the level of his mouth. "A book for Tommy," I say. "It has a blue cover and maybe there's a wolf on it and it was on TV."

A sharp laugh shoots out of Drew's mouth. "Wait, that's all he told you?"

I nod. "Yep." I crouch down to look at the shelf below.

"So are you going to look at every book in the Book Loft?" Drew asks from above me.

"Yep," I repeat.

"All right," he grunts, then he crouches down beside me, the shoulder of his pea coat bumping against the shoulder of my puffy jacket.

"Don't you have to be back on set?" I ask.

Drew shakes his head. "Nah. The next scene is just Tarah and Brody, and it's not like Tommy's going to be able to focus on anything anyway until he finds this book."

Still in my crouching position, I turn my head to look at him. "You don't have to help me. I can do this myself, and anyway this position is kind of uncomfortable."

"Ah, you forget," Drew says. "I trained for months for *The Last Apocalypse*. I have amazing thigh strength."

I look back at the shelf quickly, hoping Drew didn't see the way my face flushed when he mentioned the strength of his thighs. It's not like I want to think about his thighs. It's not like heat slowly flooded my body as a mental image of his thighs filled my brain.

Focus, Annie.

"And anyway," he says, "I can't find that *Orb of Time* book."

"*Wheel of Time*," I say, barely holding in my laughter. "Although *Orb of Time* sounds fascinating. Wait. Are you telling me you're actually going to read it?"

"I don't know," he says, looking at the shelves. "Don really hyped it up. I mean, a hero's journey, and the belief that time itself is a wheel? Who wouldn't want to read that?"

"How long were you talking to Uncle Don before I showed up?" I ask in a low voice.

He turns his head slightly to face me. "A very, very long time."

I swallow, then compose myself. "Cool. Well, you're not going to find it here in the new releases, on account of it's not even remotely new."

"That's fine. I'll grab it later. Is this what you're looking for?" he asks, holding up a green book with a bear on the cover.

"Blue. Wolf," I remind him.

"Right." He slides it back on the shelf and stands up. "I think we're gonna have to move on to the next room."

"Agreed," I say.

"We can safely assume it's not a travel guide," Drew says as we walk past the tiny room that houses them.

"I don't know if we can," I say, quickly scanning the shelves for anything blue. "Tommy doesn't even know what this book is about. Why he wants it so much is beyond me."

Drew chuckles, pushing in behind me. I instinctively take a step forward and run into the shelf. This room is more like a nook, and it's definitely not large enough for two people.

"Not here!" I say, ducking under his arm to get out.

We look through sports, business, and military history. Nothing. Drew keeps getting distracted and paging through books on personal finance and the Civil War, and I have to keep reminding him why we're here. It's a little bit funny, how he turns into an overgrown child in the presence of books.

"I wouldn't have pegged you for a big reader," I say as we walk into a small room that seems to be mostly psychology books. "Especially of epic fantasy series."

He shrugs, scanning the shelves. "I like to read all kinds of things—it's sort of like acting, you know? A way to escape into someone else's life for a moment. I always like to find a bookstore in whatever city I'm in because they're a good place to hide. Usually everyone's so interested in whatever they're buying that they don't really look at you."

I snort-laugh, and he turns to look at me. "What?"

"The attention thing again. Come on. Don't act like you don't like it."

He raises his eyebrows. "I don't."

I gesture vaguely toward him. "Look at you."

"Again," he says, mimicking my gesture in a mocking way, "these rock-solid, impressive, very attractive abs are temporary."

It would be obnoxious if he wasn't smiling as he said it.

"And anyway," he says, "I'm not an actor because I want attention."

"Then why?" I ask, sliding a blue book with no wolf on the cover back onto the shelf.

"Because I like making people happy," he says, tilting his head to look at the spines of books.

"Wow," I say. "Conceited much?"

He looks up quickly and gives me a wry smile. "I don't mean that I think my mere presence on screen causes joy."

I look away, focus on the books, and wait for him to elaborate.

"When I first started acting, I was getting some roles, but mostly small ones. Like, a background character in a sitcom, or a jock in a teen movie. Stuff like that. But then my grandpa got sick, and I went home to Shreveport."

I look at him, but Drew is still looking at the books.

"I wasn't making serious money yet, and my parents both still had to work, so I quit acting for a little bit to do all the day-to-day stuff for my grandpa. It's not like anyone in Hollywood missed Asshole Jock #2. My grandpa had bone cancer, which is pretty shitty, and it was my job to make sure he was taking his meds and eating what he could. But mostly I just hung out with him. I was used to seeing him so strong—I mean, he was a veteran, and he'd worked at a steel mill—but now he was so weak. He couldn't really do anything but sit, so we watched TV. A lot of TV. Specifically, we watched all eleven seasons of *Frasier*."

I can't help it—I laugh, then cover my mouth.

Drew looks up, a smile on his face and a glint in his eyes. "No, it's okay. Please laugh. I get that a sitcom about a Seattle psychologist was a weird choice for a blue-collar Southern guy, but for some reason it's what we ended up watching."

Drew leans back on the shelf and crosses his arms. "The thing was, it helped. I mean, it didn't make anything better—he was still dying, and we both knew it—but it made us laugh. Every time Niles did something pretentious and hilarious, we could forget for a second what was happening. It was like, for twenty-one minutes at a time, things were kind of okay because we were in Frasier Crane's apartment. And that's when I knew—that's what I want to do. Take people out of their crappy realities—out of the world where their loved ones are dying or they're getting divorced or they're losing their job—even if it's only for a little while."

He lets out a small laugh. "Anyway, that was probably way more than you wanted to know about my life," he says, shaking his head.

"My parents died," I blurt out, and he meets my eyes. I nod. I've long since forgotten about looking for Tommy's book. I don't know what it is about this moment—the tiny room, the book-lined walls, the feeling that we're the only two people in this building—but I feel not only like I can share anything with Drew but also that I *should*.

"My dad died when I was a baby, before I even knew him. Sometimes I think I have memories of him, you know? But I'm only thinking of pictures I've seen, of me on his lap. My mom died when I was in high school."

I swallow and meet Drew's eyes. He's staring at me, but with an understanding that I wouldn't have expected from him before today. He nods, just slightly, encouraging me to continue.

"And even though I never knew her and my dad together, she told me all about their relationship. They had this fairy-tale romance. They were supposed to be together forever. She told me all about how he adored her, and you could see it in the pictures, the way he's looking at her like everything she's saying is the most interesting thing he's ever heard. And he died, which was terrible, but she never, ever lost her faith in love."

"That's why you love romantic comedies so much," Drew says softly, taking a small step toward me.

I nod. "They're like my version of *Frasier*. We used to watch them all the time, and now they're comfort viewing, my reminder that everything isn't awful. There's a part of me that needs to see a world where everything works out for the best, where people are together forever, or where Tom Hanks can destroy someone's business but they fall in love anyway."

Drew smiles a little bit. "You've gotta admit, that's a pretty big obstacle."

"That's what I like about it," I say, noticing that at some point in this conversation, Drew and I have become so close to each other that I have to look up to see his face. "It's not like being in love fixes everything for them, because it doesn't fix everything in real life. It just . . . makes everything bearable. Better."

"I get it," Drew says.

"You know," I continue, unable to stop myself from talking after years of never bringing up this subject, "I always thought it would've been better if she'd died slowly instead of suddenly, because then at least I'd have closure. But honestly, it kind of sounds like it sucks either way."

Drew nods. "It's all shitty—dying slowly, dying suddenly. Life's a big ball of shit sometimes."

I smile, just a little. "But there's *Frasier*."

He smiles back. "And romantic comedies."

By this point, he's so close that his breath is hot on my face. If I wanted to—not that I do—I could reach out and touch him. Not that this is even a thought in my mind, but there are mere inches between our faces. Not that this is a movie, but if it *were* a movie, it would be very easy to close this distance between us . . .

The sound of heavy breathing interrupts us as someone else shuffles into the room . . . and since this is a tiny Book Loft room, it means that someone else is basically on top of us. Drew and I stop talking and try to move out of the way as the person in a large puffy coat reaches directly in between us to pull a book off the shelf. I bite my lip, trying not to laugh, and when I meet Drew's eyes I see that he's doing the same thing.

Then my eyes catch on the book this person has just pulled off the shelf, and I yelp.

"Wait," I say. "What book is that?"

The woman eyes me suspiciously. "I saw it on *CBS This Morning*."

"Blue cover!" Drew shouts, which seems unbearably loud in this little room.

She turns to look at him in alarm.

"It's just," I say, holding out my hands, "I've been looking for that book all day, and it's really important to me, and—"

She starts to back out of the room, clearly disturbed by us. "This obviously means more to you than it does to me," she says, handing me the book before walking away.

"Yes!" I fist pump and take a good look at the wolf on the cover. "Best assistant ever."

"What is it?" Drew asks, leaning over to read the cover. *"Mate for Life: The Science Behind Animal Romance.*

"Huh," he continues. "I guess it kind of makes sense why Tommy wants Tarah's character to have that book."

As he keeps talking about how Tarah's character is researching the science of commitment and monogamy or whatever, I finally take a good look at the books on the shelf and see *The Joy of Sex. The Complete Guide to Sex Positions. The Kama Sutra.* This isn't only the psychology room; this is also the relationship and sex room, and I'm crammed into it with Drew Danforth, sharing way too many details about my personal life.

"I've gotta get this to Tommy." I bump into the shelf and knock off a book in my haste to get out of the small room.

"Okay," Drew says, confused. He bends down to pick up the book, but the room is so small that his head brushes against my shoulder and I practically shriek.

"Bye!" I shout as I jump out of the room and try to find my way through the labyrinthine halls of the Book Loft as quickly as possible. I don't know what kind of weird moment Drew and I had back there, but I have an actual job to do, and that involves getting this book to Tommy. I don't have time to think about Drew Danforth, his surprisingly good listening skills, or his out-of-character love for a Kelsey Grammer sitcom.

Chapter Eleven

THE NEXT NIGHT, AFTER NICK'S HAS CLOSED AND I'M DONE ON SET, Chloe comes over and shares the couch with me for movie night. Since our house is lacking that all-important "open concept," I can't see Uncle Don, but I can hear him puttering around in the kitchen.

This is maybe one of the best ways to spend an evening: on my couch, knowing that the two people I love most in the world are safe and sound right here with me.

"I know you love it, but I honestly don't think I can watch *While You Were Sleeping* again," Chloe says, flipping through a magazine as I scroll through Netflix. "I find Peter Gallagher's eyebrows extremely distracting."

"Yeah," I say, "but you've gotta admit, Bill Pullman is pretty hot in that movie."

She looks up for a moment. "I don't *gotta admit* anything. He wears a reversible denim jacket."

"And it's a good look for him," I say. "What about *The Wedding Singer*? It was the last time Adam Sandler played a convincingly sweet romantic lead."

Chloe wrinkles her nose. "I'm pretty sure I have that one memorized. I can't hear Madonna's 'Holiday' without thinking of his character's breakdown."

"Oh! I know!" I say, switching over to the Hallmark app. "What about a Hallmark movie? In this one, a woman owns a pumpkin patch. Or in this one, the guy owns a Christmas tree farm."

Chloe puts down her magazine. "No! How many quirky farms can these people even own?"

"*Never Been Kissed*?"

"Creepy."

"*Groundhog Day*?"

"Too many vests."

"But it's one of the few winter rom-coms that doesn't take place at Christmas," I protest.

Unimpressed, Chloe rolls her eyes. "These are some really white and straight movies, Annie."

"I know," I say. "You're right. But Drew says that's why Tommy wanted to make an interracial rom-com so much, even though it's a way smaller movie than the stuff he's been doing lately."

Uncle Don walks in with a plate of cookies, and Chloe takes advantage of my distraction to grab the remote and start scrolling, muttering about how she's going to make me watch some documentary about serial killers.

"Are these the cookies?" I ask.

Uncle Don nods. "The cookies, indeed."

My mom always made these chocolate chip cookies with pumpkin in them, which sounds weird but is actually wonderful. The pumpkin doesn't add flavor so much as moisture, and the cookies turn out super soft and fluffy. They're the best chocolate chip cookies I've ever had (besides Chloe's, obviously), and right now, watching a movie on the couch and eating them, I can kind of pretend things are the way they used to be. The way they're supposed to be.

"You think I should bring a batch of these to the convention?" Uncle Don says. "I wonder if Tyler would like them."

I have no idea why Uncle Don cares so much if some dude thinks he makes good cookies, but I nod with my mouth full.

Uncle Don walks back into the kitchen, and Chloe, still scrolling, asks, "Do you think Don's into this Tyler guy?"

I think about it for a second. "I mean, anything's possible. I don't think he's ever dated *anyone*, but I don't know. I've seen his copies of *Heavy Metal* and there are a lot of illustrated boobs in that magazine for a gay man."

Chloe rolls her eyes and points to herself. "Bisexuals exist, Annie. We walk among you."

"I'm aware," I say, kicking her. "But I don't know, I think he would tell me. I mean, he hangs out with a gay couple every week for D&D."

But now that Chloe brought it up, I realize that I know almost nothing about Uncle Don's personal life. The only time I see him interact with people is at D&D, and I'm fairly certain he's not dating Dungeon Master Rick, since Dungeon Master Rick is married. All this time I've assumed he doesn't have a romantic life at all, but what if he does and he's not telling me?

"Anyway," Chloe says lightly, taking a bite of a cookie, "don't think I didn't notice what you said before Don walked in."

"What?" I ask with my mouth full.

"Drew said," she says in a falsetto that I think is supposed to be me, fluttering her eyelashes. "Since when are you having movie conversations with Drew?"

"I'm not having movie conversations with Drew," I say. "But we work at the same place. Sometimes we talk."

I don't mention that one of those conversations was about our pasts and took place in a small room next to some particularly racy books.

Chloe narrows her eyes. "You're such a bad liar."

I focus on my cookie. "Drew is a movie star, and I barely know him. He has also, on numerous occasions, made fun of me. And he was quite uncharitable toward Barry."

"Oh." Chloe swats at my leg. "Don't act like you're concerned about defending Barry. Nick claims he stole a roll of toilet paper."

I sigh. I don't want to explain to Chloe that yes, Drew was surprisingly nice the last time we hung out, and it felt like there was something in the air in that tiny, book-filled room. Just because I'm a rom-com fanatic doesn't mean I'm that unrealistic.

"I think he's your Tom Hanks," Chloe says with conviction.

"He isn't," I say flatly. "He's famous. He's rich. He's used to dating other famous, rich people and he doesn't take anything seriously. Tom Hanks always takes everything seriously, especially relationships."

"Yeah," Chloe says, pointing at me with the remote. "But maybe this is like *Roman Holiday*. He's the Audrey Hepburn princess, and you're the Gregory Peck journalist, and you're gonna totally end up together forever."

"When's the last time you saw *Roman Holiday*, Chlo? They don't end up together."

"Wait, what?" Chloe asks, sitting up straighter.

I shake my head. "She's a princess; she has obligations. In that last scene, at the press conference, she walks away, and he's left there alone. That's it."

Chloe sits back. "Damn. That's kinda bleak."

I nod. "I know."

"But maybe—" she starts, but I cut her off.

"He's not my Tom Hanks, okay? Maybe my Tom Hanks is a cutthroat businessman, or maybe he's on a houseboat, but he's definitely not a movie star who's going to jet out of Columbus as soon as he possibly can."

"But that's your obstacle!" Chloe says.

"Chloe."

"One last thing: love conquers all." She sits back and folds her hands. "I'm done."

"You don't believe that."

"Not even a little. But look! I picked out something for us to watch!"

I glance at the screen and barely stop myself from doing a double take. "Is this *Frasier*?"

"I know, I know, it's kinda corny, but I caught a rerun the last time I was home in the afternoon and honestly, I laughed a lot. And there's a dog, which is always a good thing. Plus, sitcoms are basically right below rom-coms on the 'comforting entertainment' scale."

"Yeah, okay, sure," I say softly as she presses play and the credits begin. But I can't even focus because, if this was a rom-com, I'm pretty sure this would be a sign.

The next morning on set, I'm trying to find Tommy while holding yet another scalding cup of coffee for him when I hear someone behind me.

"Hey."

I spin around and find myself face-to-face with Carter Reid, he of the blue eyes and the slightly curly hair and the nicely aging face.

"I'm sorry for what I said about the wires," I say in lieu of hello.

"I'm not here about the wires," he says. "The wires have very thick skins. They're not offended."

"That's a relief," I say, wondering what he could possibly want to talk to me about. What do we have besides the wires? The wires brought us together.

"So, this might be weird, but my therapist tells me I'm supposed to be putting myself out there when the opportunity arises, and meeting you seemed like an opportunity, so . . . would you like to get coffee some time?"

I take a step back and bump into someone, narrowly avoiding spilling the coffee on myself. "What?"

Carter exhales. "Did I do that wrong? It's been a really, really long time since I asked someone out. Should I have used . . . an app? Is that what people do now?"

I try to hide my smile, but I can't help myself. "No. Um . . . this is great. What you did is great. Let's get coffee."

His face breaks into a smile. "How about that place down the street? Nick's? Are you free tonight?"

Wait, am I seriously, after years of rarely going out on coffee dates or any other kind of dates, going to have two dates at Nick's in one week?

Carter misinterprets the shock on my face and stammers, "I—I mean . . . wait, is tonight way too soon? Did I make things super weird?"

"Tonight is great," I say. "And Nick's is perfect. Can I ask you a question?"

He raises his eyebrows in response.

"Do you . . . drink hot liquids?"

Carter looks at me for a moment without saying anything.

"I'm gonna need an answer," I say quietly. "It's been an issue before."

"Yes?" he answers, looking confused.

I exhale in relief. "Great. I'll see you tonight at Nick's. Eight?"

"Wait," Carter says. "While we're getting all our issues out on the table, I should tell you that I have a kid."

"Is he . . . going to be there?" I ask, imagining a baby in a high chair, kicking the table and knocking over my latte.

Carter laughs. "No. He's thirteen, so he's perfectly capable of entertaining himself if I'm gone for a couple of hours. But, you know, kids are a deal breaker for some people. I wanted to get it all out in the open."

I shake my head, thinking about sad, perfect Tom Hanks in that houseboat in *Sleepless in Seattle*, all alone with his precocious and hilarious child. And then I think about cocky, perfect Tom Hanks in *You've Got Mail*, taking his father's son and his grandfather's daughter to that carnival in New York and, again, being on a boat.

Truly, is there anything more romantic than Tom Hanks on a boat?

"No," I tell Carter, a man who I'm starting to think might actually be a character created by Nora Ephron herself and sent here to me. "Kids aren't a deal breaker for me."

"That's good." He smiles, then someone behind him yells his name. "Gotta get back to work. See you tonight, Annie."

Chloe almost drops the coffee she's holding when I tell her I'm going on a date.

"For goodness sake, Annie! You almost made me pull a Tobin!" she says, eyes wide.

"Hey. I heard that, and I don't appreciate it," Tobin says from his post, leaning against the counter and doing nothing.

"I just . . . I can't believe you did this without me, all on your own!" Chloe says, handing the coffee to a customer. "I'm *proud*. Is this what it's like to be a parent?"

"Yes," Gary says from his table, where he's reading the newspaper. "That's exactly what it's like. You're always proud of them when they accomplish something big."

"I didn't know you had children, Gary," I say.

"I have three ferrets," he says with a smile, and you know what? He *does* look proud.

Chloe widens her eyes at me briefly, then takes off her apron. "Nick, I'm taking my break!"

"You just took a break," Nick calls from the back.

"Tobin can handle it," Chloe says, coming out from behind the counter. She gestures to my usual table. "Come, sit. Tell me literally everything, in excruciating detail."

"First off, I don't get how we didn't know Gary had ferrets already. That kind of seems like something he would've mentioned," I say, sitting down.

"If you think I want to talk about Gary's ferrets right now, then you're being deliberately obtuse," Chloe says. "Spill the beans, woman."

I run through the entire story, and Chloe squeals at all the appropriate parts. "And get this . . . he has a kid," I say, leaning forward.

Chloe tilts her head, like maybe she didn't hear me. "Okay?"

"A kid, Chloe."

She continues to stare blankly.

"Like. Tom. Hanks."

"There it is," she mutters. "I thought this was maybe a step forward for you. Like, sure, you're not throwing yourself at the super-hot movie star who comes in here almost every day—"

"Drew comes in here every day?" I ask, but she keeps going.

"Even though your refusal to do so is basically an insult to me, your best friend, who would love nothing more than to hear a secondhand account of what those abs really look like in person—"

I purse my lips.

"But I thought that maybe accepting a date with an apparently hot, just-slightly-older man meant that you were committing to life here in the real world, where our interactions don't consist of banter written by Nora Ephron. However, I see now that I was wrong."

"Could you please stop talking like this? Like you're narrating a podcast about my life?"

"Hon," Chloe says. "No one's going to make a podcast about your life unless you murder someone or *get* murdered by someone. And even then, the bar is pretty high these days."

I ignore her and say, "He said he asked me out because his therapist told him to take chances. *His therapist.* This is a guy who's in touch with his feelings, like Tom Hanks in *Sleepless in Seattle.*"

"Big whoop!" Chloe says, throwing her hands in the air. "Everyone's in therapy. Gary's in therapy. That doesn't mean you need to date Gary."

"You girls know I'm happy with Martha," Gary says from across the room. I wave at him.

"Chloe," Nick says, palms on the counter. "Planning on getting back to work at any point?"

She smiles and faux-sweetly says, "Yes, sir!" then turns to me.

"Listen, babe. All I'm saying is that you need to remember this kid he has is a person, not a plot device, okay?"

"I know that."

"Do you?" She gets up and heads back to the counter. She shakes Tobin by the shoulders. "Dude. Were you asleep?"

"I was meditating," Tobin says groggily.

"Go meditate in the kitchen while you wash the forks," Chloe says.

I sigh. "Hey, did I mention that our date is tonight? Here?"

Chloe leans over the counter. "So I get to see Mysterious Hot Blue-Eyed Older Man in the flesh, hmmm?"

"Stop saying *flesh* like that. It sounds . . . lascivious."

"Good, because that's how I meant it."

"I'm looking forward to meeting your new fella," Gary says, stopping by my table.

"He's not . . . this is our first date, Gary."

Gary adjusts his hat. "But you never know what might happen."

That's what I'm afraid of, I think as Gary walks through the front door and I'm hit with a gust of cold air.

I choose a tight dress for my date. It's perhaps too tight, but Carter primarily sees me in a puffy jacket, and I'd like to remind him that I do, in fact, have a body underneath my several layers of insulation. I don't even know why I own this black dress with a neckline that's entirely too low, but it's probably a leftover from college, when Chloe and I had friends who liked to sometimes "go out," which entailed going to some weird bar with a smoke machine and dance remixes that only served to make already terrible songs even more terrible.

"Uncle Don! I'm leaving!" I call as I run down the stairs. I don't want to pull a Barry and be late to this date. For starters because it's rude, but also because I don't want to disappoint Carter. I mean, he already sees me as a girl who drops a bunch of papers all over a snow-covered street—I don't want him to think I'm a *complete* hot mess.

Although, I think as I look at myself in the hall mirror, I wouldn't mind him thinking I'm hot. I tug the neckline up a little bit.

"Whoa," Uncle Don says, stepping out of the kitchen. "Add some ears in and you're halfway to a pretty good Catwoman cosplay."

I should go change, but I'm almost running late, so I don't.

I'm grateful that my walk to the coffee shop is short, because my sheer black tights do almost nothing to insulate my legs against the cold as I carefully maneuver the brick sidewalks in my heeled booties. "I should've worn something else," I mutter as I walk-run to the coffee shop.

When I get there, I pause for a moment to check my reflection in the window, but then, through the glass, I see him. Drew. Sitting at that same table in the back, the one he was at during my disastrous date with Barry, and for a moment I forget that I'm not meeting him. For one tiny little moment, I let myself imagine that I am. That I'm rushing here in the only sexy article of clothing I own to meet Drew Danforth. I'd walk over to the table and he'd stand up and kiss me, casually, because of course in this scenario we kiss all the time so we don't need to flaunt our PDA in the middle of Nick's. And we would argue about rom-coms and everything else, but it would be fun and invigorating and not annoying, not even a little bit. And we'd eat whatever Chloe baked, and he'd love it and then, I don't know, we'd probably go back to his place and watch something on Netflix before having totally amazing sex.

A blush creeps over my cheeks as I realize that my fantasy about dating Drew Danforth, a man I find extremely infuriating, is far too detailed. And then, as if he can feel me watching him, he looks up. With that ridiculous cocky smile of his, he waves, and that's what makes me finally remember that I'm standing in front of a coffee shop window, staring like a creep, fogging up the glass with my breath after imagining having sex with a literal movie star. Oh yeah, and I'm about to go on a date with a real person, one who has emotions and also a human child.

I shake my head and walk inside.

"Decide to give Barry another chance?" Drew asks, because of course I walk straight to him, like he's a fridge and I'm a free magnet from a local health clinic.

"No," I say, standing beside his table. "Not that it's any of your business, but I'm meeting someone else. Someone who drinks hot liquids."

Drew's eyes widen. "A high bar to clear. Who is this mystery man?"

"You might know him, actually. He works on lighting for the movie. Carter Reid?"

Drew sits up straighter. "Wait—that guy? The gaffer?"

"That guy, indeed."

Drew looks distraught for some reason, but then I notice him staring at the revealing neckline of my dress. "Uh, hello. My eyes are up here. Stop staring at my boobs."

Drew's eyes shoot to mine. "I'm not staring at your boobs. I was staring into space."

"A space that my boobs happen to occupy. Convenient."

Now, Drew looks me in the eyes. "You're only a face to me now. Just a disembodied head. You might as well not even have boobs, or a torso for that matter. That's how little I notice the rest of you."

I sigh and stare back at him, but the moment starts to turn thick and heavy, the two of us staring at each other while a song by the National plays (on Nick's playlist, not Chloe's, clearly).

"I'm getting a table," I say, because I don't want Carter to walk in here and see Drew and me playing some sort of weird and unsettling staring game.

"Have a nice date," Drew says, but I don't turn around as I walk to my table.

Carter shows up right on time. Of course, he does. So would Tom Hanks.

Like many of the crewmembers, he lives here in town, so unlike certain movie stars I could name, he understands why Columbus is one of the best cities in the country. He's kind and considerate, he buys me a drink right away, and he even gets one of Chloe's tri-citrus bars for us to split.

"It's orange, lemon, and grapefruit," I say, pointing to the bar with my fork. "Chloe wanted to mix up the traditional lemon bar."

Carter smiles. "It's great. You guys seem like you're really good friends."

"Best friends," I say, beaming. "What are your friends like?"

He winces. "Working so much and having a kid doesn't leave a lot of time for friendships, you know? It sucks, but most of them have fallen by the wayside."

He takes another bite. "That probably makes me seem like an asocial loser, right?"

I shake my head and swallow. "Not at all. Lots of men have a hard time maintaining friendships. I mean, that's the entire point of the movie *I Love You, Man*."

Carter smiles. "Well, that and showcasing Paul Rudd's agelessness."

I exhale in relief. He knows rom-coms. Well, one rom-com. One extremely accessible, dude-oriented rom-com, but still, I'll take it.

"So," I say, wiping my mouth with a napkin. "What do you do on the rare occasion that you're not working?"

Carter shrugs. "Nothing all that exciting. My son is absurdly interested in monster trucks, something I never in my life imagined I'd have to know about, so we spend a lot of time going to rallies . . ."

I smile, imagining this rugged, attentive man taking a small child to a monster truck rally. It's sweet.

"And I always love to get up to the lake. We have a place up there—well, I don't want to mislead you. It's not a beach house so much as it's a small houseboat."

My mouth goes dry, and I quickly take a drink of my coffee. "A small . . . what?"

"A houseboat?" He looks at me as if it's possible I've never heard of the concept. "You know . . . a house on a boat? Like the movie *Houseboat*? Sort of like an RV on the water?"

"No, I'm familiar," I say, perhaps too loudly. "Could you hold on a second? I'm going to get a second coffee."

My coffee is still halfway full, but I book it to the counter all the same. "Chloe!" I hiss.

She closes the baked-goods case and gives me a concerned look. "What's happening? Is this a repeat Barry situation? Do I need to fake an emergency call or something?"

"Carter. Has. A. Houseboat," I whisper, leaning over the counter.

Chloe walks closer to me and leans forward so our heads are practically touching. "What?"

"A houseboat."

Chloe shuts her eyes and sighs. "Oh no."

Someone clears their throat behind me. "I thought I'd find you here."

Chloe and I look toward the sound of that voice, and I stand up straight in disbelief.

"Barry?" I ask. "Why . . . what . . . how . . ."

"Why are you here, dude?" Chloe asks, leaning on one arm on the counter.

"We've gotta stop playing this game," Barry says, gesturing between him and me. "You and me, Annie."

I blink a few times. "I was unaware we were playing a game."

He tilts his head and gives me a smile, like this is another part of our so-called game. "You know. You acting like there's no connection between us? Like we're not meant to be?"

I look at Chloe for help, but she's staring at Barry with her mouth open.

"Barry," I say, looking right into his eyes. "I want to be as gentle but as firm as possible: I can say with complete certainty that we're not meant to be."

"You don't really think that," he says, leaning forward to grab my hands, which I instantly pull back.

"We just . . . have a lot of differences," I say. "I love coffee. And water with fluoride in it. And . . . not eating bagels out of the dumpster."

"I don't even have to keep eating the dumpster bagels!" he says, his voice growing loud enough that several people, including Carter, look over. Carter gives me a look that manages to instantly communicate, "Uh, do I need to come over there?" but I shake my head.

"It's more than dumpster bagels," I say. "We just don't have a connection, and that's okay. I know there's someone out there for you, someone who likes you the way you are."

Barry sighs, then turns to Chloe. "Are you free—"

"No," Chloe says, wiping off the counter without looking at him.

"Well then," Barry says, giving me a resigned look. "You can't say I didn't try."

"I certainly can't," I say with a small smile. "Good luck, Barry."

We watch him walk out of Nick's, the bell ringing as the door swings open and closed, and I can't help feeling a little bit sorry for him. I mean, this sucks, this whole "search for a soulmate" thing. Sure, Barry was . . . well, Barry, but that doesn't mean he deserves to be lonely. I hope he does find someone, and I also hope he expands his beverage choices.

"I'll take another coffee, please. And, uh, another one of those citrus bars."

I turn to see Drew standing right beside me, not looking at me at all. I wonder if it's an intentional not looking at me or a completely unintentional "wow-I-genuinely-care-so-little-about-you-that-I-didn't-even-notice-you-there" not looking at me. Not that I would care if it were the latter, because I'm on a date with a very hot, slightly older houseboat owner.

"What do you think?" Chloe asks, and at first I think she's talking to me, but then I realize she's asking Drew about the bars. "Is it one citrus too many?"

"Not at all," Drew says. "I could, and possibly will, eat an entire tray of these bad boys."

Chloe stands up straight and smiles so hard she's practically radiating joy. How nice and not at all annoying that Drew Danforth has found the way to her heart: compliments about her baked goods.

"Not too sour?" she asks, watching as he takes a bite.

"Absolutely perfect," he says, then turns to me. "So, Barry, huh?"

"Leave me alone," I say. "Barry's trying to find a connection in a cruel world."

Drew shrugs. "It can't all be citrus bars and dates with sexy gaffers."

"Would that it could," Chloe says with a sigh, and both of us look at her. She looks startled. "Wait, I forgot that I have to do a thing in the kitchen. Bye."

"Leave my sexy gaffer alone," I say, then shake my head. "I mean, he's not *my* sexy gaffer; he's just a man. A man I'm on a date with. And I don't need you here messing everything up."

"How could my mere presence, tables away from you, be messing everything up?" Drew asks. "Unless you're distracted by me."

I blink. "Why would I . . . why would I be distracted by you?"

I guess I understood emotionally that Drew and I had some sort of annoying, angry chemistry thing going on, but I thought we were keeping that unspoken on account of he's a hot movie star and I'm a weird Ohio freelance writer and never the twain shall meet. I didn't know we were just saying it now, that he assumes I'm, like, head over high-heeled booties for him and I'm going to fall into his arms just because we had a weird moment in the Book Loft. Probably lots of people experience sexual tension in the Book Loft. It's a confined space, and there are a lot of pheromones floating around in there. It's not like it means anything.

Anyway, it's infuriating that he thinks I would want to be sitting with him instead of Sexy Gaffer, I mean Carter. Yes, I did have a sexual fantasy about him before I walked in here and yes, it is currently causing my face and other unnamed body parts to heat up, but he doesn't know about that and he never will.

"Carter and I were talking about romantic comedies," I practically spit. "He's seen *I Love You, Man*."

"Big deal," Drew says with an unconcerned smile. "Every man

who's ever had a crush on Rashida Jones has seen that movie, and FYI, that's ninety-five percent of straight men. And that's not even considering the men who also have a crush, friend or otherwise, on Paul Rudd."

I stare at him, my mouth in a hard line.

"Does that guy even age?" Drew asks, taking a sip of his coffee. "And anyway, I know rom-coms, too. I saw *When Harry Met Sally . . .*"

I stiffen. "And?"

Drew leans forward. "They were terrible for each other and they definitely get divorced years later and ruin their child's life with the bickering."

"You take that back!" I say a little too loudly, then turn to see if Carter noticed. He did, and he's giving me that "do I need to come help?" look for the second time with a second man. I shake my head and turn back to Drew.

"I have a date, so if you'll excuse me."

"I wasn't keeping you here," Drew says, eyebrows raised. "Just take that invisible body back on over to your table with Sexy Gaffer. See if I care."

"What?"

Drew draws a line across his neck. "I'm not seeing anything below your chin."

"Ugh," I mutter, then walk back to my table. I slide into the seat and force a smile onto my face. "Sorry about that."

Carter furrows his brow, opens and closes his mouth a few times like he's unsure what to say, then finally settles on, "Is it always like that for you in here?"

"What do you mean?" I ask. I go to take a sip, then realize that in all the hubbub, I didn't even get another coffee.

He gestures vaguely toward the counter. "You know. Various men fighting for your affections."

"Oh." I chuckle. "Barry. He's, uh . . . he's not exactly a threat. I mean, he's sweet, but . . . you know what? He's not even sweet. I went on one bad date with him."

"Not just Barry, though." Carter meets my eyes, then says casually, "Mr. Movie Star's got a thing for you."

My heart speeds up of its own accord. *Slow your roll, heart.* "What?"

He nods toward Drew's table in the corner. "The man's hitting on you, Annie."

I shake my head and sputter, "He's not . . . he's . . . he's making fun of me and being kind of a jerk, but he's not hitting on me."

Carter squints. "I think that might be his own weird way of hitting on you?"

I keep shaking my head, as if that will make everything he said go away. Against my better judgment, I turn to look at Drew, who's sitting at his corner table and reading a newspaper—a newspaper, instead of reading his news on his phone like every other human being in the world. The edges of his lips slightly crook up at the edges, leading me to believe that he's all too aware I'm watching him.

"No," I say, turning back around to face Carter. "Not possible."

"This is not a question I thought I'd have to ask, but since I've been totally honest with you so far, I'm gonna go ahead and ask it." Carter leans forward. "Do you and the star of our movie, Drew Danforth, have something going on?"

I smile. "No. I can emphatically say that we do not. We went to McDonald's once because Tommy made us, and that's the extent of it. I am a hundred percent mentally, emotionally, and physically present here on this coffee date with you."

Carter smiles. "Good. Because I'm having a good time, despite the fact that multiple men have apparently challenged me for your affections."

"Most of the time it's not like that for me. Most of the time I'm watching Netflix at home in my pajamas." I cringe. "I didn't mean to make myself sound pathetic."

Carter laughs that deep, throaty laugh again, the one that makes me feel like I'm curled up in front of a fire. "Trust me, nothing you say could make you sound pathetic to me."

I smile. "I'm having a good time, too, by the way."

And I mean it when I say it, and I don't even spend the rest of the night aware of Drew Danforth in the corner behind me, reading the paper with that infuriating smile on those infuriating lips.

I'm not a huge texter. Sometimes Uncle Don and I text each other reminders of what to pick up at the grocery store, or Chloe texts me about weird things Nick says, or one of my friends from college reminds me about an inside joke that feels a million years away now. But texting, with its unromantic immediacy, has never been my preferred form of communication.

So that's why I'm extra surprised when I get a text from an unknown number, and it isn't a reminder about a sale at Loft or a coupon for a pizza or yet another overdue book notice from the library. It's also not Carter, although of course he sent me a considerate follow-up text after our date to make sure I got home okay and let me know he had a good time. It's from a reporter at Hollywood Gossip.

> Hi, this is Steve at Hollywood Gossip. Could you comment on your recent sightings with Drew Danforth? Thanks ☺

It's the emoji that really puts it over the edge. What is it about strange men that they think they need to add emojis to their texts? I don't know this man; I don't know how to interpret his emoji usage! I've never talked to him, and he's assuming I'm going to send him personal details because he included a smiley face?

Another text pops up.

Of course, we do pay.

Wait, I'm supposed to share details about Drew for money? I laugh as I think about texting this guy Drew's McDonald's order. Probably not the hot dish he was expecting.

But what this means is that a) someone saw us together, b) someone presumably took a picture, and c) someone identified me. And gave this reporter my number. It's kind of messed up.

I ignore the text, obviously, but not before I get another text . . . this time, from Chloe.

Have you checked Hollywood Gossip today?

I don't know why she's phrasing it like that. Other than my shameful researching-Drew binge, I don't make a habit of reading gossip websites, and to the best of my knowledge, neither does she. Still, I pull up the page and see . . .

A photo of me.

Well, it's not just me. It's Drew and me sitting in our McDonald's booth. One of those phone-wielding teenagers must have snapped our picture and sent it in.

"Damn those youths!" I mutter, then feel approximately one million years old.

There are only a few pictures, most of them kind of blurry, clearly taken by a kid who was startled to see a movie star inside a fast-food place. There's one where I'm unflatteringly shoving a French fry in my mouth, which I don't appreciate, but you can only see the sides of our faces, so I can't complain that much. But it's the caption that really gets to me.

Even Hollywood stars need fast food once in a while! Drew Danforth relaxes with local girl Annie Cassidy in Columbus on the set of the new Tommy Crisante film. Is he finally moving on from Gillian? Let's hope so!

How do they know my name? Possibilities spin through my mind. Did Drew tell them? Does he have some sort of Kardashian-like setup where he leaks stuff to the tabloids? What's going on?

I don't know, but I intend to find out. Before closing the site, I take one more look at the pictures. There's a reason people don't do professional photo shoots in McDonald's—that overhead lighting is far from flattering—but I zoom in on Drew's face. He's grinning at me, looking genuinely happy, his eyes on my face. I think of those old pictures of my mom and dad, the ones where he's looking at her like she's the most wonderful woman on the planet. In fact, if you didn't know Drew was an actor who gets paid to look at women like this, you might even think there was something be-tween us.

It's impossible to talk to Drew on set that morning, which isn't sur-prising since he spends all his time either acting or hiding, and anyway Tommy sends me on about fifteen coffee runs.

"Our little internet star!" Chloe says as she hands me yet an-other black coffee.

"How has this guy not combusted yet?" Nick asks. "Is it pos-sible to OD on caffeine?"

"Once I drank five espressos in a row," Tobin says. "All that happened was I finished a paper and then barfed."

"Good to know, Tobin," Chloe says with a grimace. "Have you asked Drew about the picture yet?"

I shake my head. "I haven't been able to talk to him. I don't know what the deal is or how that picture got on Hollywood Gossip."

Chloe shrugs.

"Wait a second," Tobin asks. "Are you guys talking about Steve from Hollywood Gossip?"

Chloe and I both whip around to stare at him. Nick ignores us all.

"Yes," I say slowly. There's absolutely no way Tobin reads Hollywood Gossip because the only famous people he ever talks about are professional skateboarders. "How do you know about this?"

"Okay, so some guy called here?" Tobin says, his eyes darting between us like he's not sure what's happening. "And I guess he knew Drew Danforth came here sometimes? And he asked if I knew who he went to McDonald's with?"

"You didn't," I whisper.

"So I was like, sure, her name's Annie Cassidy and then he asked what your job was, but . . . I couldn't remember." Tobin shrugs.

"Tobin," Nick says. "If you're responsible for some gross dudes with cameras coming in here and harassing Annie and also peeing on the toilet seats—"

"Did I do something wrong? You guys talk about Annie's life all the time, and you're *really* loud," Tobin says. "I didn't know it was, like, confidential or whatever."

I'm annoyed, but being mean to Tobin is like rubbing a puppy's nose in the carpet it peed on.

I sigh. "It's okay, Tobin. Just . . . don't give random callers in-formation about me anymore, okay?"

Chloe wipes off the counter. "That really shouldn't have to be said."

Tobin still looks troubled, and I'm worried the stress might cause him to drop even more cups than usual, so I say, "Really, Tobin, it's fine. But if that guy calls again, hang up."

Tobin nods, then drops the latte he's holding, and then I head back to set.

Chapter Twelve

I HAND TOMMY HIS COFFEE AND I'M ABOUT TO GO GRAB A PROP HE asked for when I hear someone yell, "Hey!"

I turn around to see a woman I've noticed on set before but haven't met. "Me?" I ask, pointing to myself.

She nods. "Do you wear a size eight shoe?"

I look down at my feet and back at her. "How did you know that?"

She keeps her eyes on my feet, like she's studying them. "I've been working in wardrobe for fifteen years. I can guess all your measurements just by looking at you. You're a thirty-six B."

I cross my arms over my chest and my puffy coat. She *is* good.

She waves me over, finally meeting my eyes. "I'm Angela, by the way. I'm trying to see if these heels will work for Tarah's scenes tomorrow, but she's busy rehearsing. Can you try them on for me?"

I look over my shoulder to see Tommy talking to Brody and Drew about something. Brody is eating, again, and Drew is nodding intently, his eyes completely focused on Tommy—

"Well?" Angela asks. "Can you?"

I snap to attention. "Yeah, sure."

I pull off my boots and the thick socks I typically wear from November through March and slide my feet into a pair of red heels that have to be at least five inches tall. Even when it's not winter, I'm more of a flats girl, so wearing these makes me feel a bit like I'm swaying in the breeze.

"Hmmm," says Angela, still staring at my feet. "Could you take a few steps?"

"Uh . . ." I say, starting to walk, but it's difficult since I'm basically on stilts. I balance on my tiptoes as I walk across the bricks and—

"Crap!" I shout as my heel gets stuck between bricks and I topple to the side, my ankle twisting violently.

"Are you okay?" Angela shrieks, leaping to my side.

"I'm fine, I'm fine," I mutter. I try to stand up, but a sharp pain shoots through my calf and I buckle back down. "Maybe I'm not fine."

I look up and see that everyone is now crowded around me—Tommy, Drew, and Brody have abandoned their conversation to stand over me. Brody, however, has not abandoned his burrito, and a black bean falls on my head.

"Sorry," he says as Drew shoots him a dirty look.

"Annie!" Tommy shouts, as if I've injured my eardrum instead of my foot. "Are you all right?"

Carter appears (seriously, it's like I'm in a dream but also a hospital bed, all these good-looking men and Tommy floating above me) and kneels down. "Are you okay?"

"People keep asking that. I just twisted my ankle," I say, sliding my feet out of the heels before attempting to stand up again. This time I make it up, but I wince a little too obviously the second I put weight on my left foot.

"I'm taking you home," Carter says, placing a guiding hand on my back.

"I can't go home," I say, despite the fact that a man saying, "I'm taking you home" makes tingles run through my body, even though in a fantasy situation he'd be saying it for much sexier reasons and not because I injured myself in a particularly treacherous pair of shoes.

"We're almost done for the day anyway," Tommy says, waving a hand at me. "You go on home, put your feet up, see how you feel tomorrow."

Heat flows to my cheeks as I realize that everyone's staring at me, the little injured girl. This is my job—the one shot I have to work on a movie—and I'm not throwing it away because I fell down.

"I can stay," I say quickly. "It's not even that bad. I—"

"Annie," Tommy says, leaning forward to look me in the eyes. "I don't run the kind of sets where people have to walk around injured, okay? Go home, tell Donny to make you some soup, come back tomorrow."

His kindness almost brings a tear to my eye. "Okay," I say, then sit down in a chair Drew dragged over so I can put my socks and boots back on.

"You sure bit it, huh?" Brody asks, his mouth full.

"I sure did," I say as I slide on my boots, trying to avoid touching my ankle as much as possible. "If you're sure it's okay, Tommy, I'll head home."

"I can take her," Drew says, looking at Tommy and then me. "I've got her."

I stare at him slack-jawed, then close my mouth. Carter's hands are on my body (again, in a completely helpful and nonsexual way, but still), so you'd think Drew could see I don't need his help whatsoever.

"I've got it, man," Carter says with a tight smile.

"I'm not even in this scene," Drew says, taking another step toward me. "Whereas every scene of this movie needs proper lighting. Seriously. It's fine."

"*Seriously,* I've got it—" Carter starts, and then someone calls his name. He looks over his shoulder and groans.

"I'm fine, everyone," I say, addressing the small crowd that's rapidly dispersing. "I just have to . . . walk it off. It's only a couple of blocks." I attempt to take a step on my own and almost fall down.

"I'm not letting my assistant fall into some shrubbery because she's injured," Tommy says. "Carter, I need you here on set. Drew, make sure Annie gets home."

"You want me to order a Lyft?" Brody asks, but before he even has the question out, Drew's lifted me up.

"Excuse me!" I shriek. "What are you doing?"

"Walking you home," he says with more of a grunt than I think is absolutely necessary. "What's the point of having all these muscles if I never get to use them?"

"Oh, my God," I mutter as we walk past everyone on set, all of them staring at us. I look over Drew's shoulder at Carter and mouth, "Sorry!" as I wave. He gives me that raised-hand dude wave, a look on his face that I can't entirely decipher.

But I find it very hard to worry about Carter when I think about where I am: in Drew's capable arms.

"Wave to the people, Annie," Drew says. "Your loyal subjects await your greetings."

I groan but offer up a weak wave.

I tell Drew to keep walking down the street to get to my house, and I wonder if the German Village residents are going to be confused that a guy is carrying a woman down the sidewalk. But then the Coatless Wonder walks by, and I remember that we see weirder stuff than this most days.

Drew turns his head to watch the Coatless Wonder walk away. "Is that guy not cold? It's, like, twenty-five degrees out here."

"Hey," I say, changing the subject, because Drew's carrying me like a particularly large baby and/or sack of potatoes and it's making me feel a little awkward to have his hand so close to my butt. "Did you know there's a picture of us on a gossip website?"

Drew frowns, and since he's holding me inches from his face, I see every single line that frown creates around his mouth. The way his eyelashes curl a little more than you'd expect. The way his cheeks flush pink from the cold. The way his bottom lip sticks out when he's thinking . . .

"I don't ever look at them. What was it?"

He looks at me, our faces so close that the eye contact is uncomfortably intimate. I look at his coat as I answer. "It was some pictures of us at McDonald's. They knew my name—I guess they called Nick's and one of his employees, Tobin, didn't know he shouldn't tell them who I was."

Drew grimaces. "That happens a lot. They'll have a 'source' who claims to be very close to you, and then it turns out the 'source' is someone you went to high school with who you maybe sat beside in English once."

"It's weird knowing my picture and my name are out there for anyone to look at," I say. Swaying in Drew's strong and secure grip, I could probably go to sleep right this moment. "Do you get used to it?"

"Never," he says, so serious that I wonder how those pictures of him and his grandpa ended up online.

"I saw a picture of you and your grandpa," I say before I can think about how weird it sounds to admit that. But then again, he did see me googling him, so he already knows I'm a big creep.

I wince. "I mean, I know it was crappy of me to look you up, but I did, and I saw the picture and—"

Drew's chest vibrates as he groans. "Yeah. That picture. I can't even tell you how much I wish that wasn't out there."

"Then why is it?" I ask. "Turn left here."

Drew sighs, and the air from his mouth hits me right in the face. "Kind of a long story, but I was dating someone a while ago, and we had . . . I guess you could say different priorities. I liked my privacy, and she was always thinking about how she could spin stories from our personal lives into an interesting angle for *People* magazine."

I don't know for sure, but he must be talking about Gillian Roberts.

"She'd never met my grandpa, since he died before we got together, so I told her about him and showed her that picture. For her eyes, not everyone's. But she thought it would show people . . . I don't know, that I'm not some ridiculous asshole who doesn't take anything seriously, I guess? She hated the shit I did on red carpets and in interviews. So she sent it out to magazines, and long story short, that was the final straw for us."

"Oh," I say. "Go through the park here, okay?"

As we walk though the park, underneath the trees with bare branches and the piles of gray snow, Drew says, "I just hate this part of the job. It's so boring. Like, those articles with random facts about celebrities . . . do I actually need to know George Clooney's favorite color? I don't even think George Clooney cares about George Clooney's favorite color."

I try to shrug, but it's kind of hard to do when someone's carrying you.

"Anyway, I know it makes me look like an asshole sometimes or like I don't take anything seriously, but that's why I do all that stuff in interviews."

"Like wearing a fake mustache," I say softly.

"Wow," he mutters. "You really did google me, didn't you?"

"Sorry."

"Or, like, whenever I see someone following me with a camera, I just fall down. I learned how to do pratfalls in high school, and I'm legitimately good at falling down without injuring myself—a weird skill, I know. I wish I remembered something more useful from school—but then they stop taking pictures and they rush over to see me and we usually end up having a conversation, instead of them taking a picture of me so internet commenters can talk about what kind of sunglasses I'm wearing."

He sighs. "I know this probably doesn't make a ton of sense to you, and I sound like some spoiled rich dude whining about how hard his life is—"

"No," I say with such force that he glances at me, surprised. "I think you know how hard life is." After all, like he told me in the Book Loft, it's why he makes things—to make people forget about their miserable moments.

"Okay, this is my street," I say. "Just a couple of blocks. You didn't have to carry me to my house, you know. I could've managed it."

"Yeah," Drew says, shifting my weight a little bit, "but then I'd be kind of a dick, wouldn't I?"

I meet his eyes again and see that he's smiling at me, looking for all the world like . . .

Well, like someone who's probably played a scene like this in a movie. A damsel in distress, a strong man who's able to carry her, a moment where their faces are so close that they just . . . might . . . kiss. Because that's his job, I remind myself. Being charming. Acting.

And then his grip feels less solid, and I realize I'm falling. I shriek, and his grip tightens again as his smile gets wider.

"Just kidding," he says. "I'm not gonna drop you."

"What the hell?" I ask, smacking his arm. My hand lingers there for a moment, and I'm basically clutching him as he carries me. I pull my hand back and cross my arms in front of my body. "That wasn't funny," I mutter.

"It was a little funny," he says.

"You're kind of an asshole, you know that?" I say.

Drew laughs. "I can tell you think that, but in my family, being an asshole is how you show you like someone. I've never hugged my brother, but I put him in a headlock every time I visit home, and I love him more than anybody. And every time my mom sees me, she doesn't bother to tell me that I'm doing a good job, but she *does* make fun of how ridiculous I looked when I had to do a sex scene."

"Your mom watched your sex scene?" I ask, appalled.

He raises his eyebrows. "What, *you're* disturbed? Trust me, I'm more horrified by it than you could ever be."

"Your family sounds weird," I say, but the truth is, his family sounds nice. The idea of coming home to two parents, to a little brother, to a group of people who know you well enough to make fun of you. It sounds wonderful.

But I don't have a chance to think about it anymore, because we're in front of my house.

"This is it," I say. "You can let me off here."

"And what?" Drew says. "Make you hobble up the stairs? My Southern mother would never stand for that."

"Is this situation in your official Southern Manners Guide?" I ask. "What to Do When You Encounter a Poor, Pathetic Girl Who Tried to Walk in Heels?"

"Maybe not in those exact words," Drew says as we climb the stairs. I shift my weight a little to find my keys in my coat pocket and slide them in the door.

Drew easily maneuvers me inside and suddenly, I'm seeing our house as a stranger—or a movie star—would.

"I know it's nothing special," I say in a rush. "It's messy and cluttered and that couch is about a million years old, but—"

"Annie," Drew says with a laugh, and I'm struck again by the way my name sounds coming out of his mouth, like no one's ever said it before. "This is amazing. I've been living out of a hotel room; this looks like paradise to me."

He walks around the living room, still carrying me, inspecting the artwork and the knickknacks, of which there are many. I notice everything now; the way our outdated wallpaper is slightly curling right there at the corner, the way that throw pillow is threadbare, the way the TV is covered in a thin layer of dust.

"Your parents?" he asks, gesturing with his head toward the framed wedding photo on the wall.

"Yep," I say, and he gives me a smile, a tiny, sad one, one that says he understands.

"Your mom was really beautiful," he says. "I mean, your dad was beautiful, too. Don't wanna leave him out."

I laugh a little. "You can put me down now. You've safely de-livered this damsel to her house, and your Southern duty is over."

"Annie?"

I hear Uncle Don's voice before I see him. He walks down the stairs, then stops when he sees us. Maybe some other person would wonder why a popular actor was carrying his niece through the house like a giant baby, but Don acts like all of this is normal.

"Drew! Good to see you again!" he says, smiling as if Drew is here on a purely social call. "Did you find the book?"

I snort, about to explain that there's no way Drew would have the chance or inclination to finish a book that's almost a thousand pages long, but before I can say that, Drew answers, "I'm reading it now."

"And?" Don asks, eyebrows raised.

"It's great," Drew says. "But I've gotta ask . . . does Rand ever—"

"Shhh!" Don waves his arms, then points at me. "No spoilers. She hasn't read it yet. I'll lend you my copy of the second book so you're ready to go when you finish this one."

I turn my head slowly to look at Drew, my mouth open, and he shrugs. And then I remember, once again, that he's still holding me and I say, "Okay, I'm getting down now."

As Drew gently places me on the floor, Uncle Don finally no-tices that something is amiss. "Oh, Annie. What did you do? Do you want Dungeon Master Rick to look at it when he gets here? You know he's an EMT."

"No!" I shout, then my eyes bolt to Drew's face. He's looking at me with wide eyes. "I just tripped and hurt my foot. It's the very definition of 'no big deal.'"

"Can you carry her upstairs?" Don asks, turning to Drew, who's apparently his new book bestie and most trusted friend now.

"I'm here to serve," Drew says jovially.

"Oh, I don't require any further assistance," I say. "I'm capable of walking up the stairs." Because the thing is, I really, really don't want Drew Danforth to see the state of my bedroom and my tiny bed, when he probably has, like, a California King that's covered in a million-thread-count sheets. Did I even make my bed today? Is there underwear on the floor? I'm not in the habit of leaving any clothing on the floor, but I'm sure this is the one time that all my underwear flung itself out of the drawers and onto the floor for the express purpose of embarrassing me in front of Drew.

I take one step and almost fall into the sofa.

"I'm not sure you are, actually," he says, picking me up again. I don't bother resisting. He carries me up the flight of stairs, then nods toward the first door on the right. "This one?"

I sigh. "Yes."

"Ah," Drew says as he pushes open the half-closed door. "This is it, huh? Where the magic happens?"

"If by 'magic,' you mean articles about hemorrhoid relief, then yes."

"You're still insisting that was for work, then?"

"Put me down." I already had to have one conversation about hemorrhoids with Drew; I'm not having another one in my bedroom, of all places.

He places me gently on the bed, like I'm a doll he's sitting on a shelf, like I weigh nothing at all.

"Thank you," I say primly, trying to regain a modicum of dignity, which is hard when a man you barely know has just deposited you on your unmade bed (but, like, not in a sexy way). But Drew isn't paying attention to me; he's looking over everything on my desk.

"Are you working on something?" he asks, riffling through a few printed-out pages of my screenplay, and I forget about my foot and leap across the room.

"No!" I shout, grabbing them out of his hands. The pain catches up with me, and I wobble before he catches me. "This is . . . nothing. It's nothing."

"Is it a screenplay?" Drew asks, squinting and trying to read the words on the pages in my hand, his hand still on my arm.

I narrow my eyes and take a painful step back. "You're really annoying, you know that?"

"It's been said before," Drew says, shoving his hands in his pockets. "Fine. Don't talk about it."

"Great." I stack the papers and place them back on my desk.

"But what's it about?"

"Oh, my God," I mutter. "Do you really want to know?"

"More than anything in the world," he says, the slightest bit of a smile playing across his lips. Maybe when I first met Drew I would've thought this was sarcastic or mean, but I'm starting to understand him.

I shuffle through the papers on my desk. "It's a romantic comedy. Obviously. It's kinda loosely based on Chloe and Nick at the coffee shop, one of those banter-y, love/hate relationships where one of them doesn't believe in commitment but you just know they're gonna end up together."

"So you're the next Nora Ephron?" Drew asks, pointing to my framed photo of her.

I snort, loudly. "No one is the next Nora Ephron. She was one of a kind."

Drew leans closer to inspect the photo. "What is it about her that you connect with so much?"

I look at the picture instead of at him. "It's a lot of things. She worked hard. She was smart and funny and tough, and even when life knocked her down she kept going."

"Like you," Drew says. *Hardly*, I think, but I keep talking.

"That's not it, though. I think the main thing I love about her work is that it's sad. Everyone thinks of romantic comedies as being these sappy, unrealistic stories where love conquers all and everyone ends up happy at the end. But that's not what her movies were at all. Like, in *Sleepless in Seattle*, you can't really get any sadder than Tom Hanks missing his dead wife. And in *You've Got Mail*, Meg Ryan misses her mom and she loses her store. None of that gets resolved by the end. It's not like Tom's wife comes back to life, and Meg Ryan still loses the business her mom built."

"Wow," Drew says, widening his eyes. "When you put it that way, it sounds like a laugh riot."

"But then they find love!" I say, my voice rising. "The things that suck still suck, but they're allowed to be happy. And maybe it means so much more that they're happy, knowing that they still carry all that sadness with them."

Drew nods, slides off his coat, and sits down on my bed. There is a very large, very attractive man here in my childhood bedroom, *on my bed*, a place where large, attractive men usually are not. I wonder, for a second, if he would even fit in my bed, lengthwise. Probably not. I'm afraid Drew can read my thoughts all over my face, so I'm glad when he breaks the silence.

"But your rom-com isn't that sad, is it?" he asks, leaning back on his elbows. His sweater rides up the slightest bit, showing off those much-praised abs. I can't even imagine being that comfortable with my body, but he's so casual about it. "Chloe doesn't seem very sad."

I pull out my desk chair and sit down. "I know she's always listening to upbeat music from the seventies and putting sprinkles on lattes and knitting striped scarves, but her life is hard. Her dad has early-onset Alzheimer's and her mom split a long time ago, so she's in charge of him. Whenever she's not working, she's usually at his assisted-living place. That's where all her money goes, and that's why she's still going to school."

"I didn't know that," Drew says. "I wasn't trying to be a jerk."

I shrug. "How would you know? She doesn't like to talk about it."

"Now that," Drew says, "I can understand."

I look at him reclining on my bed and he looks at me and there's a moment, a slightly too-long moment, where we're just looking at each other. And then he says, "Hey, I'm sorry I made fun of romantic comedies."

Our argument at Nick's flashes through my mind, and I flush with embarrassment. "No, it's okay. I shouldn't have yelled at you. I was just upset because I was on the world's worst date with the world's stinkiest man."

Drew sits up and shakes his head. "I was being an asshole. Like, I thought we were . . ." He gestures back and forth between us. "Bantering or whatever. I didn't realize how important they were to you. I didn't know you were taking it personally."

"Yeah, well. Imagine if someone was making fun of *Frasier* to you."

Drew makes a fist. "I swear to God, if anyone said even one ill word about David Hyde Pierce . . ."

He stands up then, takes a step toward me. "You thought I was a jerk, didn't you?"

I consider lying, but Drew's being honest with me, so instead I nod. "Yeah. I really hated you."

He laughs. "Wow. That was . . . candid. I like it. Why did you hate me?"

I stand up and roll my eyes. "Come on, dude. You made fun of my job. You made fun of romantic comedies. *Coffee Girl*."

"What about Coffee Girl?" Drew asks, taking another step closer.

"You gave me an embarrassing nickname in front of other people, like I didn't have a job or dreams or a name. Like I was just some lowly employee who exists only to get coffee."

Drew snort-laughs, but when he sees the look in my eyes, he sobers up. "Wait, you really don't like the nickname?"

I shake my head. "No!"

"I thought it was our fun inside joke, since you spilled coffee on me."

I shake my head again. "Uh, maybe if you're trying to establish a fun inside joke with someone else, you should first determine if the other person finds what you're saying a) fun and b) a joke."

"I won't call you that anymore, but I wasn't trying to make you feel bad. I told you, Annie," he says, taking another step toward me, and my name on his lips still sounds like a lovely foreign word. "Not taking things seriously is the Danforth way. We mock those we like."

"Like pulling a girl's pigtails when you have a crush on her?" I ask, and then I try to laugh but it comes out as a squeak. Drew is very close to me now, and my body is at war; part of me wants to run away from him, from this moment, but my eyes can't look away from his.

He smiles, then reaches out, grabs one of my unruly curls, and pulls on it oh-so-gently.

This can't be real. It can't. This is a weird dream, and any minute now Uncle Don is going to burst through the door but he's going to look like RuPaul and he's going to tell me that I forgot to do homework for my ninth-grade math class. And then I'll wake up and tell Chloe about this at Nick's, and she'll say, "Wow, what's going on in your subconscious, anyway?"

"What are you doing?" Drew asks, looking at my arm.

"Pinching myself," I say. I pinch myself harder, but I'm not waking up.

Drew laughs, a tiny little sound. He takes another step toward me, so now there's really and truly no space between us. His chest is against mine, and I'm once again in a situation where I realize how tall he is, a full head above me. I look up at him and start to shake, so I pinch myself again.

"Annie," Drew says, and he puts his hand over mine. "What does Sexy Gaffer think of your screenplay?"

I shake my head.

"Does he not know you're a writer?" Drew asks, his low voice incredulous.

"We haven't talked about it," I whisper. "Yet."

Drew shakes his head, the disbelief written across his face, which I can see quite clearly because it's mere centimeters from mine. We're so close that I've started converting things to metric. "That's bananas, because I could tell you were a writer from the moment I met you. Well, not the moment when you didn't speak and I temporarily thought you were French. But after that, I could tell. You have the vocabulary of a writer, and you just . . . seem like you have something to say."

I get that these words in this configuration wouldn't mean much to most women. Maybe other women would like to hear that they're beautiful or irresistible or flawless, but for me, for someone who's spent years feeling like she had nothing to say, this might be the kindest thing anyone's ever said to me. That Drew saw that in me before he really even knew me . . . it means more to me than anything.

He leans even closer. Another beat and closer still. How is there even still space between us? How much longer can this keep going on? How long do I have to wait before his lips touch my lips and—

"Hey, sweetie?"

The door creaks open and Uncle Don pokes his head into the room. I yelp, jump back, land on my injured foot, and crash into my desk before bouncing off and landing on the floor.

Uncle Don, oblivious as always, doesn't notice that he interrupted a tension-filled moment in which I think a kiss might have actually been about to happen. Or at least it was a moment in which I *wanted* a kiss to happen, a thought that fills me with an exciting feelings-cocktail made up of excitement, despair, dread, and just a dash of nausea.

"Annie, honey!" He crosses the room and kneels beside me.

Drew does the same. "Are you okay?"

Drew reaches out, and I pull away. "I'm good. I—actually, can you guys go downstairs? I want to get changed. I'll be down in a second."

Uncle Don nods. "I came up to ask Drew if he could help me put a leaf in the dining-room table. The guys are about to come over, and Dungeon Master Rick always complains that the table's not big enough."

Drew shoots me that look again, reminding me that I never explained the whole D&D thing to him; he probably thinks he's helping Uncle Don set up for some weird sex party. I just shake my head and give him a look that I hope communicates *I'll explain later.*

"Sure," Drew says. "I couldn't live with myself if Dungeon Master Rick was disappointed."

"He's a difficult man to please," Uncle Don says with a sigh, which really doesn't help the whole "this looks like a sex party" situation.

I listen as Don and Drew walk downstairs, and as soon as I'm in the clear I pull my phone out of my pocket and call Chloe.

"What's wrong?" she answers.

"Nothing!" I say. "I mean, I'm a little injured, but that's not the issue. I think . . ."

I trail off, unable to even put what just happened into words.

"What??" Chloe practically shouts.

I look at my photo of Nora and gulp. "I think Drew and I almost kissed."

Chloe screams for a full ten seconds, which doesn't sound like that long but is actually a very long time to scream.

"Are you done?" I ask.

"Yeah. Wait . . . no, yeah, I'm done. What the hell, Annie? How did this happen? How did things go from you being all, 'Nooooo, *Roman Holiday* is a bummer' to 'Sure, let's bone a movie star'?"

"We haven't *boned*, Chloe. We didn't even kiss. Uncle Don walked in and I fell over and now they're downstairs getting ready for D&D."

"Back up. Why is he at your house? What's going on?"

I tell Chloe the whole story, and she's silent for so long that I start to think the call dropped. But then she says, "So how many times, total, have you fallen over today?"

"Twice."

"Okay. And you've also run into Drew and spilled coffee on him."

"Yes."

"And didn't you run into Carter when you met him, while carrying a comically large stack of papers?"

"Right. Your point?"

"Girl," Chloe says, and I can practically see the expression on her face. "There are two men fighting over you—three if you count Barry—"

"Which I don't."

"—And you're in a rom-com of your own making."

"I am not, Chloe."

"You're the charming, klutzy heroine and you're in the midst of a lopsided love triangle, and you need to go down there and kiss Drew right now," Chloe says with bravado.

"In front of Uncle Don?"

"Don doesn't care," she says. Her voice grows muffled before she comes back to the phone. "Sorry, Nick's being a total pill. Like, 'there are customers' and 'I don't pay you to talk on the phone' and 'your screaming is upsetting Gary.'"

"Gary doesn't like loud noises. You know that. And anyway, this feels wrong. I mean, I'm sort of dating Carter—"

Chloe snorts. "Um, you have been on *one date* with Carter. I'm ten thousand percent sure he hasn't put his entire dating life on hold just because he got coffee with you. Just promise me we can dissect this moment a million times tonight."

"Promise. Don't get fired."

"Bye."

I take a look at myself in my vanity, the same one I used to stare into in elementary school when I wished I had boobs. And in middle school when I wished I didn't have braces. And in high school when I wished, more than anything, that my mom was here.

And now I'm looking into it, wondering what's happening. I

almost kissed Drew—there's no denying it. I run my fingers over my hair and hastily apply a little more blush and lipstick. But wait, that's way too obvious; tinted lip gloss is my typical daytime look, and lipstick screams, "Hey, look at me, I'm trying to look hot." But what's wrong with trying to look hot? Maybe I want to look like I put some effort into this.

Ugh. I grab a tissue and wipe off most of the lipstick, then put some clear gloss on over it.

I study my reflection. I look okay—like a woman who's about to walk downstairs and find a movie star with her uncle's D&D friends, and *oh shit*, Drew is going to meet Don's D&D friends.

I hobble downstairs as quickly as I can, round the corner into the dining room, and find . . .

Uncle Don patiently explaining the rules of D&D to Drew while the rest of the D&D guys look on.

Drew looks up and sees me, his face breaking into a smile so big that I would have a hard time standing up even if I wasn't injured. "Hey," he says. "You were supposed to let me help you down the stairs."

"I just thought," I say, looking around the table, shocked at how well Drew's fitting in, "that you might want to learn everything there is to know about D&D."

"This is actually pretty interesting," Drew says.

"No duh," says Dungeon Master Rick.

"Drew was telling us about the guy, weren't you, Drew?" Earl says, nudging Paul. "The guy we saw in the movie. Tatum Channing?"

"Channing Tatum," Drew corrects him, and I stifle a laugh.

"Yeah," Earl says as Paul nods. "We like that guy."

"He's a nice dude," says Drew, and I barely have time to wonder what Channing Tatum movies these guys are watching before he says, "Well, this was really fun, but we have an early call time tomorrow so I've gotta get to bed."

I try to stop myself from imagining Drew in his hotel-room bed, but I am unsuccessful. He shakes everyone's hand, and Uncle Don says, "Come back anytime; we'd love to have you play with us."

"We can't bring in a new character at this point—" Dungeon Master Rick starts.

"We can do whatever we want!" Paul says gleefully. "That's the fun of D&D!"

"I'll walk you to the door," I say, shooting Uncle Don a look. He shrugs.

"By walk," Drew says, grabbing my arm to steady me, "you mean limp-hop, right?"

"Maybe." I let myself lean into him and embrace the weirdness of this moment. I reluctantly let go of Drew's arm when he opens the front door. He pulls on his coat and shoves a beanie on his head as he steps out onto the porch.

"Oh," he says, turning around as I lean on the doorframe, and I think he's about to go back to that conversation we were having in my room right before Uncle Don burst in and I fell over. That gloriously sexual-tension–filled conversation.

"Definitely thought the dungeon master was some weird sex thing," Drew says, walking down the stairs and looking over his shoulder. "This makes a lot more sense."

I laugh, both relieved and disappointed.

He turns around. "Good night, Annie." And then he walks away.

I close the door and lean back against it. The sound of rolling dice comes from the dining room, then Dungeon Master Rick saying something about the party entering a tavern.

I sigh and cover my face with my hands, even though no one

is around to see me blush. You know how in every romantic comedy, there's a scene where the love interests almost kiss? They're so close, their faces mere inches apart, their bodies practically radiating heat, when some precocious child or rude elderly woman interrupts them and they spring apart?

Well, sub in Uncle Don for a child or old woman and you've pretty much got what happened in my room.

I thought Drew Danforth was nothing more than an irritating jerk, but maybe I was misreading the signs. Maybe this entire time, we've been bantering and I didn't even notice. Maybe this is an enemies-to-lovers situation, and we've been gradually building sexual tension that will have no choice but to explode in a scene so explicit that it would change the movie of my life from a PG to a hard R rating.

Chloe might be right. I might actually, finally, be in my romantic comedy.

Chapter Thirteen

I STAY UP LATE INTO THE NIGHT WORKING ON MY SCREENPLAY. WRITing is often like plugging in one word after another, willing them to make some sort of sense, but this is different. My fingers attack the keyboard, and words appear on the screen before I even notice I wrote them.

I drift off to a dreamless sleep, then wake up before my alarm goes off (which is very, very early). *Drew was in here*, I think to myself as I get ready. *He saw my room.*

Despite Chloe's reassurances, and despite the fact that Drew and I didn't even kiss—I mean, I'm pretty sure no one would qualify "getting coffee with one man and then having a sexually charged conversation with another man before falling over" as morally dubious behavior—it's still weird for me. Carter and I aren't dating, per se, so much as we are People Who Have Been on One Date in Which Barry Was Present. What do we owe each other at this point? I haven't dated enough to know, and romantic comedies didn't prepare me for this. In movies, usually one guy is comically terrible—he's cheating on the heroine at his bachelor party or using her connections to get a job. It's easy for us to yell at the screen, "JUST DUMP HIS SORRY, TWO-TIMING ASS!"

But it turns out real life isn't like that. Yes, I have strong and confusing feelings for Drew, but a) he's leaving town soon and b) doesn't everyone? And perhaps Carter's presence doesn't cause my breath to quicken or my brain to scramble, but I don't know him that well yet. Maybe what we need is another date.

Maybe what we need is a kiss.

Luckily for me, Carter and I have a date scheduled for the night after my weird bedroom conversation with Drew. Carter seems like an old-fashioned guy, but I'm pretty sure even he would agree that a second date is a perfectly acceptable moment for a first kiss. And maybe, probably, when we do kiss, it will be so good, so intense, that I'll know instantly that he's the one for me.

That's how it often works in the movies, right? In *The Wedding Singer*, Drew Barrymore and Adam Sandler don't understand their true feelings for each other until they have to pretend-kiss in front of her best friend under the guise of Drew practicing for her upcoming wedding. But when that kiss is over, they just stare at each other, entranced. It turns out their true love was there all along, like some sort of virus that's only transmitted via saliva.

I intend to find out the secrets contained in Carter's saliva tonight.

He suggests an Italian restaurant in German Village. I don't know if he's actually a fan of Italian food or if he's trying to avoid the sort of situation that happened last time when we were at Nick's, but whatever it is, I'm happy to be going out with him. Not just because of my aforementioned kiss plan, but also because it's nice to have a distraction from the weird Drew situation yesterday, which makes me feel altogether unsettled whenever I think of it.

He offers to pick me up, but since I live a few blocks away (and my ankle feels much better after a night of icing it) I walk. The restaurant is one that Don and I have been to a few times for special occasions, like our birthdays and the days on which particularly exciting *Star Wars* news is announced (we would never go on an actual premiere day, because Don spends those days in the theatre eating an absurd amount of popcorn). It's nice, with white table-cloths and piped-in, soft instrumental music and a lot of dramatic-looking busts that I assume are Italian, but I wouldn't know. It all comes together to create an ambiance that is decidedly not Mc-Donald's.

Carter stands up when I approach our table, and after an awkward shuffle, he pulls me into a hug. I like the way he feels—solid, strong, dependable.

"You're like an oak tree," I say into his shoulder.

He pulls back and looks at me. "Thank you?"

"It's a compliment," I say as we sit down. "Trust me."

We've seen each other on set today, so he knows my ankle is mostly better, but he asks about it anyway. We order some wine and soon I'm pleasantly buzzed enough to wholeheartedly dig into the bread basket. As I chow down on the delicious rosemary focaccia, Carter tells me about weekends spent on the lake, how his divorce turned him into a better dad, and how he got started in film. Throughout our meal, he asks me all sorts of questions, about my parents and Uncle Don and my favorite movies.

Don't get me wrong, it's a good conversation. I mean, it's a *great* one. He's polite and he's interested in me and not once has he mentioned dumpster bagels. But it's hard for me to concentrate when all I'm thinking about is kissing him and how that will make everything fall into place.

"Um . . . Annie?"

I blink a few times. Carter stares at me, concern evident in his furrowed brow. His eyes search my face, and I realize I've been staring off into space as I daydreamed about our hypothetical kiss.

"Are you okay?" he asks.

"I'm fine!" I say. "I'm good. Great. Awesome. Perfect."

"Well." He laughs. "Who could argue with that?"

I don't want to waste any more time. Less useless chitchat, more making out; that's my motto. I survey the restaurant, taking in the Italian busts and the waiters milling about. No, this is not the place for a mind-blowing, destiny-deciding kiss.

I toss my napkin onto the table. "Are you ready to get out of here?"

Carter raises his eyebrows in surprise. "I do have to pay first."

"Oh." I nod. "Right."

I almost bounce in my seat as we wait for our server to return Carter's credit card. I'm like a child on Christmas morning, except that I'm a grown woman and now my present is a hot dude. When it's finally time to leave, Carter's hand on my back lightly guides me around the tables full of couples on dates and families celebrating who knows what. His hand transmits warmth and strength, but it doesn't produce even the tiniest of tingles. *Yet.*

I wait until we're on the sidewalk, the glow from the restaurant windows illuminating Carter's face. "I had a nice time tonight," he starts to say, but I don't let him finish his sentence before I launch myself at him.

I close my eyes and mentally prepare myself for the moment that will decide my future; the moment that, years from now when I'm speaking to Carter's son and the many children we've had since then, I'll say, "And that's how I knew your father was the one . . . it was right there, in front of a tiny Italian restaurant while cold rain misted from the sky, that I kissed him and knew we were meant to be."

But my daydream ends when I realize I'm not kissing Carter's lips at all; I'm kissing his cheek, because he turned his head at the last minute.

"Annie," he says, putting his hands on my shoulders and pushing me gently away.

"Whoa," I say. "Did I—did I misread something? I thought you wanted to kiss me. I thought that's what was going on."

"I do want to kiss you."

"Oh no," I say, placing a hand over my heart. "Am I . . . Barry?"

Carter laughs. "You're not Barry."

I press my hands to my hot cheeks, trying to cool them down. "I'm a total Barry. You don't even want to be here tonight, do you?"

"Hey." Carter puts a hand on my arm until I look at him, and the understanding in his blue eyes calms me down immediately. "I want to kiss you. I really do. But I have to ask you something first."

"Okay," I say with a little apprehension. It's not like I have a ton of kissing experience, but I don't think the act is usually preceded by an interview portion.

"I'm not trying to freak you out or anything, but you know I'm older than you."

"Late-thirties isn't that old."

He winces. "Mid-thirties, okay?"

"Sorry," I whisper.

"Anyway," he continues. "I'm having fun hanging out with you, and I think you're having fun, too, right?"

I nod.

"But at my age, I can't just have fun forever. I'm not asking you to marry me after a couple of dates or anything, but I have a kid. I can't keep dating someone if I don't think we have a future, so I guess what I'm asking you is . . . are you really into this?"

I freeze, then stare at a random couple coming out of the restaurant. His arm loops around her shoulders and she leans into him with the comfort of two people who've been together for a long time and plan to stay together. It looks nice. I glance back at Carter, who hasn't taken his eyes off me, and I think about what it would be like to have that sort of life with him. Because the thing is, Carter is great. He's nice and funny and, okay, super hot in a slightly-older-than-me way. To paraphrase Melanie Griffith in *Working Girl*, he's got a head for lighting films and a bod for sin.

But have I ever once fogged up a coffee shop window while fantasizing about those strong, solid, dependable arms ripping off my clothing?

I open my mouth but don't say anything, my heart breaking just a little as this one possible future dies.

"You can be honest," Carter says gently.

"I'm sorry," I say, as deflated as a helium balloon a week after a three-year-old's birthday party. "I do like you, I swear, but—"

He holds up a hand. "You don't have to justify yourself, really."

"It's just," I continue trying to justify myself, despite his protest. "You're great. You're perfect. You're literally everything I ever wanted in a man. You own a *houseboat*."

"Still not getting why that's such a thing for you," Carter says.

But then I stop for a moment and think of the way I felt when Drew and I were alone in my room, when he was talking about my writing and standing so, so close to me and I know that what I feel for Carter is not the same. Sure, it's absolutely ridiculous to turn down a real-life guy because of a movie star, like saving myself for one of the Jonas Brothers in junior high, but it's how I feel.

"It just . . . wouldn't be fair for us to keep going out," I say quietly.

Carter nods. "I wanted it to work, but I could tell there was something holding you back. I think . . . maybe both of us wanted a connection, so we were trying to force one."

I cover my face with my hands. "I feel bad for trying to force it."

"I don't think either of us should feel bad. We're just two people trying to find someone . . . there's nothing wrong with that."

I nod. "Like Greg Kinnear or Bill Pullman."

"Um . . . sure?" Carter's knowledge of rom-coms apparently doesn't extend to the Ephron canon.

He tilts his head, like he's weighing what he's about to say, but then he goes for it. "Listen, Annie. This might be overstepping a bit, since I don't know if we're at the level where we can give each other advice, but we've been pretty honest in the short time we've been hanging out."

I nod, wondering what he could possibly be about to say.

He ducks his head a little bit to look me directly in my eyes. "If you're as head over heels for Drew as you seem, you should go for it."

My jaw drops like I'm a cartoon character. "Excuse me?"

Carter chuckles. "It's . . . pretty obvious. You guys have something going on."

I shake my head but don't say anything.

"I'm not telling you what to do or anything, but I've never heard anything bad about Drew. And if you're lucky enough to connect with someone in a world where that's pretty hard to find . . . well, I think you should grab life by the balls. Metaphorically speaking."

It's alternately thrilling and misery-inducing that my feelings for Drew, the ones I don't even entirely understand, are being broadcast so loudly that anyone can see them. This is how I felt in junior high when I heard someone talking about my crush (again, one of the Jonas Brothers and no, I don't remember which one), just ecstatic and alive to even hear his name. But I'm also a little ashamed that I've been mooning around like a lovesick teenager.

"Do you think I'm an idiot?" I ask softly.

Carter shrugs. "The heart wants what it wants."

"Like Selena Gomez said about Justin Bieber."

Carter stares blankly at me.

"In her hit song . . . You know what, don't worry about it," I mutter.

Carter laughs again. "You're really something, Annie Cassidy. I'm sorry this didn't work out."

"Yeah," I say as he takes a step away from me. "Me, too." And I mean it. I *am* sorry I can't be with Carter, with his strong arms and his ready-made family and his politeness. It would be so nice to want a life with him. I wish with all my foolish, film-addled heart that I could fall for him, instead of pining over an almost-kiss with a cute and aggressively flirtatious man who recently met Dungeon Master Rick.

"Hey," I say, just before he turns around. "One last thing."

Carter stops moving. "Yeah?"

"We call you Sexy Gaffer," I say. "Drew and I."

Carter pauses, tilts his head to the side. "You know what? I'm gonna choose to be flattered by that."

We look at each other for a moment, and then I say, "Bye, Carter."

"Goodbye, Annie," he says with a small wave, and then he turns and walks down the sidewalk, not looking back.

. . .

Since my date with Carter ended sooner than I expected, I head over to—where else—Nick's. There's a bounce in my step that you might not expect from someone who essentially got dumped after a mere two dates. But as breakups or almost-breakups go, that was about as good as it gets. I mean, that was a Nora Ephron–level, Greg-Kinnear-and-Meg-Ryan–caliber breakup—just two people who aren't right for each other, doing what they know they have to do before they move on and find out that Tom Hanks has been their secret pen pal all along.

I may not have a secret pen pal, but what I do have is a man who demonstrated clear interest in me in my bedroom before having a lengthy conversation with my uncle. Yes, Drew and I had a rough time getting to know each other, but so did Tom and Meg, and look what happened there. A romantic kiss in the park, while a golden retriever ran around them. I'm not saying things with Drew are necessarily going to end like that . . . but, well, I haven't spent all this time waiting for Tom Hanks for nothing.

It's ridiculous, I think as I approach the coffee shop, all of German Village lit up and glowing in the dark, that someone decided twinkle lights are Christmas-only things, when we desperately need them to get through the bleakness of the post-holiday winter. January is almost over, but we still have February and March and possibly April full of darkness and snow and ice. Twinkle lights should be everywhere all the time.

That's what I'm thinking about when I open the door, the bell jingling to announce my arrival over a Hall and Oates song.

"Twinkle lights!" I announce, and Chloe looks up from the textbook she's reading at the counter.

"Is that your new greeting?" she asks. "Idiosyncratic, but I kinda like it."

"Why don't you have twinkle lights, Nick?" I ask, walking to the counter. "Don't you think they'd really add something?"

"Yeah," he says, handing me a cup. "Extra cost to my electricity bill. Here, try this lavender hot chocolate Chloe made."

"It's good, right?" Chloe shuts her textbook, then leans over the counter and peers at my face, gauging my reaction. "Like, Nick should put it on the menu, shouldn't he?"

I take a sip. "I like it. It's—"

Gary appears from behind me and grabs the cup from me. He takes a drink and says, "You know, I thought this was gonna taste like potpourri, but I actually like it."

"Gary," Nick says patiently. "We've talked about this. You can't sample other customers' food and drinks."

"This isn't a customer," Gary says, handing the drink back to me. "This is Annie."

"I'm not even offended," I say. "Just think about the twinkle lights, okay?"

"I think Annie's right," Chloe says. "Like, put them around the front window, so everyone on the street sees them, and it will make this place look like it's glowing."

Nick squints at me. "You're in a good mood."

"I had a breakthrough on my screenplay last night," I say with a smile.

"And she's currently enmeshed in a love triangle, like she's the heroine of a dystopian YA trilogy," Chloe says.

"Chloe . . ." I start, wanting to talk to her about my Carter breakup away from Gary and Nick.

"Wait, with that guy who was in here the other day?" Nick asks, wiping down the counter. "The one who smelled bad? He stayed here for two hours after you left, not even drinking that water and talking to Gary about fluoride."

"It's a conspiracy," Gary says, shaking his head. "I didn't even know."

Chloe tilts her head and gives me a smile that says, *What sort of people have we chosen to surround ourselves with?*

I sigh, then decide to go ahead and tell everyone. "I'm not in a love triangle. Carter and I broke up."

"Oh no," Chloe says, reaching over the counter to put her hand on my arm. "Are you okay?"

"Yeah, actually," I say, and I sort of can't stop myself from smiling. "I'm . . . kind of ridiculously okay."

Chloe leans back over the counter and crosses her arms. "Well," she says softly. "Maybe it wasn't such a love triangle after all."

"Love can be other shapes, you know," Gary muses. "Square. Rhombus. Octagon."

Tobin comes out of the back room, and everyone's attention turns away from me. "Hey, Annie," he says, pushing his hair out of his face.

"Where have you been, young man?" Chloe demands.

"My mom called," Tobin says. "She and my stepdad are on their honeymoon in Costa Rica, and she wanted to make sure I've been watering her plants."

"And have you been?" I ask.

"No," he says unapologetically. "But every day is a new beginning, you know?"

"But possibly not for your mom's plants, which may already be dead," Chloe says.

Tobin turns to Nick and points to the speakers. "Seriously? Chloe can play yacht rock again? When is it gonna be time for ambient whale sounds?"

Nick busies himself at the espresso machine. "Shut up, Tobin."

"This is unfair," Tobin mutters.

With a laugh, I sit down at the table closest to the counter and pull out my phone. I type an "H" into the search bar, and Hollywood Gossip pops right up. Looking at the site has become my dirty little secret, especially now that I know how much Drew hates this stuff, but I can't help it. Now I'm invested in the lives of celebrities I don't even know, and as a bonus, I can rank the Kardashians in order of favorite to least favorite.

But it still feels gross to read gossip, so my eyes shift back and forth from the counter to my screen, like I'm looking at porn in public (which I would never do, mostly because *eww* but also because Nick once had to kick out a guy for watching porn at full volume and then no one would sit at that table for weeks). Chloe is giving Tobin a lecture about how important plants are for our health, both mental and physical, when I see the headline.

Drew Danforth's new love? The heartthrob was spotted getting cozy with costar Tarah Thomas on the set of his new film!

I'm vaguely aware of the espresso machine running and of the Steely Dan song that starts playing. I sort of hear Nick tell Chloe that one song was fine but now she needs to turn it off, and Chloe argue that hardly anyone's here right now and she should be able to play something happy for the book club meeting in the corner. But, for the most part, the sound around me fades into nothing.

"Chloe," I say, and it comes out strangled.

"What?" she asks, running around the counter and rushing to my side.

Without looking at her, I hand her my phone.

"Oh," Chloe says. *"Oh."*

"This doesn't look good," says Gary, who I didn't even realize was standing beside Chloe, reading over her shoulder.

Tobin walks over, grabs the phone, and lets out a low whistle. "I think you got played, Annie."

"What happened to cleanup?" Nick asks from behind the counter.

"Drew might be hooking up with another woman," Gary says.

"See?" Nick points at all of us, accusation in his voice. "This is why I said I didn't want any movie stars around. This is what happens. At least Bradley Cooper had the good sense not to date any of my customers."

"We weren't dating," I say, taking my phone back from Tobin and sliding it into my purse. "We were just . . . I don't know, we were just flirting. I shouldn't have assumed anything."

"Oh, Annie," Chloe says, wrapping me in a side hug. "This isn't your fault. You know what this is? Some sort of fun misunderstanding. Like, you know how in romantic comedies the heroine always thinks the hero is cheating on her but it turns out he's been talking to his sister or something?"

"I'm fairly certain Tarah isn't Drew's sister."

"It's just an example. What I'm saying is that this is your rom-com misunderstanding, and you'll resolve it and then ride off into the sunset and get married. There aren't even any pictures, so who knows if this is true? It's an anonymous tip."

I shake my head. "Thanks for the pep talk, Chlo."

Then Tobin wraps me in a hug from the other side, and Gary says, "Oh, all right," and hugs all three of us. I steal a glance at

Nick, and although he would never join in on a group hug, even he looks at me with eyes full of sympathy. It's all too much.

"Actually," I say, wriggling out of the hug, "I have to get home. I have a lot of work to do."

"Okay," Chloe says, watching me with concern. "I can come over tonight if you want?"

"Thanks, but I'm just gonna work and go to bed," I say, and then I give her one more hug. "Bye, guys."

The bell jingles as I walk out the door and into the night, where the street that looked so charming and lit up before now looks dingy and dark. This is it, I tell myself. This is your life.

It felt good to think, even for a day, that something magical could happen to me. That a movie star could come to town, and he could not only be good-looking but also sweet and sad and complicated, and that we would have a connection. But this is real life, not a movie, I remind myself as my boots hit the brick sidewalk. Drew Danforth is probably used to dating whoever he wants, whenever he wants, and anyway he'll be gone in a couple of days.

And then, my sadness starts to morph into something more akin to rage. Because I broke up with Carter over this jerk. Sure, Carter didn't make my heart flutter, but maybe that's not what I wanted. Maybe I don't need to feel like I'm constantly having heart palpitations! Maybe I should've gone for someone who was strong, steady, dependable, and I don't know, NOT A MOVIE STAR.

"This is exactly why Hugh Grant should've stayed away from Julia Roberts," I mutter under my breath as I step into the house.

"What's that?" Uncle Don calls from the couch, where he's working through yet another rewatch of the *Merlin* television series.

"Nothing!" I call as I hang up my coat.

I head to my room and stop as soon as I walk in. The thought that filled me with giddy elation this morning—"Drew was in this room!"—now fills me with incandescent fury. If I'd never met him, maybe what I had with Carter would've been enough. Oh, poor hypothetical Annie, forced to date a hot man with big arms who knows how to properly light a film set. How would I ever have survived?

But no. I had to meet stupid, flirty prankster Drew Danforth, a guy who will pull on your hair and make you think you're having a movie moment even though he's probably just thinking about making out with an impossibly beautiful actress.

I look at myself in the mirror, slumping when I see the sad remains of the lipstick I hopefully put on earlier, back when I imagined it would be smeared all over Carter's face by the end of the night.

The only thing that cheers me up is the buoying effect of my own anger, which reminds me that I'll be able to tell Drew exactly what I think of him tomorrow in a speech worthy of a movie.

"I hate you, Drew Danforth," I whisper to my reflection with a smile.

Chapter Fourteen

IN MOST ROMANTIC COMEDIES, THE FIRST SCENE ESTABLISHES WHY THE female lead needs a change in her life. Maybe she's barking orders at an assistant and sleeping at the office, so we know she's a workaholic who needs to find love! Or maybe she's on yet another terrible date, so we know she wants to get married and she needs to find love! Or maybe she lives alone and watches TV while eating dinner, so we know she's lonely and she needs to find love!

The common denominator here (besides, you know, the whole "finding love" thing) is that no romantic comedy heroine's life is perfect when the film starts. In fact, it's usually pretty screwed up. Maybe it's sad, or maybe it's lacking meaning, or maybe there's just a lot of bad sex. Either way, something is off, and we find out what it is right away, usually set to music and possibly in the form of a montage.

I thought I was already in my love story—at first I thought Carter could be my perfect man, and then I thought he was a romcom red herring, meant to distract me from Drew. But I was wrong both times, because my love story hasn't even begun yet. This is all backstory, yet another thing in a seemingly endless list of humiliations that will endear me to viewers, and while that might sound disheartening, it's not. It means that my meet–cute and happy ending are still out there, waiting, and they'll mean so much more because of everything I've gone through.

I just have to wait.

I walk downstairs, my ankle supporting my weight like a champ, and see Uncle Don standing with his arms crossed, staring at the Chewbacca costume spread out on the floor.

I stand beside him and look down at the costume. "What are we looking at?"

He looks over at me. "Is it a cliché to dress as Chewbacca for a con?"

I tilt my head. "Sometimes clichés are clichés for a reason . . . because they work. Maybe it's just a great costume."

He nods. "That's what I thought. Dungeon Master Rick told me he thought it was hacky, but he's only five foot six. I'm six foot two."

"A much better height for Chewbacca," I agree.

"The guys and I are leaving tomorrow morning for Chicago," Don reminds me. "But tonight's still D&D night."

"Well, don't stay up too late." I head into the kitchen to grab a banana. "You don't want to be crammed into Paul's Subaru with a tired, cranky Dungeon Master Rick."

I walk back into the room and see Uncle Don gathering the costume up off the floor. "You know what? I'm gonna go for it. I refuse to let Dungeon Master Rick get in my head."

"Stay strong," I say, toasting him with my banana. "Well, I have to get to work. See you tonight."

As I walk down the street, I can't stop myself from humming.

After an endless winter, today's warm weather feels like a gift made especially for me. The sun beats down on my head, and the sad piles of gray snow are turning into puddles. It's easy to imagine I'm Meg Ryan in *You've Got Mail*, walking purposefully with a Starbucks cup while the Cranberries play.

Except that I would never go to Starbucks because I wouldn't want to hurt Nick's feelings.

"How about this weather?" I burst through the door to Nick's, the bell jingling in my wake. I slam my hands on the counter. "God, I love Kenny Loggins."

Chloe side-eyes me. "Shush. Nick hasn't noticed that I put on an all-Kenny playlist this morning, so don't bring attention to it. Are you . . . okay?"

"Never better." I smile. "One for me and one for Tommy, please."

She fills two cups, still watching me out of the corner of her eye. The dulcet tones of "Whenever I Call You 'Friend'" start playing, and I can't help swaying back and forth.

"I'm saying this as your BFF," Chloe says, popping lids on the cups. "You're acting super weird. Weren't you just, like, heartbroken?"

I shrug as she sets the cups on the counter. "Yeah, but then I realized: Drew is nothing. He's insignificant. He's the guy in the rom-com who treats me horribly before I meet Tom Hanks."

Chloe thinks about this for a minute. "Yeah, but Greg Kinnear was pretty nice in *You've Got Mail*. Like, he was boring and loved typewriters too much, but he wasn't mean."

"Not in that movie."

"And Bill Pullman was okay in *Sleepless in Seattle*. Again, kind of boring, and he had a lot of allergies, but it wasn't like that was his fault."

"Not the point, Chloe! We've seen other romantic comedies, okay? I'm not talking about Tom Hanks specifically in his Nora Ephron roles. I'm talking about the broader concept of Tom Hanks and what he represents."

Chloe nods. "Tom Hanks as a symbol. Got it."

"Anyway, I'm going to be fine." I pick up the coffees with what I imagine to be an air of insouciance. "My rom-com hasn't even started yet. Or maybe it has and this is still the opening montage where I fall down a lot and injure myself and meet terrible men and—"

A customer bumps into me and the coffees fall out of my hand, splashing all over the floor.

"Oh, for God's sake," I say as a few customers clap.

"Tobin!" Chloe calls. "Clean up!"

Tobin emerges from the back room, mop and bucket in hand. "On it."

"Wow," I say as Tobin starts cleaning up the mess. "What's gotten into him?"

"I think he feels bad about killing all his mom's plants," Chloe says.

"I can hear you," Tobin says. "I'm just working on my karma."

I glance at the giant clock on the wall. I'm due on set basically now, and the thought of seeing Drew makes me feel as if a small but unusually active animal has taken up residence in my stomach. "Crap," I say. "I have to go."

"Hey," Chloe says, carefully handing me two new cups. "Did you hear that we're supposed to get a huge snowstorm tomorrow night?"

I shake my head. "I refuse to process that information. It's fifty degrees right now, summer is here, and we're about to bust out our bikinis and start playing the Beach Boys."

"Are you *sure* you're okay?"

"Never better!" I say, although to be honest, a slightly manic energy is radiating off of me. "Now, I'm off to work. My montage continues!"

Chloe offers up a wave, her brow still furrowed. The bell jingles as I push my way through the door.

Okay, so I may be slightly exaggerating my good mood, but the point is: I'm fine, and I don't want Chloe to worry about me. I *am* hurt, and I *am* sad, but this is okay.

But one thing's for sure: if I talk to Drew Danforth today, he'd better watch out.

My eyes drift over to Drew and Tarah, who are filming a big fight scene today. Not, like, a punching-bad-guys fight scene—this isn't that kind of movie—but one where their emotional barriers finally come to the surface, and she yells a classic rom-com line at him: "And you know what? Maybe that's your problem. You care so much about your past that you never think about your future."

I'm a little bit jealous, because there are a few choice lines I'd like to yell at Drew Danforth. Not that one, of course, but maybe: *You know what? Maybe that's your problem. Hollywood Gossip caught you canoodling with your costar.*

You know what? Maybe that's your problem. You pretended like you were jealous of Sexy Gaffer, but apparently it was all some big game for you.

You know what? Maybe that's your problem. You and your ridiculously perfect abs that you don't even care about and that annoyingly swoopy hair and . . .

Oh, God. This isn't helping, because now I'm feeling less "c'est la vie" and more "I want to dropkick Drew Danforth into the sun." But honestly, I have very little lower-body strength, so I probably couldn't even do that. Maybe I need to start going to self-defense classes or something.

Instead of thinking about every one of Drew's infuriatingly perfect features that I now hate, I watch Tarah. While I wouldn't say that we're friends, we are on a friendly basis. Once she gave me an extra taco when she ordered too many from the taco truck that parks at the corner sometimes, and I can't help but like anyone who shares their food.

But there's no denying that we're pretty different people. I mean, she's almost impossibly beautiful, like a painting or a doll. Obviously I've seen her on screen, but in person she emits a glow that normal people don't have. I search my heart for some sort of jealousy or anger toward her, and I can't find any; how could I compete with her anyway? She's a famous, talented, beautiful actress. We're not on the same playing field. We're not even playing the same sport—it's like she's in the WNBA, and I'm playing with a child-sized Fisher-Price basketball hoop.

As the scene cuts and they pull away from each other, I watch them for some sign of chemistry, for some evidence of the canoodling Hollywood Gossip talked about. But they step away from each other immediately and get absorbed into a conversation with Tommy.

I guess Drew's always good at hiding his real intentions.

Drew catches my eye and smiles, that ridiculous, lopsided smirk, and I look away before it can affect me.

I mean, it still affects me a little, but I tell myself I'm immune to it now. Getting so close to him in my bedroom was like getting exposed to chicken pox when you're young, and now I can't get it again.

Except that I just wrote an article about chicken pox, and I know that sometimes it comes back as shingles when you're much older, but that's not the point here.

When Tommy asks me for another coffee, I'm glad to go get it.

"Hey," Drew says, sidling up to me as I attempt to open another phone charger for Tommy—the third one I've bought him, since he's always losing his.

"Oh, hello," I say, pretending that I'm running into a political canvasser whose opinion differs from mine, but I still have to be polite because we're both human beings. See? Drew Danforth isn't the only one who can act.

"This weather, huh?" He bumps his shoulder into mine.

"Please don't use your impressive bulk to knock me over." I try to focus on the phone charger, but it was pretty easy to open and doesn't really require any more concentration. I wind the cord around my hand a few times, pretending that this is an important task.

"Whoa." He reaches out and puts a hand on my arm so that I'm forced to stop wrapping the phone cord around my hand. "Whoa, whoa, whoa. What's . . . going on?"

I turn to face him and raise my eyebrows. "*What's going on?* Are you serious?"

His eyes search my face. "Annie, I—"

I hold up my hands. "Don't say my name like that, okay? I just . . . obviously, this meant nothing to you. That . . . moment, or whatever, in my bedroom. Carrying me home. Being so nice to my uncle. It was all a game for you."

Drew shakes his head slowly. His hand is still on my arm, so I pull away. "I have no idea what you're talking about."

"Have you checked Hollywood Gossip today?"

He snort-laughs. "I never check Hollywood Gossip for the same reason I don't repeatedly hit my head against a brick wall."

"Well then," I say, vindicated, "I guess you missed the article about how you and Tarah are hooking up."

His mouth drops open.

"And you thought I wouldn't notice," I continue. "You thought, 'Oh, this little rube from Ohio won't even know that I'm just flirting with her for fun.'"

"Annie." Drew grabs both my arms now and leans down so he's right in front of my face. "That's not true. That's . . . that's all made up."

"I broke up with Carter for you, you turd!" I whisper-shout, not wanting everyone nearby to hear us but also kind of wanting everyone nearby to hear us, so they'll all know exactly what type of person Drew is.

"You—what? You broke up with Sexy Gaffer?" Drew's mouth drops open and I hate to admit, even an expression of dopey surprise looks good on him.

"Like you even care, you asshole," I hiss, and oh, this is satisfying. Really letting it rip, letting out all my frustration, using a few choice but still tame curse words because the movie of my life is destined to be PG-13, I guess.

"I care, Annie." Drew leans toward me, his voice low.

I roll my eyes and step back, willing myself not to be moved by the way Drew sounds exactly like a rom-com male lead apologizing and trying to win back the heroine's heart. He's not Mr. Darcy over here, I remind myself. He's the before. The Bill Pullman, but a jerk. The montage.

"You have to know most of the stuff on those sites is fake.

That's why Jennifer Aniston is perpetually pregnant with twins. Tarah and I are friends and maybe someone saw us talking and—"

"Oh, no thank you," I say, taking a step back. "I'm so not here for whatever excuses you're going to give me. With your big speech in the Book Loft about *Frasier* or whatever and trying to help my uncle with his table and pretending to be all nice. I don't trust you, Drew Danforth, and you're just part of a montage."

He blinks. "Why do I get the distinct feeling that I should be insulted by that?"

"Because you should." I turn away and start walking. "Good-bye, Drew."

The thing about telling someone off in real life versus in a movie is that I didn't really have any great lines. If I were to script this, I would've added something a lot more poetic and dramatic, and I definitely would've explained the whole montage thing to him first so that it would've been properly insulting in the moment.

I text Chloe that I won't be at Nick's tonight. What I want to do is curl up in bed and watch whatever rom-com I can Netflix on my laptop . . . but, seeing as internet content never sleeps, I'll have to settle for curling up in bed and writing SEO-optimized articles.

The creak of the front door and the rumbles of male voices alert me that the D&D guys are here. I smell Uncle Don's famous spinach-artichoke dip, and my stomach growls in response. Still, I'm in no hurry to go downstairs. The guys were so smitten with Drew (well, not so much Dungeon Master Rick) last time, and I don't want to deal with all their questions about him. When your potential flirtation with a celebrity fizzles out, the last thing you want to do is talk about it with a group of middle-aged gamers.

Still . . . that spinach-artichoke dip is *so* good, and I know for a fact that Uncle Don made his special paprika chips out of baked pitas. I roll my eyes and squeeze myself out of my blanket cocoon. A quick glance in the mirror reveals that I look objectively awful. I'm wearing yoga pants (sidenote: I have literally never done yoga) with a hole on the thigh and a T-shirt that reads PIZZA SLUT. Chloe bought us matching ones as a joke because we order a lot of pizza for our movie nights, but it's one of the most comfortable shirts I own so I tend to sleep in it.

Whatever. It's not like the guys will even notice what I'm wearing, and maybe if I creep downstairs quietly I can slip into the kitchen unnoticed.

I tiptoe down the stairs, which, since this house is over a hundred years old, creak pretty much all the time. Still, the guys are deep in a D&D discussion, so they don't hear me. As I step into the kitchen, I hear the sound of the dice and Dungeon Master Rick saying something, then a comment from Uncle Don, and Paul and Earl laugh and—

Wait a second. Is there a fifth voice? They would never let someone else join in on D&D. Unless . . .

I push the swinging door between the kitchen and dining room open just a little. Dungeon Master Rick scowls as Don leans over and explains something to . . .

Drew Danforth.

"What the hell?" I whisper before I can stop myself, and all five heads swivel toward me. I step back and let the door swing closed.

I run toward the fridge, open the door, and stand there as casually as possible, like, "Oh, me? Yeah, I came downstairs to get a snack. I definitely wasn't spying on you from behind a door like we're in a sitcom or anything."

The door swings open and I hear a quick snatch of conversation from the dining room, a snippet of Dungeon Master Rick complaining about too many breaks in the game, but I barely notice because Drew Danforth is in front of me. Here. In my kitchen.

I stand up straight and shut the fridge. "What are you doing here?" I ask with as much dignity as I can muster.

Drew gestures toward the dining room. "Well, the guys invited me over to game with them, and I was kind of curious, so . . ."

I deflate a little. I mean, it's not like I thought Drew Danforth came here for me—not that I even want him to!—but there's something slightly pathetic about taking second place after D&D.

I nod. "Right."

"But . . . okay, I'll be honest." Drew runs his hands through that outrageously fluffy hair, and it falls back into place as soon as his hands leave it. I can't help myself from imagining the softness of that hair between my fingers, and . . .

I shake my head.

"I didn't just come here to learn about tabletop gaming," Drew says, looking down at the island.

I try to say "Oh, yeah?" but it comes out as a strangled groan.

"I came here because I wanted to explain to you, and you wouldn't listen to me today," he says, meeting my eyes and taking a step toward me.

I take a step back, reminded of my earlier anger. "You don't have to explain anything. I get it, okay?"

He shakes his head. Another small step forward. "I don't think you do."

I step back again. "It was nothing. You're a grown man; you're allowed to flirt with or do whatever with whoever you want. And I'm a grown woman. I can handle it. Forget about it . . . it didn't even mean anything."

Drew shakes his head again and takes yet another step toward me. Now there's nowhere else for me to go; I can't back up any more unless I want to knock over the recycling can, which is full of empty Mountain Dew cans because that's what the guys drink on D&D nights.

"It wasn't nothing, and I don't want to forget about it. Tarah and I don't have anything going on. She's married."

"Wait," I say. "She is? But Hollywood Gossip didn't—"

"Please," he groans. "Stop getting your news from Hollywood Gossip. No one knows she's married because she's pretty secretive about her private life, and they haven't thought to look into it. Maybe someone saw us talking or filming a scene, but we weren't *canoodling.* Canoodling is— God, why did they have to use the word *canoodling?* It sounds so terrible."

"Like you're sharing a noodle, like in *Lady and the Tramp*," I say quietly.

"What? I mean . . ." Drew gives me a narrow-eyed, skeptical look. "I'm not trying to get into the origin of the word *canoodle.* That's not what I came here to do."

"You came here to kill some dire wolves," I say, trying and failing to pry my eyes off his brown eyes, which are somehow even more beautiful than they are on screen.

"No, Annie," he says, my name still sounding special and magical when he says it. "I came here to see you. Did you really end things with Sexy Gaffer?"

"He has a name."

"Fine. Carter. Did you really end things with Carter? Because I know I was kind of a dick about him. I'm sorry. He's an okay guy."

I shrug. "We weren't right for each other anyway. You don't have to be sorry about that."

"Well, good," Drew says, taking another step toward me. "Because I'm actually not sorry at all that you broke up."

I take that extra step back and the trash can tilts over, Mountain Dew cans crashing onto the floor. I immediately crouch down and start picking them up, and Drew follows suit.

"This," I mutter. "This is a mistake."

"Tell me about it," Drew says. "There's no way this much Mountain Dew is good for those guys. Once I knew this dude in high school who drank so much Mountain Dew that his stomach lining literally corroded and—"

"No." I shake my head, meeting his eyes. "I know you came here to see me and that's nice but—I can't."

Drew drops a Mountain Dew can into the recycling bin and it lands with a satisfying thunk. "What are you talking about?"

"I mean . . ." I sigh. "Obviously I think you're attractive. Obviously."

"Obviously," he repeats, giving me that smirk that makes me scowl.

"But you're done here tomorrow night, and then you're off to God knows where—"

"New York," Drew supplies. "I'm taping a morning show appearance on Monday morning to promote my next movie, but I have my hotel here booked through the weekend. Let's hang out. Let's get dinner. Let's—"

I hold up my hand and almost fall out of my crouching position, but Drew's hand shoots out to steady me. It's infuriating that he's always around to catch me when I fall.

"But I don't want to hang out for a couple of days with any guy. Do you get that?" I ask, searching his eyes. He looks back at me, waiting.

What I want to say is that Tom Hanks doesn't just *hang out*. My parents didn't just *hang out*. I want the real thing—the rom-com love, the forever love, the "let's start a family" love. But that's a little too much to say right now, even for me, so I settle for, "We have really different lives. You make movies, and I write about hemorrhoid relief."

"So come out and visit me sometime," Drew says, excited. "You'd like LA. There's this thing called sunshine there; maybe you've heard of it? And people get hemorrhoids all over the world, you know. They're the great equalizer."

I smile a little. "No. It's just—I'm glad we met, okay?"

Drew looks at me, his eyes poring over my face so slowly that it almost feels like he's touching me, and I have to stop myself from either pulling away or throwing myself at him. He's not even doing anything; he's just *looking* at me. That's the effect this guy has on me, and that's why I know I made the right decision not to make out with him or go to dinner with him or whatever.

Even though I really, really want to make out with him.

Someone like him—famous, confident, perfect—can't possibly understand what it's like to be rejected and alone. The way I felt when I saw that article about him and Tarah? I don't ever want to experience that again, and I know that if this weird, amorphous, flirtation-type *thing* with Drew progresses any further, I definitely would.

I'm not putting myself in a situation where I could lose someone else. When I meet my Tom Hanks, and it's real, then I'll know: there won't be any risk and I won't ever have to be afraid of a broken heart.

Drew looks like he wants to say something else, but finally he says, "If that's what you want," with no trace of frustration or malice in his voice.

I stand up, my knees cracking, and Drew follows.

"We're friends, okay?" Drew asks. "If you ever want to send me your screenplay, please do. I'd love to read it. Seriously."

I nod. "Thanks."

"I'll see you on set tomorrow," Drew says. "Oh. And at the wrap party."

"Oh yeah," I say, remembering that Tommy promised to take us all out for drinks after we finish tomorrow.

"I'm glad we met, too," Drew says, his hand reaching out as if he's about to touch me, but then his fingers hover before falling back to his side. "And Tarah and me—we're really not—"

I shake my head. "No. I believe you."

"Well, I better get back to the game," Drew says, gesturing over his shoulder. "Dungeon Master Rick runs a pretty tight campaign."

"Tell me about it." I smile. I wave as he walks toward the dining room door, but right as the door swings open, he says, "Nice outfit, by the way."

The door swings shut. I look down at my Pizza Slut shirt and groan.

Chapter Fifteen

ONE OF THE REASONS I LOVE *WHILE YOU WERE SLEEPING* SO MUCH (besides Sandra Bullock being impossibly charming and Bill Pullman being unexpectedly sexy in that reversible jacket Chloe made fun of) is the family. At the beginning of the movie, Sandra Bullock works on holidays because she has no one. She's as alone as a person can be, which in a rom-com means that she has a cat. But then, through a series of misunderstandings, she ends up pretending to be comatose Peter Gallagher's girlfriend and goes to a Christmas celebration at his family's house. It's big and loud and everyone's yelling and arguing and *she loves it.* No longer is she surrounded by only her apartment building's weird tenants; now she's part of a family that envelops her and makes her one of their own and gives her a stocking, and that's why it's so hard for her to tell them the truth . . . that she's not really Peter Gallagher's girlfriend.

Of course, things work themselves out because his brother, Bill Pullman, proposes to her with the entire family in tow and it's very sweet and I always cry, but the point is, I get it.

It's not that I'm alone. I have Uncle Don, and he counts for a whole lot. I have the best friend ever in Chloe, and I have the warm, caffeinated comfort of hanging out at Nick's and the way his wacky patrons make me feel like I'm part of a sitcom.

But right now, when Uncle Don's getting ready to leave for the convention and Chloe's busy studying at her place and I know the house will be silent and lonely all weekend, I yearn for that big family in *While You Were Sleeping.*

I wish I could meet my Tom Hanks *now* and we could have five kids, enough people that we would never be lonely. And maybe that's pathetic. Maybe I should only care about my career—but the thing is, I want a family. I want love, and I don't think it makes me a weak or bad person to not want to be alone. You know how, in wedding vows and engagement-party speeches, people say that their partner is their "other half," and we all either swoon or roll our eyes? Yes, it's so cliché that it borders on meaningless, but pieces of me went missing when my parents died. Those pieces will never be replaced, but what I want is someone who can help me patch up the broken places. Maybe my person and I won't fit together like two halves of the same whole, but neither did Tom Hanks and Meg Ryan in *You've Got Mail* or *Sleepless in Seattle.* They didn't erase each other's pain; they just made it bearable.

As I sit on the couch, Uncle Don walks past me, his Chewbacca costume in his hands. "I'm gonna go shake this thing out on the porch," he says, holding it like it's a rug.

I know Chloe's studying, but I need to tell someone about what just happened, so I pull out my phone and text her. One of the perks of living on the same property as your best friend is that she can get to your couch in about 2.5 seconds.

After I explain everything that happened with Drew tonight, Chloe says, "I will never, as long as I live, understand anything you do."

"He isn't my Tom Hanks, Chloe."

She throws her hands in the air in frustration. "Who cares about Tom Hanks right now? If I had the chance to bang a movie star who has a body like that . . . I mean, Annie, for God's sake, this is like you have a chance to eat at Chez Panisse and you're like, 'Nah, I'll wait' or you have a chance to see a once-in-a-lifetime meteor shower and you're all, 'Eh, I'll catch it next time.' Can't you take this chance for me?"

I bite my lip to stop myself from smiling. "Sure, Chloe, I'll hook up with someone so I can tell you all about it later. That sounds like a great reason to form an emotional attachment to a man who's leaving town in a matter of days."

Chloe sighs and looks at the ceiling. "Okay, can I present a theory?"

I narrow my eyes. "What sort of theory is this?"

"What, do you think it's about the origin of the universe? It's about you. Duh." She shifts her position so that she's sitting on her feet. "Why do you like rom-coms so much?"

I tilt my head. "You know why, Chlo. Because they're funny and there's kissing and they're full of hope."

"Right." She nods. "And you watch all these movies, and you say you want that Tom Hanks kind of love, but do you really?"

My eyes widen. "I mean . . . yes. Of course. If I didn't care about finding true love, like my parents, like a movie, then I would be making out with a hot movie star right now."

Chloe points at me. "Exactly."

I blink a few times. "What point are you trying to make?"

"You have a reason to reject every guy you've ever met. Every date you go on, there's some nitpicky reason why he's not perfect."

"Barry didn't drink hot liquids, Chloe."

"Not just Barry! Everyone. They don't have the perfect quirky job, or they don't have the perfect quirky hobbies, or they don't have the perfect quirky living situation. For whatever reason, you didn't even fall for Carter, and that man was basically a cardboard cutout of a rom-com hero. You find something wrong with every guy, and I wonder—"

She stops, sighs, and crosses her arms.

"What?" I ask.

"I just wonder . . . you watch all these movies and you say you want love, but do you, really? Or are you hiding behind rom-coms because you don't want anything to change?"

I sit back and try to take a breath. "What do you mean?"

"Love is a risk, right?" Chloe widens her eyes and nods, like she's explaining simple arithmetic to a small child. "Loving someone means you might lose them. And God knows you've already lost a hell of a lot, Annie. But I don't want you to be so afraid of anything changing that you don't take a good opportunity when it's right in front of you."

I bite my lip. "If I didn't know you, I might take you for a hopeless romantic instead of a total cynic."

"Hey," Chloe holds a hand over her heart, mock-offended. "The opportunity I'm referring to is the one to jump Drew Danforth's bones, okay? My status as your friendly neighborhood relationship cynic remains intact."

I laugh.

"Seriously, though." Chloe reaches out and squeezes my knee. "Romantic comedies are great, okay? And I know you're writing a perfect one. But sometimes real life is a little more messy and confusing and you can't necessarily plot it out with *Save the Cat*."

"Do I really talk about *Save the Cat* that much? It's just that it's a great book and—"

Chloe holds up a hand. "Not helping. Just . . . I hope you're able to open yourself up a little bit. This isn't a sad rom-com montage, because you're not a sad, lonely person. You always have me and Don, no matter what, because we're not going anywhere."

"Aw, shucks," I mutter, looking at my feet on the sofa.

Don walks back in, dripping wet. "Well, it started raining and now the costume's soaked, so we're gonna smell like wet Wookiee all the way to Chicago."

Chloe looks at me and I look at her and we both burst out laughing.

Don's costume drips onto the living room floor as he looks at us, bewildered. "What? Did I say something funny?"

So it's not like I'm going to listen to Chloe and attempt to hook up with Drew before he heads off to New York, but maybe she's right about one thing. I might be lonely once in a while, but I'm definitely not alone.

Chapter Sixteen

I AM, HOWEVER, ALONE WHEN I WAKE UP ON FRIDAY MORNING. Uncle Don left way before the crack of dawn, and although it's not like we always have conversations in the morning or anything, the house is strangely silent knowing I'm the only person in it.

I shuffle around the kitchen, grabbing an apple and thinking about how quiet it is here. When my mom was alive, there was always music playing or her off-tune humming or her laughter ringing through the house.

I know Chloe was right when she said that I wasn't alone, but I hate this. This quiet. This solitude. I let my thoughts stray to what would happen if I didn't live here anymore, if I moved to some other city or even some other house . . .

But no. Then Uncle Don would be by himself, rattling around in these empty rooms, and what way would that be to treat the man who dropped everything in his life to take care of me?

I crunch into my apple and think about it. Maybe I can't leave or make a big change, but could I make a small one? I wouldn't ever go off to LA or New York, but I could take Drew at his word—maybe he really could take a look at my screenplay, unfinished as it is. Sure, he's not a writer, but he's had a whole lot more experience in movies than I have.

See? I say to Chloe in my head. I'm not afraid of change or rejection. Look at me, asking change to come into my life! Courting rejection! Taking chances!

I toss my apple core into the garbage can and head off to set.

We're even busier and more frantic than usual, since Tommy is trying to cram a lot into one day. It's not the last day of shooting, since some of that will take place in other locations, but it is the last day of shooting here in German Village. I'm so busy running around and grabbing things for Tommy that I can barely even think, let alone focus on Drew.

At one point, Carter catches my eye from across the street. He waves and gives me a tiny smile before turning to do whatever it is he does. I never one hundred percent figured out what his job entails, which *might* make me a bad person, but that was probably a sign that we weren't meant to be. It still stings just a little bit to see him, though, like lemon juice on a paper cut.

The last scene we film isn't even an exciting one; it's some conversation between Tarah and Drew on the sidewalk, and I watch it, watch him lean toward her and watch her smile up at him, and wonder.

And then, all of a sudden, it's over. People clap and pack things up and I help Tommy with a million things. He grabs his beloved megaphone and yells, "Seven P.M.! We're going to Victory's, and we're celebrating a job well done! If you can hear me, you're invited. Well, not you." He points to a person across the street. "But everyone else."

"Are you going to be there tonight?" Tarah asks me, stopping me before I head off to Nick's.

I nod. "Yeah, I think so." My breath puffs out into clouds; even though it was warm and sunny yesterday, the air has turned bitterly cold, and the sky hangs heavy with the promise of snow.

"Great!" she says, with one of those megawatt smiles she's known for. "I'm glad you understood that me and Drew—we're not—" She shakes her head and grimaces. "I mean, I'm married. I'm not trying to move in on your guy."

My eyes widen and now it's my turn to shake my head. "Oh, no. He's not my— I'm not— We're not—"

She raises her eyebrows and laughs, a tinkly, wind-chime sound. "Whoa! I'm sure that defensiveness is definitely not a sign of any underlying feelings."

"It's not— I don't—" I continue to stammer.

She reaches out and puts her hand on my arm. "I'm kidding, Annie! I'll see you tonight!"

And with that, she turns and walks away, and I'm left alone. How does she even know anything about me and Drew? All of our weird, sexual-tension-filled romantic-comedy almost-kisses have taken place at my house, not in public. Is Drew talking about me to people? WHAT IS GOING ON?

I look to my left and see Drew and Brody deep in conversation about something, and right then they both turn and look at me. Brody waves as if this is totally normal, as if two famous men turn to stare at some random Ohio woman all the time.

I ignore him, look away, then turn and walk-run to Nick's to dissect this entire day with Chloe.

"Come with me, Chloe!" I beg later that night. "Don't you want to see what a Hollywood wrap party is like?"

"First off," she says, handing a cup to a customer, "this isn't

Hollywood, it's Columbus. Secondly, no way am I going to a party to be your female version of a cock block. Wait, what is the female version of a cock block?"

She pulls out her phone and scrolls through it.

"You won't be my female cock block because you're not blocking anything, metaphorical or otherwise," I say, leaning against the bakery case. "I just want to ask Drew to take a look at my screenplay, but things are really weird between us and—"

"You mean that the air between you is full of sexual tension, and for some reason you won't just put your mouth all over his," she says, then looks back down at her phone. "These are—oh, God, these are really dirty. I can't even say these out loud in here."

She hands the phone to me, and I scroll through them. "Yeah, no, some of these don't even make sense. 'Pussy pass' doesn't remotely sound like 'cock block.'"

I hand her phone back to her right as Nick walks behind the counter. "What are you doing?" he asks, leaning in and looking at her phone. "Wait, what—are you looking at porn at work?"

"No!" Chloe screeches, and Nick plucks her phone out of her hand.

"I'm gonna have to confiscate this," he mutters, but he's smiling as Chloe leaps onto him to grab it back. I make a mental note of their body language to include in my screenplay.

"Nick!" she wails, pretend-hitting him on the arm. He doesn't seem to mind the extra physical contact.

"Fine, fine, fine," he says, handing it back to her. "But I'm not paying you to look at BuzzFeed, okay?"

"What are you smiling so dopily about?" Chloe asks me when Nick walks into the back room.

I know better than to mention her getting together with Nick, because Chloe is like a small child in that she will immediately reject any idea given to her by someone else. She needs to come to it on her own, so she thinks it's her idea. I just shrug.

Chloe glances at her phone once more before sliding it into her pocket. "Isn't your super-sexy party starting, like, right now?"

"I'm trying to be fashionably late," I say, shifting my weight from one foot to another. "That's still a thing, right?"

"Nick says no," Tobin says, walking behind me with a load full of dirty cups and tiny plates. "At least, that's what he said last week when I was late for every shift."

He disappears into the back room and I'm forced to admit that I've stalled long enough. It's time to go to this party, have a drink, ask Drew if he's serious about looking at my screenplay, and then hightail it home to my big old empty house.

Chloe looks at me with concern, like she can read my mind and see how worried I am. "You're gonna be fine! Promise. But be careful; aren't we supposed to get, like, the blizzard of the century tonight?"

"Yeah, I guess," I say, but snow is hardly the first thing on my mind right now. Mainly I'm thinking: if this is the last time I'm going to see Drew, then what should I do? I should play it safe, be professional, leave it at that. Right?

Or. Maybe Chloe's right. Maybe this, all of this confusion, was our rom-com obstacle and I'm going to, improbably, have a happily-ever-after with this beautiful man who—

Is going to New York at the end of the weekend, I remind myself. After which he will definitely not be back in Columbus, because he doesn't live here. I, meanwhile, have built my entire, unchangeable life here. I may not have access to a Magic 8 Ball right at the moment, but I know that if I were to shake it, it would say "Outlook Not So Good."

Or maybe it would say "Ask Again Later." I tended to get that response a lot at sleepovers.

"What are you wearing?" Chloe asks, leaning over the counter.

"Um, this?" I say. I unzip the puffy black coat I wear from November through March and reveal the large gray sweater I'm wearing under it.

Chloe tilts her head and squints. "I can only assume you intend that sweater to function as a sort of chastity belt."

I give her an angry look, but the truth is . . . well, kind of.

But at this point, I can't stall any longer. "Well, I'm off, I guess."

Chloe reaches across the counter and grabs my hands. "Good luck. Maybe you can drink so much that you get really sick and barf everywhere and Drew has to take care of you and in the process of nursing you back to health you'll realize that—"

"Chloe! How have you absorbed so many rom-com plotlines?"

She shrugs. "Just text me if you guys hook up, and make sure to include lots of details. Circumcised, uncircumcised—"

"I'm not going to text you about his penis," I say. "And on that note, I'm leaving."

I wave as I walk past Gary, who gives me a salute, and out the door.

A few tiny flakes of snow are hitting the sidewalk, but nothing like the huge snowstorm that's been promised. Either way, I'm glad that Uncle Don arrived safely in Chicago—he sent me a selfie of all the guys and their gear in their hotel room.

It's one of those magical nights in the city, when the lights make the darkness look cozy instead of bleak. Those few snowflakes look almost like glitter raining down, and people walk past me holding coffee cups and bags of macarons from the bakery Pistacia Vera. The

Coatless Wonder strolls by, hands in his pockets, unconcerned as ever about the cold.

At the bar, I hesitate with my hand on the door. I see the dim lighting inside, silhouettes of people moving, and I hear the clink of glasses and the gentle hum of conversation punctuated by an occasional sharp laugh. What if Drew says something like, "Ew, no, I don't want to see your screenplay, I was only asking because I wanted you to sleep with me."

Which, to be fair, doesn't really sound like him, but you never know.

"Oh, hey."

I turn around to see Brody standing behind me, a beanie shoved on his head and a scarf wrapped around his neck.

"Hi. Hey. Hello," I say, startled.

"Are you, uh . . . not going in?" he asks, gesturing toward the door.

"Oh!" I look at the door as if it suddenly appeared and, wow, there's a door here! Who knew! "I'm going in. I'm just . . ."

He leans forward. "Do you want someone to walk in with?"

That *is* what I want. Maybe one of the worst minor awkward situations is walking into a room where you know no one, or, in this case, walking into a room where you know a few people and searching the crowd for them with your eyes while trying to act like you're totally comfortable.

"Yeah," I say. "Actually, that would be really nice."

His smile takes over his face and I can see why he's famous. He's a lot shorter and stockier than Drew, but he has an honest, open expression.

He walks around me and holds open the door, gesturing for me to go inside. The wave of sound crashes over me, the conversations and glasses much louder than they were outside. Brody places an arm lightly on my back, guiding me through the crowd, careful to keep his hand high. He's wearing a strong and spicy cologne that actually smells good, even though typically I hate cologne on men.

But Brody's nice-smelling cologne aside, he isn't who I care about tonight. No matter how much I lie to myself, I know I'm looking for Drew.

Which is why I think he might be a figment of my imagination when he materializes right in front of us, looking down at Brody with steely eyes. "Hey," he says.

"Annie's here," Brody says, his hand dropping from my back.

"I can see that," Drew says, and still no one's looking at me.

"Um," I say, and both of their heads swivel to look at me. "Am I missing something?"

"I'm gonna go get a drink," Brody says, shooting Drew another look. And then he's gone.

Drew finally turns to me, and the second his eyes hit my face, he smiles, and it makes my heart break open. This is how I feel when Tom Hanks says, "Don't cry, Shopgirl." This is how I feel when Bill Pullman proposes to Sandra Bullock. This is how I feel when Billy Crystal gives Meg Ryan that impassioned New Year's Eve speech about all of her weird and wonderfully annoying quirks. There's a lifetime of wishing and hoping and dreaming in each one of Drew's smiles.

You came here to tell him about your screenplay, I remind myself, so I say, "Hey, can we sit down for a sec?"

I head toward a high-top table while he grabs us drinks from the bar. As I wait for him, I look around the room, which is packed full. I see Brody taking a selfie with a cute girl and Tarah laughing with Angela, the wardrobe woman, about something. Even though this is just one movie, and even though my main contribution to it was keeping Tommy fed and hydrated, I'm still proud. *I did it, Mom, I say in my head. I made a movie.*

"Annie!"

I look to my left and see Tommy, giant beer stein in hand, his mouth wide open in a genuine smile.

"What are you doing over here all by yourself?" he asks in mock disapproval. "This is a party!"

"Drew's getting us drinks," I say, pointing toward the crowded bar.

"Ah," Tommy says, then takes the seat across from me. "We have a second, then. So Drew told me you've got a screenplay."

Warmth floods to my face, the way it does whenever anyone finds out I'm a writer. It's so personal, to have someone else know that I like to sit by myself and transfer my deepest, darkest desires to the page. "Um, yeah."

Tommy throws his hands in the air, exasperated. "Why didn't you tell me? We work on this movie together for two weeks and you don't even mention you're a writer?"

I shake my head. "I mean . . . it's not . . . it's not finished."

Tommy leans forward, looking at my face until my eyes meet his. "Send it to me. I wanna read it, okay? No obligations, no strings, I just wanna see it."

I nod quickly, my heartbeat speeding up. "Okay."

Tommy takes another drink of his beer. "But that's not why I'm here. I wanted to talk to you about something."

My stomach drops as I think he's about to fire me, but then I remember that filming is over.

"What are you doing after this?"

I pause. "Going home?"

Tommy shakes his head. "No, I mean after this job. What do you have lined up next?"

Startled, I laugh. "I hadn't even really thought about it. It's not like another movie's going to film in Columbus anytime soon, so . . ."

Tommy narrows his eyes and looks irritated for the first time I can remember. "You're good at this job, Annie, and a good assistant is hard to find. Sometimes even when you do find one, they leave you for an underwear model."

"Truer words," I say, assuming this conversation is over.

"I'm not saying you can't work in entertainment at all in Columbus, but if you want to get serious, you need to go where they make TV and movies. You've gotta move to a bigger city."

"Thank you for the suggestion," I say, even though, in true Tommy fashion, he didn't suggest so much as demand. "But I don't think I can leave Columbus."

Tommy leans forward and looks into my eyes with a level of scrutiny I find unnerving. "What's here for you?"

I blanch. "Uh, my life? Don?"

"Nah," Tommy says, grimacing like he's got a bitter taste in his mouth. "Donny doesn't want you to spend your whole life waiting on something to fall into your lap. He'll never have this conversation with you, and that's why I'm doing it. Tough love. You want to work in movies, right?"

I nod.

"You're never gonna get a job on a movie set if you don't leave the house. Move somewhere else, get a job."

Perhaps I should be annoyed at Tommy for overstepping his professional boundaries, but maybe he's right. Uncle Don wouldn't ever have a conversation like this with me. We primarily talk about his feelings regarding spoilers for new *Star Wars* films, not the state of my employment opportunities. I wonder if, this whole time, Uncle Don has been waiting for me to make a move, thinking I'm some big loser for spending so much time writing internet content.

"But it's not that easy," I say to Tommy. "I can't just move somewhere and poof, someone offers me a job."

"Not to toot my own, but . . ." Tommy holds up his hands in an exaggerated shrug. "Toot toot, I won an Oscar. I have connections. I make a damn fine recommendation."

I can't help laughing.

"Listen, Annie, I'm not saying this is your only chance, but you've got some experience now. If you want to try something new, you can. All right, then." He slams a hand on the table. "How are things going with Drew?"

I raise my eyebrows. "What do you mean?"

Tommy smiles. "Ah, come on. You think I haven't seen the way you two have been looking at each other since the first day on set? You're talking to a guy who makes love stories for a living. I know one when I see it."

I shake my head. "Drew and I are not— Wait. When you sent us to dinner together, was that like . . . a setup?"

Tommy smiles. "Just call me your fairy godmother, sweetheart."

Emboldened by our conversation, and uncomfortable by the way Tommy has been meddling in my love life like he's turning me into his own personal rom-com, I say, "You know, you really shouldn't call women sweetheart. Or honey. Or dear."

He looks at me in confusion. "You mean you don't like that?"

"No," I say. "We're having a cultural moment, Tommy. You've gotta keep up."

"Huh." Tommy leans back, drumming his fingers on the table. "You learn something new every day."

"An old-fashioned for the lady," Drew says, appearing with our drinks. "And, Tommy, can I get you anything?"

"No, no, no," Tommy says, vacating Drew's seat. "The old man's getting out of here to let you kids have a good night. But promise me you'll think about it, Annie."

He looks at me meaningfully, and at first I think he's talking about Drew. But of course he's talking moving, about taking a big risk, and a wave of something—excitement? nausea?—washes over me. I just nod, and then he walks away.

Drew gestures toward him with his bottle. "What the hell was that about?"

"Why did you tell Tommy I'm working on a screenplay?!" I ask.

Drew takes a drink. "Uh, because you are, and because friends help each other out with their careers?"

Friends, I think. *Right.*

"But now I have to send it to him," I say.

"The horror! Forced to let a world-famous director read your screenplay." Drew reaches across the table and grabs my hands. "Annie, will you ever accept my apology for ruining your life?"

I hold back a smile. Even though Drew's joking, he kind of *is* ruining my life. In a couple of days he won't be around anymore, but I'll be stuck here, forced to see him occasionally on TV or movie posters, a constant reminder of what I kind of, sort of, almost never had.

"I forgive you," I say softly. To my chagrin, he lets go of my hands.

We each have another drink and talk about things other than my screenplay. About how Drew doesn't think Billy Crystal and Meg

Ryan are right for each other in *When Harry Met Sally* . . . ("They're annoyed with each other, like, most of the time!"), even though he is *obviously* very wrong. About how I heard a rumor there's going to be a *Frasier* reboot, and Drew says he would do just about anything to get cast in the smallest part.

I've had two old-fashioneds, and for a lightweight like me who's only had an apple and a bagel today, that's a lot. I'm already feeling it when Tarah comes over to say hi and, from the way she's utterly unfazed by Drew's presence, I can tell that they weren't lying to me. There's definitely nothing between them.

"I'm gonna run to the bathroom," I say, and tilt myself off the chair. I float rather than walk toward the back hallway to the restrooms.

When I'm done, I inspect myself in the mirror. I'm not drunk, not yet, but I'm definitely on the road there. I'm right at that alcohol crossroads where if I don't have anything else to drink I'll sober right up, but if I have another I might become really and truly plastered. I should probably leave now, before I have another drink and embarrass myself in front of Tommy and ruin any chance I have to use his connections and promise of a recommendation.

My phone buzzes, and I expect to see a text from Chloe demanding updates, but instead it's another text from Hollywood Gossip, asking if I have anything to share with them about Drew and reminding me that they pay for tips.

"Not now, Steve!" I mutter, shoving my phone back in my bag. If this is annoying for me, I can't even imagine how terrible it must be for Drew.

I pat my fingertips under my eyes, cleaning up my smeared eyeliner, and dab on the tiniest bit more lipstick. Satisfied, I turn to leave and open the door just as Drew turns the corner into the hallway.

A very large part of me wants to turn around and run back into the bathroom, but I'm trying to act like an adult here, and part of that involves not hiding in public restrooms.

"Oh," I say, brushing my hair out of my face. "Hello."

"I almost punched Brody earlier," he says, as if we're in the middle of a conversation.

It's quieter back in this hallway, so I can hear him even before he slowly takes a few steps toward me.

"Why?" I ask, flashing back to that weird moment when we first showed up.

"Because I thought you came here together," he says, a self-deprecating smile on his face. "You guys walked in, his hand was on you, and even though I'm a modern guy and my parents raised me to be a feminist, it activated this caveman part of my brain."

"He was only being friendly," I say. "Trust me, I've lived in a world full of pervs for a long time, and I know when someone's being a creep."

Drew holds up a hand. "I know. I know. And it's not like you have to explain anything or defend yourself to me. I'm not even the type of guy who gets into fights—unless it's in a movie—but in that second, I could've punched him in the face."

I laugh. "You would've destroyed him. I mean, look at you."

And then I do look at him. He's wearing this gray, long-sleeved thermal that clings to his chest in a way that is, frankly, obscene, and I'm struck by the desire to reach out and rub my hands across his torso. I shake my head quickly.

Drew leans down. He's much closer to me than he should be. "I shouldn't have worried. Brody knows about us."

My mouth drops open. "Knows what about us?"

"That we're friends," Drew says, his voice low in an almost Bill-Pullman-in-*While-You-Were-Sleeping* growl. "Very, very good friends."

Someone walks past us, headed to the men's room, and Drew scoots even closer to me to let the man pass. I force myself to keep my eyes on his, to not let my gaze stray down to his lips or his chest or his anything else.

"I'm glad you didn't come here with Brody," Drew says, never taking his eyes off mine. I can hear all the sounds from the bar, the laughs and shouts and clinks. I swallow, hard.

The dude who went into the bathroom comes out and brushes past us, and Drew takes the opportunity to get even closer to me, so that our bodies are now fully touching.

"I'm fairly certain that guy didn't even wash his hands," I whisper, which isn't the sexiest thing to whisper in this circumstance, but I'm not trying to be sexy here. Am I?

I gasp when he reaches out to touch my hand, and it's easier for me to watch our hands than it is to look into his eyes. He circles his fingers on my palm, and even though we're in a public place and I'm wearing the world's largest, grayest sweater, it feels so outrageously sexual that I know I'm blushing.

"I know you said you wanted to be friends," Drew says in a low murmur as I watch his fingers move. "And I respect that. But would it be okay if I—"

His face is so close to mine that it's no effort at all for me to close the gap between our mouths and press my lips onto his. Both of his hands press into my back, pulling me toward him with urgency. His tongue is in my mouth and, God, we're in a hallway directly beside bathrooms, but I don't even care. *I'm kissing Drew Danforth.* I'm kissing Drew Danforth and he's beautiful and he's everything and he's gone in two days and—

"Oh, God." I pull away from him and shake my head. "I can't believe I did that."

"Let's keep up this streak of unbelievable activity," Drew says, his eyes on my mouth as he leans in again. I kiss him back and then break away again.

"We are *in public*!" I whisper-hiss. "By *bar restrooms*."

"Well, you have fully scandalized me," Drew says with the hint of a smile on his face. "I was a good Southern boy before you, Ohio temptress, kissed me in this most sordid of places."

"Drew!" I slap his arm. "I . . . I . . ."

There are a million things I want to say. That I don't normally kiss guys in bars. That I'm not looking for a one-night (or two-night, or three-night) stand. That there aren't a lot of rom-coms about people who live hours away from each other, and even in *Sleepless in Seattle* we don't get to see how they work out the logistics of being together. That I don't even know if he wants to be together, or if I even want to. That kissing him made me almost forget about everything else I wanted to say.

"I should go home," I say finally. "Before I embarrass myself any further."

"I don't consider this embarrassing," Drew says. "That time you threw coffee on me? A little embarrassing. This? Not so much."

I look up at him, since he's a half foot taller than me and he's leaning over my face, and shake my head. "What are you even doing?"

"Wow, if that's not obvious, then I'm striking out pretty hard. Maybe this *is* embarrassing. I'm kissing a pretty girl."

"Is that a line from a movie?"

"Maybe your problem is that you spent so much time thinking about your past that you didn't spend any time thinking about your future," Drew says with sudden passion, then relaxes into a smile. "*That's* a line from our movie."

I give him another small smile. Oh, I like this guy. He's funny and he's sweet and he's a good kisser with a body that makes me want to rub my hands all over it the same way I compulsively need to touch those sequined mermaid pillows when I see them at Target. Why does he have to be a famous actor who's only in town for a short period of time?

"I'm gonna go," I say, pushing myself off the wall. I don't look back at him as I walk toward the bar, because I know if I do I'll never leave. I'll just make a new home there by the bathrooms, kissing Drew Danforth and pausing only to eat the occasional buffalo wing.

I find Tommy and say goodbye. He gives me a hug and a pointed, paternal look, reminding me of our conversation from earlier. "You're a good assistant, Annie. Unlike certain assistants I could name, who left me for underwear models."

"He says that to all the girls," says a voice from behind me, and I turn to see Brody.

He gives me a quick hug, says it was nice to work with me, and then says, "Listen, be gentle with Drew, okay?"

I cackle-laugh at that, but he continues giving me a serious look. "Wait, you're not kidding?"

Brody shrugs and turns to talk to someone else.

I'm grabbing my coat from coat check when Drew appears. "I'm gonna walk you home," he says, getting his coat as well.

A full-body tingle washes over me. This is a bad idea, or maybe it's a good one, but all of a sudden I don't care because I want it to happen. Drew Danforth is walking me home. A beautiful, funny, smart man who kissed me in public is walking me home and maybe this isn't a romantic comedy and maybe it's going to end with me being a lot more upset but right now, I just don't care.

Chapter Seventeen

D REW OPENS THE DOOR FOR ME, AND AN HONEST-TO-G OD BLIZZARD greets us. "Holy moly," I say.

"Holy moly," Drew repeats with a smile. "You're so Midwestern."

"Don't make fun of me," I say as I start walking toward home.

"I'm not making fun of you." Drew bumps his shoulder against mine. "It's cute."

I think about heading back toward Nick's with Drew to blow Chloe's mind, but she'd be able to tell we kissed just by looking at me (and she'd ask me too many questions about his penis that I don't know how to answer). I'll tell her tomorrow, but for now, I want to keep this one thing to myself, something private between me and Drew. One little moment that's a bit like magic.

But this, right now, is a little magical, too. We walk down the sidewalk, the bricks covered in fresh snow, the kind that's so fluffy it makes a satisfying crunch under our shoes. The snow tumbles down underneath the streetlights, getting caught in my eyelashes and my hair. As we turn to walk through the park, it all seems so cinematic. This is the scene in my rom-com when the characters realize they love each other.

"This is really pretty," Drew says. "I kind of love snow."

"Spoken like someone who grew up without it," I say. "It's beautiful right now, but tomorrow, when it's all packed down and brown and covering your car, it kind of sucks."

He brushes a snowflake off my face. "That's fine. I'll take it, if it means I get to walk through the park with you right now when it looks like this."

I don't know how to respond to his comment, so instead I try a classic Drew Danforth tactic and ask a question. "Hey, that thing you do when people are taking your photo, when you fall down?"

"Pratfalling." He shoves his hands in his pockets.

"Yeah. When did you learn to do that?"

He laughs. "In junior high. Pretty impressive, right?"

"It's actually a little—"

I scream as Drew drops to the ground, looking for all the world like his feet go over his head.

"Are you okay?" I ask.

He pops back up and brushes the snow off of his coat. "I'm fine. Don't worry—I'm a professional."

"Oh, my God." I smack him on the arm. "You scared me! Why do you even do that?"

He smiles as we start walking again. "Kind of a long story, but believe it or not, I wasn't always this perfect specimen of manhood."

He gestures to himself, and I can tell he's kidding, but . . . well.

"In junior high, I was awkward in just about every way a kid can be awkward, and it wasn't like kids bullied me, necessarily, but they definitely made fun of me on a regular basis and made me hate going to school."

"I think that's the definition of bullying."

"Perhaps. Anyway, nothing I could do would make them stop laughing at me, so I thought, what if I was *making* them laugh? Like, what if I was so weird and so goofy that they thought I was hilarious and laughed with me?"

"And that worked?" I ask, incredulous.

"Were you or were you not amazed by my ability to pratfall back there?"

"Amazed. Terrified. Same difference."

Drew shrugs. "Now that kids at school are bothering Ryan, I keep telling him to make it a joke. That all of this doesn't matter in the long run. But the thing is, it's kind of hard to tell a kid that what they're experiencing won't always be happening, because it's all they know. But maybe when he grows up one of his bullies will send him a Twitter DM to try to get tickets to his movie premiere, and he'll get to be like, 'No way, loser.' "

"Is . . . that a personal example?"

"Maybe."

We exit the park, and I don't even have to tell him which way to turn to get to my house, since he's been there twice already. "You're pretty close to your family, huh?"

He nods. "Very close. Perhaps too close. My grandparents on my mom's side are still around and on that side alone I have six aunts and uncles and I don't even know how many cousins, and it all makes for very loud, chaotic Christmas dinners where my aunt Robin ends up getting drunk and attempting to start a sing-a-long of Christmas carols she swears are real but we're pretty sure she just made up."

I smile, but on the inside my heart is breaking because *I want that*. I want that so bad. This past Christmas, Uncle Don and I ate a wonderful beef brisket that he made, along with a bunch of sides and pumpkin, pecan, and chocolate silk pies. We opened presents by the tree and then ended the night by watching *Love Actually* by the fire (which was a little awkward because of that porn scene, but it was fine). And it's not like we didn't have a good time, but I can't pretend there wasn't a part of me that didn't want, say, five to twenty more people there. I wanted a bunch of stockings and kids yelling and so many dishes to wash that I sighed while looking at them and thinking about all the work it would be.

"Do you want to have a big family of your own some day?" I ask, even though this is a very personal question that isn't any of my business. "With a lot of kids and a golden retriever?"

"Yep," he says, no hesitation. "I want to have a million kids, give or take a few, and have my own huge holiday dinner. But no to the golden retriever. I want a rescue greyhound named Charlie."

"That's very specific," I say with a smile.

We're at my door now. Drew stays on the sidewalk as I walk up the steps, and I know he's not going to ask to come in. I look down at him standing there, looking up at me, his hands in the pockets of his coat and the snow turning his hair white, and I don't want this to be goodbye. I don't want this to be how it ends. I don't know if this is the love story or the montage, but I don't care right now, because all I can think about is families and Christmas and a rescue greyhound named Charlie.

"Drew," I ask. "Do you want to come inside?"

Chapter Eighteen

"YEAH, SO . . . I ACTUALLY DON'T KNOW HOW TO DO THIS."

Drew volunteered to build a fire as soon as we took off our coats, but after staring at the fireplace he stands up.

"I thought if I just, like, looked at it for a while the secrets of the fireplace would reveal themselves to me."

"Turns out that's not how fire works," I say, brushing past him. "And there aren't really any secrets. I mean, cavemen figured this stuff out."

"Sheesh. What a burn," Drew says.

"Hmmm." I look over my shoulder at him. "Not sure if you can use the term 'burn' since you can't start a fire."

Drew clutches at his heart. "Damn. You're ruthless."

As I get the fire going, Drew asks, "Where did you learn to do this?"

"In Ohio, where it gets cold, because I'm one of two people in a very old, very drafty house." After a couple of minutes, the fire crackles away and I turn around to face Drew, who's sitting on the couch.

"Do you . . . want to watch a movie?" Drew asks, then grimaces. "Wow. I swear I wasn't asking you to Netflix and chill. I just . . ."

I laugh. "That's okay. I mean . . . yeah, I would love to. Do you want some wine?"

He practically slumps over in relief. "That would be great."

In the pantry, I pull out my phone and text Chloe. "Emergency. Drew Danforth is currently in my home."

She texts back immediately. "OMG. WHAT. HOW. Please tell me you're naked right now."

"It's not like that," I respond. "Drew walked me home and now we're going to watch a movie. Also, I have never and will never text you while I'm naked."

"Netflix and chill. I see," she responds, and wow, I wish that phrase had never become part of the cultural lexicon.

I grab a bottle of wine and two glasses and head back into the living room, where Drew is scrolling through channels. He looks so at home on the old couch with the remote in his hand that my chest expands with a yearning I can't even define.

"So listen," he says. "I know I said I wanted to watch a movie, but there's a *Chopped* marathon on. Which isn't that surprising, since *Chopped* is always on, but still."

When he sees my blank expression, he slowly says, "Wait. Do you not like *Chopped*?"

I shrug. "I've never seen it. I don't really watch cooking shows."

"Oh, no no no," Drew says. "Annie. *Chopped* isn't a *cooking show*. It's an immersive experience. It's a lens through which we view American culture. It's a lifestyle."

I eye him skeptically, then sit down on the other side of the couch, leaving one cushion between us. "Um, okay?"

Several episodes later, we're opening our second bottle of wine, and I'm shouting, "No! Don't try to use the ice-cream machine! You just said you've never used one!" at a contestant who is most certainly about to get chopped for abusing mascarpone.

"This is what always happens in the dessert round!" Drew says, sloshing a bit of wine out of his glass. "They either make a boring-ass bread pudding or they go buckwild with that damn ice-cream machine."

I snort-laugh and send wine flying out of my mouth. "I don't think I've ever heard you talk about something so passionately."

"Oh," Drew says, "I'm plenty passionate. About lots of things."

I steal a glance at him out of the corner of my eye as the chef on TV complains about his ice cream not freezing properly, which, duh, of course it didn't. Drew's cheeks are flushed from the wine, and he looks like a little kid who just came in from playing in the snow. It's unexpectedly endearing.

The episode ends, and our wine-drunk *Chopped* spell breaks.

"It's late." He takes a look at his phone. "I should . . . I should probably go."

"It *is* late," I say, drawing out the words. "And you *should* probably go."

Because he probably should. But the real question is, do I want him to?

No, I answer my silent question in my head. I want him here, with me, because this house is so not empty when he's here. I don't want to be alone and I want to be with Drew and my thoughts are running around each other in tipsy circles, but he's already standing up and walking toward the door.

I don't know how long we've been here—that's the wonder of *Chopped*, I'm realizing, that it renders time meaningless—but when he opens the door, we both gasp.

There's easily a foot of unshoveled, unplowed snow on the steps, the sidewalks, the street. A black lab and his owner walk down the center of the street, past buried cars, but other than that no one's out. A blanket of silence hangs heavy over everything.

"It . . . snowed," I say, watching the flakes fall in the light from the streetlamps.

"It sure did," Drew says, holding his coat but making no move to put it on.

I don't know what it is—if it's the confidence I got from Tommy's pep talk, or the way-too-much wine I had, or the fact that Drew and I kissed tonight and I would really, really like a repeat performance, but I'm feeling bold.

"Well, um." I clear my throat. "That's a lot of snow, and you might get stuck in it."

"Get stuck?" Drew asks with a smile, turning to me.

I nod vigorously. "Frankly, this looks pretty dangerous. I think you need to stay here tonight. For, you know, purely safety-related reasons."

Drew nods, shuts the door. "Are you sure?"

"Do you want more wine?" I ask. "And we can watch more *Chopped*."

Because that's the thing about *Chopped*. It's always on.

I'm honestly not sure how many episodes of *Chopped* we've watched by the time we finish the second bottle of wine. It all runs together in a stream of chefs who are trying to prove something to their parents, judges who don't think dishes are well-executed or creative, and contestants forgetting to put all their basket ingredients on their plates.

At some point we ate an entire frozen pizza and a bag of microwave popcorn, but the abundance of wine is making my tongue pretty loose.

"Where's Don, anyway?" Drew asks.

"Oh!" I say. "A convention in Chicago. He's a Wookiee."

"Of course he is," Drew says. "He's got the build for it."

I nod once, but my head keeps nodding of its own accord. "If you've got it, flaunt it. That's what I always say."

Drew laughs and I put my feet in his lap. "Why do you have to go to New York?" I ask.

"Because." Drew puts his hands on my feet and rubs them. "God, your feet are cold. I have to be on *Good Morning USA* to talk about the zombie movie I have coming out this week. We actually made it two years ago, but it took forever to find distribution and . . . this is boring. You don't care."

"What's it called?" I squint, trying to remember. "*A Zombie for Christmas?*"

He snorts. "No. That sounds like a weird Hallmark movie. It's called *Winter of the Undead.* It's . . . I'm gonna be honest with you, it's not a very good movie."

I dissolve into laughter, then slap his shoulder for emphasis. "See? This is why you should only make rom-coms."

"Well," Drew says, looking right into my eyes. "This one certainly turned out pretty well for me."

"You are very good-looking, you know," I say, wiggling my toes.

Drew smiles at me. "You're a little drunk, you know."

"How are you not drunk? How much wine did you have?"

"Well, for starters, I'm six foot two, not five foot five."

"I'm five foot five and three quarters," I protest, because the distinction seems important to me at the moment.

"Do you want some water?" Drew asks. "I'm kind of worried about your hydration."

I nod slowly. This, oh, this is nice, someone here to look out for me. Not that Uncle Don doesn't care about me, and not that I need someone to look out for me, but all of a sudden I'm struck with the desire to always have Drew here to make sure I don't drink too much and tuck me in at night and take care of me when I'm sick.

"Water," I say. "Good idea."

In the kitchen, I grab a glass out of the cabinet. I turn to go to the sink but before I can, Drew is there, and he easily picks me up and places me on the counter.

He kisses me, his hands on my face and in my hair, and I pull him to me. I wrap my legs around his waist and run my hands up under his shirt. "God, you have, like, no body fat," I say into his mouth.

"It's not always like this," he says, his words vibrating into my mouth. "A few more weeks of McDonald's and wine and you'll be disappointed."

"I don't think I could ever be disappointed in you," I say, and I'm too far gone to even be embarrassed.

Drew pulls back, and for a second I think that must've been too far, that I've said too much, but he puts his hands on my face and looks into my eyes.

"You're pretty drunk," he says, both a statement and a question.

I think about arguing, but it's pretty clear, so I nod.

"I don't want to do this right now," Drew says. "I mean, I do want to do this. I really, really do. I think I've made that pretty clear. But I would like both of us to not hate ourselves or each other in the morning."

I look at him and blink a few times. He rubs his thumb over my cheek.

"I like you, Annie," he says, and the thrill of hearing that statement tingles through my entire body, starting at my head and going all the way to my toes. "And I've been wanting to kiss you ever since you ran into me on the sidewalk."

"Wait," I say, pulling my head back and looking up at him. "What? Are you joking?"

He shakes his head, still not taking his eyes off mine. "Not about this. I know I made fun of your romantic comedy obsession before you explained it to me, but something happened the second I saw you. It was like I knew you were—"

I kiss him again before he can say anything else because this, this is too good to be true. There's a charming, funny, goofy man in my kitchen telling me that he's had a thing for me ever since we had a meet-cute, and he's so kind and respectful that he doesn't want to hook up with me because I've had a little too much wine. This can't be real, but it is real. The movies never lied to me; Nora Ephron, my mom, and Hollywood were telling the truth. I found my Tom Hanks.

"What?" Drew asks, pulling back, and I realize I've said this last part out loud. "Tom Hanks is an American treasure, sure, but why are you talking about him right now?"

"Don't worry about it," I say, kissing him harder, and he pulls away with a groan that is quite possibly the sexiest thing I've ever heard in my life.

"I'm gonna sleep on the couch," he says, stepping back and leaning against the island. "You go get some sleep, too."

"Sleep is for losers," I mutter, crossing my arms.

"Water," Drew says, taking my glass and filling it at the sink. He goes into the pantry, then tosses me a granola bar. "Eat."

"Boo," I say.

"Very mature." Drew unwraps the granola bar. Part of me wants to be upset that we're not making out right now, but another part of me is tired and hungry and ready to crawl into bed.

Drew hands me the granola bar, and I put my head on his shoulder, which is easy to do because I'm still sitting on the counter. "Sleepy," I say.

"Go to bed." Drew kisses me on the forehead, and I think about how nice this could be, forehead kisses and granola bars and a human being looking out for me.

I follow him into the living room, where he pulls the blanket off the back of the couch. "I'm perfectly comfortable down here, so don't worry about me," he says. "But come get me the second you wake up, okay?"

"It's late," I say. "Don't you have someplace to be?"

He shakes his head and walks over to me. "My flight doesn't leave until Sunday night. I have nothing to do this weekend except focus on you."

He leans in to kiss me softly, and that full-body tingle is back. I want him to keep going but he stops, pulls back, and gestures toward the stairs with his head. "Sleep. Go."

I brush my teeth and put on pajamas (I do not own sexy pajamas, but I do manage to find some pug-printed pajama shorts that are at least cute, although pairing them with my Pizza Slut shirt is maybe not the most inspired fashion choice). Just before I slide into bed, I glance out the window at the snow blanketing our tiny backyard, covering the bird feeder and the garden gnomes and the steps up to Chloe's apartment. Nothing has ever been so cozy as being snowed in at my house with Drew Danforth downstairs (well, maybe if we were in the same bed . . . a minor detail). Nothing has ever felt so safe and warm. I want to keep thinking about Drew, letting all the things he said wash over me, but I'm so tired that I fall asleep the second my head hits the pillow.

I jolt awake, one thought in my mind: Drew Danforth. Here. In my house.

I look at my bedside clock—it's 5 A.M. Still dark, but the sky outside my window is turning from black to blue. My mouth is dry and tart, so I get up and brush my teeth.

Part of me doesn't believe Drew could be here—that must be a dream I had, one where an impossibly good-looking man wants to feed me granola bars (listen, there have been weirder fantasies). Before I can question this any more or talk myself out of it, I tiptoe down my stairs.

He's on the couch, but he's not asleep. He's scrolling through his phone, and he looks up at me, the screen glowing blue on his face in the dark. The way his eyes change when he sees me—that has to mean something, right? That what he said last night was true? That this isn't just a one-time thing for him?

"Are you feeling better?" he asks.

I nod, then realize he probably can't see me in the dark. "Yes."

"Good." He throws his phone on the floor, crosses the room in a few steps, and picks me up.

Chapter Nineteen

THERE'S PLENTY OF SEX IN CURRENT ROMANTIC COMEDIES, BUT I wouldn't call Nora Ephron's films particularly racy. Yes, in *When Harry Met Sally . . .* you see Billy Crystal and Meg Ryan when he's in a post-sex panic, but you're left to imagine the actual act. In *Sleepless in Seattle*, they're all the way across the country for most of the film, so there isn't even physical contact, let alone sex. And in *You've Got Mail*, the chemistry between Tom and Meg is so intense, so crackling, that we can only assume they're having intense, crackling sex in her cozy apartment right after the credits roll. But we don't need to see it to know it's real.

Which is why, about my night with Drew, I will just say this: we totally had amazing sex.

I stand at the foot of my bed, marveling at how cute Drew is when he sleeps. At some point he put his gray thermal back on, which is somehow even sexier than him with his shirt off (although that's plenty sexy too, as I now know). His face is smashed into my pillow on my twin bed and his feet dangle off the edge, just as I imagined they would. *This is real.*

I snap a photo on my phone to send to Chloe, because if a picture is worth a thousand words, then a picture of Drew Danforth in my bed is worth, like, a billion. She's going to lose her shit. I include the caption "Drew Danforth is currently asleep in my bed," in case she isn't clear on what's happening. And then I add, "He's circumcised btw," because I know it will make her laugh and also because he is.

I want to crawl back into bed and curl up next to Drew's warmth. Instead I walk into the bathroom to take a shower, because I would like to not be totally gross when Drew wakes up and sees me in the full light of day, and also because I'm hoping I can sort of wash away my white wine hangover. I think about what we'll do today, places I can take Drew. Maybe he wants burgers and we could go to Thurman's, or maybe he's feeling pizza and I could take him to Harvest. Is this what it's like to have a person, someone to do things with, someone who isn't my uncle?

I may no longer be drunk on white wine, but my head is spinning with this feeling.

Drew said a lot of things last night. That he wanted me to come visit him when he's back in LA, that he wants me to come with him to New York on Sunday, that he wants me to meet his family in Shreveport. And each one of those things made it clear: this *is* my movie. Chloe was right; everything before this was a misunderstanding or a miscommunication and now it's all worked out. He's my Bill Pullman with the large, lovely family in *While You Were Sleeping* and my Julia Roberts in *Notting Hill* (but, again, much less of a jerk). He's my Tom Hanks. I found him.

I get dressed in something that I think says "casual yet cute," which is just leggings and yet another large sweater, because apparently all my style icons are from '90s movies. I don't put on makeup, and I walk into my bedroom with my hair still wet.

The bed is empty, the sheets and quilts rumpled, and the indentation from a head visible on the pillow.

My heart surges. Maybe Drew went downstairs to make me breakfast. I mean, we haven't talked at all about whether or not he can cook, but wouldn't that be a perfect detail in a romantic comedy as a way to show that he's the ideal man? There he is at a skillet, effortlessly flipping pancakes while the coffee brews!

I walk downstairs, sniffing the air for the telltale scent of breakfast, but stop at the foot of the stairs when I see Drew pulling on his boots.

Maybe he's going out for coffee, I think, but some of my optimism drains out of me.

"What are you doing?" I ask, and he stands up.

"Are you kidding me right now?" he asks, his voice measured and bland in a way that I haven't heard before. He walks to the door and pulls his coat off the hook.

I follow him, telling myself not to look too much like an eager puppy. "What do you mean? Are we talking in questions now?" I smile, hoping it comes off as cute but afraid it comes off as frantic.

He raises his eyebrows as he puts his coat on, and then thrusts his phone into my face. "I woke up to a lot of texts and notifications."

I lean in to look at his phone. Hollywood Gossip is on the screen, and it's a photo of Drew in my bed. It takes a moment for things to click into place, for me to figure out what's going on here. How is there a picture of Drew in my bed? The picture I just took? That I sent to Chloe? Did Chloe send it to Hollywood Gossip? But why would she do that?

Oh no. Oh, no. I pull my phone out of my pocket and go to my texts.

There it is. The picture I just took of Drew, the one I thought I was sending to Chloe? I sent it to Hollywood Gossip in my sleepy post-sex haze. Chloe is almost always my most recent text, so I must've responded to the first one without thinking about it.

"Oh, my God, Drew, this was an accident," I say. "I took . . . okay, so this sounds weird, but I took a picture of you to send to Chloe because she's been wanting us to get together and I knew she would be so excited and you just looked so good, but then I had a text from Hollywood Gossip, and I guess I accidentally replied to that one." I take a breath.

Drew shakes his head, not looking at me. "How much did you get?"

I stare back at him.

"For the picture, I mean. Was it worth it?"

"I didn't get anything!" I shout.

"You knew," he says, holding out his phone. "You knew how much this stuff bothered me, and you did this. Was this all some ridiculous long con for you, some way to get yourself on this website?"

"No! I don't care about Hollywood Gossip!" I shout, tears springing to my eyes. "You're my Tom Hanks."

He holds up a hand. "Okay, spare me the Tom Hanks bullshit, please. I don't particularly care what Tom Hanks would do in this situation, because he's an actor who plays fictional characters, and I'm a real person. And now everyone's going to see a picture of me sleeping next to details about my dick."

Oh, God. I forgot I included that thing about him being circumcised.

"I'm sorry," I say, trying hard not to cry. "It was an accident. Please believe me."

Drew won't look at me, and I just want him to look into my eyes and know that I'm telling the truth. *Just look at me*, I will him with my mind.

He does, but then he shakes his head. "I need some time, Annie."

The way he says my name normally makes my entire body feel like a lit-up string of Christmas lights, but right now, with his voice so disappointed and defeated, it just hurts.

He turns and walks out the door, closing it behind him. I think about running after him, but I don't want to look desperate and anyway, I'm pretty sure no one's shoveled the sidewalks.

Instead, I start to cry.

Chapter Twenty

It's not like I would've cried onto Uncle Don's shoulder if he were here, but at least then I wouldn't be all by myself. Even though I know Chloe's studying, I text her and she comes over immediately, wearing leggings and her own Pizza Slut T-shirt.

"I'm sorry for interrupting you," I say through sobs. "But I messed everything up."

"Babe!" Chloe says, pulling me into a hug. "Don't apologize. Remember that time I needed to pass a test and you helped me make flash cards about the core functions of marketing until two A.M.?"

She pulls back and appraises my face, squinting. "You are actually covered in snot, you know."

"Ugh." I lift my sleeve and wipe my nose.

"Wow." She winces. "We've reached a new low. Sit down and I'll find you a box of tissues while you tell me everything."

I run through the story for her—the kiss, the wine, the sex, the fight. I show her the picture, and she gasps.

"God, he looks amazing," she says. "Even asleep and with his mouth open. What's his chest hair situation like?"

"What?"

"I'm trying to get a good mental picture of what he looks like naked."

"Chloe! This is quite possibly my soul mate who now hates me, and all you care about is what he looks like naked?"

She rolls her eyes. "Annie. He doesn't hate you. You pulled a reverse 'Baby, It's Cold Outside' and he loved it. If he's anywhere near as nice as you've made him sound, he'll come to his senses and march right back here and apologize to you."

I sniffle. "You think?"

"Yes!" Chloe smiles. "Now *this*. This is the Big Misunderstanding, after which he'll make some sort of Grand Gesture to apologize, and then you guys will have your Climactic Kiss as the cover of a '90s song plays and the camera pans out."

"Whoa." I blow my nose. "You really have watched a lot of rom-coms with me."

She shrugs. "You never want to watch my preferred genre, TV shows about murder. Speaking of which, do you want to watch a rom-com right now?"

I think about it for a second. On one hand, I've just been brutally abandoned by a kind and funny man. On the other hand, *Sleepless in Seattle* always makes things better.

"Yes," I say. "But I want to watch it on VHS."

Chloe narrows her eyes. "Um, okay?"

Typically I stream rom-coms, or rely on DVDs for those rare movies I can't find on any streaming service. But when I was little, Mom and I used to watch them on VHS, and she kept all her favorites on the shelf by the TV. They've long since been put away in the attic to make room for Uncle Don's *Lord of the Rings* collector's edition DVDs (which, unsurprisingly, take up a lot of room), and I haven't seen them in ages.

"I just think it might make me feel better to see the tapes," I say, and Chloe nods encouragingly, even though I can tell she doesn't get it.

If my mom were here, she could talk me through this. I could tell her all about what happened and she'd comfort me, like she did in second grade when Taylor McNaughton made fun of my multiple speech impediments (I ended up correcting them in speech therapy, and Taylor McNaughton got kicked off the volleyball team our senior year for drinking, so, you know . . . boom).

But she's not here, so she doesn't know about Drew. She'll never meet him or hear about our meet-cute or our many awkward almost-kisses or our very non-awkward real kisses (although, let's be real, I would edit that part when talking to my mom). In fact, she'll never even see me as an adult woman, one who grew up and fell in love, and that stings way more than Drew storming out of here this morning.

Maybe holding those VHS tapes won't bring her back, but this morning, I need something that will help me feel a tiny bit closer to her.

I leave Chloe on the couch with a mug of coffee and one of her Spicy Cinnamon Brownies and go up to the attic. It's one of those perfect movie attics, with the ladder that pulls down. Of course, the attic itself isn't filled with anything magical like any good '90s children's movie would be; instead, it's mostly filled with Uncle Don's action-figure collection (all still in their original packaging, obviously). But, as I climb up, I can't help feeling like something magical could happen up here, like I could find these VHS tapes and suddenly, miraculously, things would get better.

It turns out Uncle Don has been storing way more stuff up here than I thought (like, does he *need* these *Star Trek* commemorative dinner plates that I can guarantee we're never going to eat off of?), and it's hard to know where the tapes are. In the faint light coming through the tiny, fogged-up window, I brush dust off boxes and try to read what they say.

My mom was never one for organization or tidiness, so many of the boxes are labeled "stuff" or "various knickknacks." Uncle Don's, in contrast, have labels like "Star Wars magazines 2000–2016." I paw through a few boxes, coming across things I'll want to properly pore over later, but right now I'm on a mission.

I open a box labeled "things from bedroom" (helpful!) and am greeted with a tiny lamb-printed onesie that must've belonged to baby me. There's a pair of baby shoes, a hairbrush, and then a stack of letters.

These must be love letters between my mom and dad; I just know it. The way mom talked about their relationship, it was epic and poetic and although I never knew my dad, I somehow know he was the type of guy to write a love letter. This is the framing device of a great romantic drama—a girl finds her parents' old love letters, then we flash back to their relationship. Sort of like *The Notebook*, but not as cheesy.

I'm running through plot points in my head as I unfold the first letter on the stack and start reading. These letters are addressed to my mom, but as I glance at the name on the return address, they aren't from my dad. They're from someone named Edwin Smith.

These must've been from before she met my dad. I pick up the first letter off the pile and start reading.

This will be the last contact I have with you. I say this knowing full well that it will break your heart, but I have decided not to leave Marie. She found out about us, and she was upset, but we've decided to work on our marriage—or at least attempt to. This means that I have to stop meeting with you, calling you, everything. As much as that hurts, it's the only way.

Please don't call me, at work or at home, as I won't be able to answer. You know I'll always love you. I've mailed you all of our correspondence, because I can't have it in my home but I can't bear to throw it away.

Edwin

And then, I see the date written at the top of the letter. These are from the year before she died.

Chapter Twenty-one

I READ THROUGH THE REST OF THE LETTERS ON THE STACK, EVEN though I'm nauseated and almost unable to breathe. I never knew my mom was dating someone before she died—let alone a married man.

"Knock, knock," Chloe says, poking her head into the attic. "I've watched an entire episode of *Dr. Oz* since you went up here, and now I know way more than I wanted to about superfoods and—oh, my God, are you crying?"

She pulls herself into the attic and runs over to me, floorboards creaking under her feet.

"What's wrong?" she asks, kneeling beside me. "Are you thinking about Drew again? Because I promise he's going to come back here any minute, sad and sorry and ready to bang the living daylights out of you."

I shake my head and wave the letter I'm holding. "My mom was having an affair with a married guy. Right before she died."

Chloe shakes her head. "That . . . doesn't sound like your mom."

"It's right here, Chlo, in these letters. It was some guy named Edwin, and he didn't leave his wife, and . . ." I trail off, not even sure what else there is to say. I look at Chloe. "I thought she believed in true love, like her perfect relationship with my dad. And now I know that not only had she totally moved on from him, but she was having an affair!"

I watch Chloe read the last letter, her lips moving slightly and her eyes widening in shock. She looks up at me and exhales. "This is . . . a lot."

"I know."

She reaches out and strokes my arm. "I'm sorry, hon."

"There is no romantic comedy where this happens. Like, I can't name a single rom-com that begins or ends with a person carrying on an affair with a married man, then getting her heart smashed to smithereens."

"Maybe a Mike Nichols movie," Chloe says, raising a shoulder, but when I glare at her she says, "Okay, okay, you're right. This isn't funny."

"It's really, really not."

Chloe lowers herself from her crouching position until she's sitting beside me on the dusty attic floor. "So this sucks. There's no way around that."

I nod and wipe my nose on my sleeve again. Chloe cringes.

"But all it really means is that you found out your mom was a human being. It's shitty, but we all have to learn that at some point. For me, it was when my mom ran off to Ann Arbor to meet her online boyfriend when we were in elementary school. And then it happened again when I had to put my dad in a memory-care facility because he wandered out of the house and was missing for an entire hour."

I nod, chastened, because I tend to forget how hard and lonely Chloe's life has been.

"And listen," she continues. "I'm not saying my problems are bigger than yours, because sure, my mom's still alive out there somewhere. But at least your mom didn't totally suck when she was alive. I get that you want to have this perfect image of your mom in your mind, to remember her as this angel who was pining away for your father and believing hopelessly in true love, but no one's flawless. All this means is that your mom was like any of us—kind of a fucked-up person who made bad decisions sometimes. That doesn't mean she loved you any less."

I nod. "You're right. You're totally right."

She leans into me and wraps me into a side hug, putting her head on my shoulder. "Listen, there are some brownies down there with your name on them, and I'm pretty sure there's an entire hour of *Family Feud* coming up. Instead of a rom-com, do you wanna let Steve Harvey cure your ills?"

I nod again. "Yeah. Okay."

Chloe smiles at me, concern still written on her face. "I'll go slice you off a brownie and pour you a glass of milk while you clean up, okay?"

"Okay. Thanks, Pizza Slut."

"Anytime, Pizza Slut."

I watch Chloe's head disappear as she crawls down the ladder. She is, really and truly, the best friend I could ask for. She's been buoying me lately, and always, even though she has more than enough on her own plate to worry about—her dad, her classes, her job, the endless stream of apparently very sexually satisfying dates she goes on. And it's not like what she said wasn't true or helpful, so I didn't want to make her feel bad by rejecting it.

But this is like when I was eight and I figured out that Santa Claus wasn't real. The kids at school had been talking about it all winter, and in person I'd agreed with them. Like, yeah, of course—a bearded guy slides down your chimney and gives you presents? I'm not buying it! But in my own mind, I still believed in Santa fiercely and absolutely. I knew he was real, the same way I knew my favorite food was pepperoni pizza or my favorite movie was *Beauty and the Beast*. But then that Christmas, I noticed that Santa used the same red-and-white-striped wrapping paper that my mom did, and their handwriting looked eerily similar.

I asked my mom about the wrapping paper, and she told me that Santa must shop at the same store she did, but I knew that didn't make sense. Santa had elves, and surely they were capable of making a simple paper product. I knew then that Santa wasn't real, that there was no magic behind these presents. I finished opening them and acted happy, but inside I was hollow, because if there was no Santa, then everything I'd believed was wrong.

The same hollowness expands in my belly now, the knowledge that my entire belief system, everything I needed to get through the day, is a lie. I've believed in romantic comedies all this time, relying on their promise of hope and love, *knowing* that there was a happily-ever-after waiting for me.

But what if I was wrong? Maybe movies are just that—movies, nothing but fictional tales to delude people into spending a happy hour and a half before returning to the misery of their lonely lives.

Drew's gone, and he's not coming back. My mom died with a broken heart after having an affair with a married man. I had a perfect, houseboat-owning single dad right in front of me and I couldn't even muster up enough feeling to make *that* work. There's no reason why my life will ever be anything other than this—alone, in my childhood home, fooling myself by watching ridiculous movies over and over.

I crawl carefully down the ladder, clutching the letters in one hand. Chloe is still in the kitchen, and before she comes back into the living room, I throw the letters into the fire, then watch as they curl and turn black.

Chapter Twenty-two

My phone buzzes, and through the haze of sleep, I reach for it on my nightstand. But when my hand grabs on to nothing, I open my eyes. I'm not in my bed; I'm on the couch, and when I try to move my legs, I realize that Chloe's head is at the other end, her legs draped across mine. My phone buzzes again, insistent, but Chloe doesn't stir—she's always been a heavy sleeper, the kind of girl whose face you could draw things on during a sleepover.

After some digging and trying to avoid jostling Chloe too much, I find my phone under one of the couch cushions. My blurry eyes see the time on the phone before the text registers. Two A.M. We must've fallen asleep after watching the most ridiculous TV we could find late into the night, drinking too much wine, and eating an entire pizza.

Of course, I'm the person who doesn't make reckless romantic decisions while heartbroken . . . just indigestion-inducing ones.

I rub my eyes and focus on the text, then almost drop my phone when I see that it's from Drew. "Holy moly," I say at full volume, and Chloe moves a little bit. With my hand over my mouth, I open the text and read the full thing.

> Annie, I'm sorry about the way I left. I know you're
> not the kind of person who would send my picture to
> some gossip site. Can we talk?

And then, as I'm still trying to comprehend that text, another one:

> Please?

Before I can even think of a response, I throw my phone across the room. It clatters to a rest somewhere near the TV (thank God I didn't hit the TV—Uncle Don would be seriously pissed).

I rest my head in my hands. There is a part of me that wants to respond to Drew, that wants to hear what he has to say. Part of me wants to think that, sure, we'll kiss again as a stirring instrumental score plays and everything's going to magically work out, because love conquers all or some bullshit like that. Part of me still wants to believe that this is a movie, that he'll give me some big speech about the depth of his feelings for me and I'll fall for it.

But the rest of me knows that this doesn't mean anything. Soon he'll head off to New York or LA or wherever he's going and he'll be surrounded by people who have personal trainers and professional hair and makeup teams and he'll forget all about the sad, lonely girl in Ohio whose hopes he trampled all over.

I know what believing in love did to my mom. It left her heartbroken, right before she died. And frankly, I wasted too much of my life watching a bunch of ridiculous movies that gave me some pretty unrealistic ideas about life to let myself end up like her.

There's a tiny pang, a sharp inkling that I might be doing the wrong thing by ignoring Drew's text, but no. I don't want to deal with this. Now that the curtain is pulled back, now that I'm no longer wearing my heart-shaped, rose-colored glasses, I can't believe in this anymore. I can't believe that love or like or whatever this is will be enough.

And who knows? With my luck, Drew doesn't even want to apologize or make out or ride off together into the metaphorical sunset. Maybe he wants some closure, to tell me in person that it's never gonna happen. And that is, perhaps literally, the exact last thing I need right now.

I let out a loud, frustrated groan, and Chloe rolls over. Without opening her eyes, she croaks, "You tell Dolly Parton I'm not making her any donuts."

It's been a while since Chloe and I had a sleepover, so I'd forgotten about her habit of a) sleep talking and b) having vivid, nonsensical dreams.

I stand up and pull a blanket over Chloe. "I'll tell Dolly to leave you alone."

I switch off the lamp and head upstairs, thinking, just for a moment, about how I did almost this exact same thing with Drew last night.

But that was before I knew what love really did to people.

Chapter Twenty-three

WHEN I WAKE UP, THE AIR SMELLS LIKE CINNAMON AND NUTMEG, butter and bacon. Even from my bedroom, I can hear pans clank and the telltale gurgle of the coffeepot. A glance at the clock shows that it's already 4 P.M.; apparently, I was exhausted from staying up half the night, or my brain was trying to avoid thinking about the shitshow of my life.

In the kitchen, I put my arms around Chloe. "Have I told you lately that I love you?"

She pretends to think. "Not frequently enough, actually. Anyway, I know that basically the entire day is gone, but I made you breakfast for dinner because I think you need it."

"Wait a second." I step back and look at her. "Aren't you supposed to be working all day?"

She flips a pancake. "I called off. Tobin was happy to fill in for me, and Nick understood. I said it was a family emergency."

"He probably thought something was wrong with your dad!"

She waves me off, unconcerned. "He knows you're family, too."

Maybe this is what my movie should be about, I think as I lean against the counter and Chloe hands me coffee in Uncle Don's favorite TALK WOOKIEE TO ME mug. Maybe it should be about the power of female friendship, not an unbelievable love story. Because this I can count on; at least I know Chloe isn't going anywhere.

"Oh, PS, your phone kept buzzing, and I crawled around on my hands and knees looking for it and finally found it under the TV cabinet." She hands it to me with eyebrows raised.

I grab it, a little too quickly, and scroll through my texts. They're all from the library, reminding me of the books that are due this week.

"Expecting something?"

"Nope." I slide the phone into my pocket. "Certainly not."

"Convincing. So," she says, her eyes on the pancakes, "how are you feeling?"

I take another sip of coffee. "Like I've had way too much wine two nights in a row and I'm not twenty-one anymore."

"No." She looks up. "I mean, about . . . Drew. And the whole thing with your mom."

I shrug. "It is what it is."

She drops the spatula. "Whoa. You must really be feeling bad, because the writer I know would never use a terrible cliché like that."

I sigh. "Give me a break."

"No, I'm serious. What does that even mean? *It is what it is?* Like, of *course* it is what it is! No shit!"

"Okay! Fine! I meant 'it *is* terrible and shitty but I have to deal with it because that's life, dude.'"

Chloe nods. "Better, but definitely isn't gonna fit on a throw pillow."

"Are my pancakes ready yet?"

"Patience!" she says, and I sip my coffee and she cooks in companionable silence until we hear the front door opening.

"Is someone breaking in?" I whisper.

"Oh no." Chloe waves the spatula in faux-concern. "They're going to steal all the pancakes."

"Hide! Turn off the oven! Seriously, why are you not more concerned?"

But before I can duck behind the island, Uncle Don walks into the kitchen.

"Hey there, girls," he says, gesturing to a petite purple-haired woman in horn-rimmed glasses who trails behind him. "This is Tyler."

I can't say anything for a few moments. Tyler is a woman—a woman who, if I'm judging correctly, appears to be about Uncle Don's age but considerably prettier. I'd always assumed Tyler was a man, but now that I think about it, Don never specifically said so.

"But what are you doing home?" I ask, because 'why is there a woman with you?' seems like a rude question. "I thought you weren't getting back until Monday morning."

"I decided to leave early," Don says, his eyes cutting to Chloe.

"I called him," she says, and gives me a not-all-that-apologetic shrug. "I figured he'd want to know if his niece was having a crisis of faith."

"Tyler was nice enough to come with me," Uncle Don says, putting his hand on her elbow in a way that seems *very* familiar, "so we caught a flight home and left Earl, Paul, and Dungeon Master Rick there. They've gotta bring the Wookiee costume home, but oh well."

"But . . . why?" I ask.

Don looks around the kitchen, then says, "Ladies? Could you give me and Annie a moment to talk privately?"

Realizing that there are things that should be said privately is kind of new for Uncle Don, so I'm worried about how bad this conversation is going to be, but Chloe winks and leads Tyler out of the room. Chloe could make conversation with a cast-iron skillet, so I'm not at all concerned about leaving her alone with a relative stranger.

"So," Uncle Don says, leaning against a counter and crossing his arms. "Chloe told me you found some letters."

I cock an eyebrow. "Some letters. Yes. Some letters that informed me I never really knew my own mother."

He nods, and then I get it. "Wait. Did you also know that she had her heart trampled on by a married man?"

Don nods again. "She was my sister. Sometimes we talked."

"But why didn't I know?"

Don smiles gently. "You were a kid. Most parents—most good ones, anyway—probably don't have in-depth discussions with their kids about their romantic lives."

"This doesn't make any sense!" I say, throwing up my hands in exasperation. "Mom believed in love. In true love. The kind she had with Dad and the kind that was in movies. Why would she have put herself in this shitty, not at all cinematic situation?"

Don shrugs. "I try not to judge people who face situations I've never faced."

"Well, how wonderful that you're so nonjudgmental," I mutter, then add, "Sorry. That was unnecessarily mean."

He shrugs again. He's doing a lot of shrugging today.

"I don't get it." I slump over the counter. "This doesn't even sound like Mom. I spent my entire life holding up her and Dad's relationship as this ideal, of watching and rewatching the movies she loved because I thought they held some sort of secret, you know?"

Uncle Don doesn't say anything, just waits for me to go on.

"Like if I could star in the perfect montage or have the ultimate sympathetic backstory, then that meant I would find love. And sure, there would be one big miscommunication, but nothing that couldn't be solved with a romantic grand gesture set to a really great song."

Uncle Don smiles a little.

"But that's not how it worked out for Mom, is it?" I ask, my voice growing quiet. "She fell in love with someone who couldn't even love her back, and it didn't matter that she had the ultimate sympathetic backstory or whether she attempted any sort of grand gesture."

"Your mom did have a great love story," Uncle Don says. "I wish you could remember more about your dad, kiddo, because he was really one of a kind. When your mom met him, she told me, 'I just met the man I'm going to marry.' She really knew. And you could tell whenever they were around each other that he adored her."

"But he died," I say flatly.

"And that sucks Ewok balls," Uncle Don says. "But that doesn't make their love any less real."

"Do Ewoks even have balls?" I ask, eyebrows raised.

"It's not explicitly discussed, but I assume. All I'm saying is . . . just because your mom's love story ended doesn't mean it wasn't real or that it didn't mean something. It meant everything to her."

"But then she died heartbroken," I say. "And almost ruined another woman's life."

"She died with one heartbreak, sure," Don says. "And you know what? All of us are gonna deal with a bunch of heartbreaks throughout our life. But she also died knowing that she was truly in love once, and not everyone can say that."

"Geez," I say. "What happened to you? You meet a woman and all of a sudden you turn into a relationship expert?"

Uncle Don smiles, not meeting my eyes.

"Speaking of which," I say, way too eager to change the subject away from me, "you never told me Tyler was a woman."

Uncle Don shrugs. "You never asked, and I didn't think it was important. She's an important person in my life regardless of her gender."

"But is she . . . you know?" I wiggle my eyebrows. "An important part of your life?"

"I like her quite a bit," Uncle Don says, which for him is basically an admission of love. "We like the same things, and she's a kindhearted person."

"Well, good," I say, although I'm preemptively worried about what will happen on the eventual day that Uncle Don's heart gets broken.

As if he can tell what I'm thinking, he says, "I know you're worried about me, because I have . . . limited dating experience."

"Try no dating experience," I say. "Sorry for the burn."

"I don't think it's a burn if it's the truth," Don says. "And I know there are risks to falling in love. But a lot of the time in D&D, you know a situation is dangerous and you walk right into it anyway. Because who knows? Something pretty great could happen, too."

I nod slowly.

"Or you could get eaten by dire wolves," Uncle Don says. "Either way, you can't stay in a tavern talking to people all the time, or the game would be pretty boring. Sometimes you have to get out there and take a chance."

I bite my lip. Maybe Uncle Don's weird D&D metaphor is hitting a little closer to home than I would like. And then I remember the conversation that Tommy and I had at the wrap party, about how Don doesn't want me to spend my whole life waiting for an opportunity to fall in my lap.

"Do you . . . want me to leave?" I ask quietly.

Don tilts his head. "Do I *want* you to leave? Of course not!"

I look down at my feet. "Tommy was talking to me about taking risks and chances or whatever and he said I really need to move away from here if I'm ever going to get anywhere in film, and . . . well, he's probably right."

I look up and see that Don's nodding.

"But I don't want to leave you here," I whisper, once again to my shoes.

"Annie," Don says, crossing the room to stand by me. "I love living here with you. You're the best roommate a guy could have. You eat everything I make, and you never complain about Dungeon Master Rick coming over on a weekly basis, which would likely annoy most people."

"He's an acquired taste," I admit.

"So no, I'm not exactly looking forward to the day you leave. But I know—and I think you do, too—that you can't stay here forever. And I don't want you to be worried about me, because I'm not alone. I have my job; I have the guys."

I nod toward the living room. "And Tyler."

He smiles, and it hits me how little credit I gave him. I always thought Uncle Don needed me, like he would fall apart from loneliness if I wasn't around, but he has his own life, full of friends and work and Wookiee costumes and a girlfriend. It turns out he never really *needed* me so much as he just liked hanging out with me.

"So where's Drew, anyway?" Don asks, not even bothering to segue into the question.

"We, um . . . we had a fight." I cross my arms.

"Did he do something wrong?" Don asks.

I shake my head, unable to meet his eyes. I'm not up for explaining how gossip sites work to Uncle Don, so I go for an abridged version of the story. "No, he didn't. He thought I did something bad, and I tried to explain it was an accident. But then I ignored his texts when he tried to talk to me, and . . . I think I might've been kind of an asshole."

Don sighs. "Well, listen, kid . . . we all mess up. All the people you love are gonna let you down at some point. But until it's game over, you can always fix your mistakes."

I stand up straight, thinking about Uncle Don's words. About love being worth the risk, about taking chances, about knowing that heartbreak awaits most of us around every corner but about walking around that corner anyway.

"You're right," I say, my voice full of confidence. "I need to go talk to Chloe."

We walk into the living room, where Chloe is talking animatedly to Tyler. "And then I said, Nick, you're wrong, the Doobie Brothers are one of the greatest rock groups of all time and—"

She breaks off when she sees me and makes a face when she sees my smile. But all I'm thinking about is how great it's going to be when she figures out she totally has a thing for Nick.

"What are you smiling about?" she asks, and I motion for her to join me upstairs.

"Listen," I say when we're sitting on my bed. "I think I might've screwed things up with Drew."

She shakes her head. "He'll come around and apologize. You'll see."

"The thing is, he might've been trying to apologize already. Or not. I don't know. He texted me."

She tilts her head. "And what did you say?"

I study my cuticles. "I might not have responded."

Chloe grabs my shoulders and shakes me. "Were you out of your mind, woman?"

"I got scared after reading Mom's letters! Like, who am I to say that this isn't going to end in heartbreak?"

Chloe sighs with her whole body. "No offense, but duh. Any relationship could end in heartbreak, but that doesn't mean it isn't worth trying."

I nod. "Yeah, that's pretty much what Uncle Don told me."

"Don said that?"

"Well, he was talking about D&D, but I think it was supposed to be a metaphor."

Chloe sits up straight, pushing a pillow out of her way. "So where is Drew right now?"

I check the time on my bedside alarm clock. "He said he has a flight late tonight because he's doing a morning show tomorrow in New York to promote *Christmas Zombies*. I mean, *Winter of the Undead*. So . . . probably at his hotel?"

Chloe shrugs. "So go see him."

"What, I'm just supposed to . . . show up? At his hotel? And be like, 'Hi, I fucked everything up, but love is a crapshoot, so we might as well give this thing a shot'?"

"I mean, you're the writer, so I'm sure you can come up with a better speech than that, and you might wanna tone down the language if you want a PG-13 rating, but yeah. That's basically it."

We sit in silence for a moment, then Chloe says, "Listen. You know I love you, right?"

"Uh-oh," I say.

"So please take it in the spirit of love when I say that you need to get your head out of your own ass right now."

"Um, okay. Go on."

Chloe grabs my hands. "You have a chance right now to do something truly amazing. To go get a guy who's hot and good in bed and totally into you—"

"*Maybe* still into me," I correct her.

She snorts. "Okay, sure. But here's what I'm saying: I don't want this to be another chance you don't take. You're worried that things with Drew are a big risk, but guess what? Life is a risk, and you can't protect yourself from heartbreak by refusing to go after what you want. You think Meg Ryan wasn't taking a risk when she went all the way to Seattle to stare at Tom Hanks?"

"I don't really know if stalking is the risk I want to take here."

"Whatever. I don't want you to spend five more years moping around this house because you're waiting for life to happen to you. You aren't stuck here, Annie. Some of us have obligations and people we need to take care of, but not you. Look at Uncle Don—he scored a hot purple-haired girlfriend. He doesn't need you to look after him."

"Fair point."

"You're in love with Drew, so go tell him that," Chloe says, looking at me like she's simply telling me to order a pizza.

I sit up straight. "I can't be *in love* with him. I've only known him for two weeks."

Chloe shakes her head at this minor detail. "A lot can happen in two weeks. How many rom-coms have you seen where people fall in love in one wacky, caper-filled night? Maybe it's time you stopped waiting around for Tom Hanks to show up. Maybe this time you have to be your own Tom Hanks."

I don't entirely know what that means, but I do know that Chloe's right. I've cocooned myself in this house, the one I shared with my parents, because I miss them so much and I'm surrounded by their memories. But would they want me to stay here forever, afraid to try something new? I'll never know for sure, but I think Mom would want me to go for it. Nothing in my life will change unless I take some chances, like actually trying to find a job (hopefully with Tommy's help) and moving away from the only home and city I've ever known.

But first, there's something else I need to do.

"I have to go talk to Drew." I pick up a pair of leggings off the floor. "I was an asshole. A huge asshole."

"That's a good line for your speech," Chloe says. "Oh, my God, this is so exciting. I can hear the dramatic music swelling now! I'll take Don and Tyler over to Nick's for some coffee while you're professing your undying love."

"But you just made coffee."

She wrinkles her nose. "Yeah, but . . . the coffee at Nick's is much better."

I narrow my eyes. "You sure you don't just want to see Nick?"

She puts her hands on her hips. "Annie Cassidy, what exactly are you insinuating?"

"He's going to find out you didn't have a family emergency, you know."

"It was a quick emergency," she says, still eyeing me skeptically. "Go focus on your own love life and stay out of mine, okay?"

"Okay," I singsong, not bothering to tell her that I'm writing an entire screenplay about her life. And anyway, focusing on her life is a lot better than focusing on mine, because when I think about what I'm going to do, I'm afraid I might barf.

"Okay, people!" Chloe says when we walk downstairs. I try to avoid noticing that Uncle Don has his arm around Tyler as they watch TV, because it's so weird to see him in a romantic relationship. I mean, good weird, but still weird.

"We're going to Nick's to get coffee while Annie professes her love to Drew Danforth, star of screens large and small," Chloe continues, pulling on her coat and winding her scarf around her neck.

Don stands up and pats me on the back. "Good for you, sweet pea. It's always a good idea to tell people how you feel about them. I told Tyler how I felt about her while I was still in my Chewbacca costume."

Tyler puts her arms around his midsection and beams up at him. "I had to ask him to repeat himself three times, but I was so happy once I heard him."

"That costume really muffles everything," Uncle Don says, looking at her as if I'm not even there. "Also, it doesn't breathe at all."

Chloe glances at me and raises her eyebrows. "Okay, guys, let's get a move on."

As they put their coats on, she whispers to me, "Before they start hard-core making out right here in front of us."

Chloe, Don, and Tyler head off in one direction while I head off in the other, Chloe blowing kisses to me as I go. She tries to insist that I run toward the hotel because it's more cinematic, but there's still a lot of ice on the unshoveled sidewalk, so I elect to walk.

I try to practice what I'm going to say as my boots stomp through the now-smushed-and-gray snow.

I think I like you. Ugh, what am I, twelve?

I'm in love with you. Okay, let's not come on too strong.

See, I found these letters from my mom that made me question whether love was even real and if the foundation I'd built my belief system on was full of lies, but then Uncle Don used a D&D metaphor as a way of convincing me that maybe love is real. Wow, way too much and kind of a bummer.

By the time I reach the hotel, I still don't have any great speech in mind, but you know what? I bet Matthew McConaughey's character didn't have a speech planned out when he got on his motorcycle to catch Kate Hudson's character on that bridge at the end of *How to Lose a Guy in 10 Days*. And what he said was passionate and kinda profane, but it ended with a kiss and a slow camera pan-out, so I *think* it worked out okay for him.

I walk into the lobby, the sliding doors whooshing shut behind me, and realize I don't even have a plan for finding Drew. What am I going to do, wander the halls calling his name?

"Annie?"

I turn to see Tarah, standing up from one of the lobby's stylish sofas, next to a few decorative palm fronds that are trying but failing to convince us we're not in Ohio in the middle of winter.

"Oh! Um, hey. How's it going?" I stall, trying to come up with a reason I'm in the lobby of Drew's hotel.

But she sees right through me. "You're here for Drew?"

"Yes," I say, the sound of his name filling me with hope.

She frowns, which on her still looks beautiful. "He left for the airport about an hour ago."

"He . . . he did?" I try to form more words, but everything is crumbling. This was it—my chance to tell Drew how I really felt, my big speech. And now . . . it's nothing.

"He seemed upset," Tarah says. "Not that it's any of my business, but . . . did something happen?"

"Uh, yeah," I say. "Something happened."

Tarah sits back down, and I sit down beside her, and that's how I end up spilling my entire sad life story to a famous movie star right there in the lobby of a hotel.

"Wow." Tarah leans back. "That's a lot, but you know what? This is fixable."

"How?" I ask. "He left."

She shakes her head and pulls out her phone. "Drew and I were supposed to be on the same flight, but I switched to a later flight because . . ." She looks around, then whispers, "My husband came into town to surprise me, so we're staying an extra night."

As if on cue, the lobby doors swoosh open and a man who bears more than a passing resemblance to John Cho walks through the doors holding two bags of food. My breath is temporarily taken away.

"I couldn't decide between burgers and Thai," he says, holding up the bags. "So I got both."

Tarah looks at me and smiles. "I know, I know. A cute guy who brings me multiple food options. I got lucky."

She introduces us, and he heads up to their room. I assume she's going to follow him, but then she holds out her phone. "This is his flight number."

I glance at the phone screen, then at her face. "Okay?"

She raises her eyebrows. "Do with this information what you will. His flight leaves in forty-five minutes, so . . ."

It dawns on me what she's saying. "I can go talk to him before his flight leaves."

She shrugs. "I mean, I didn't say it. But listen. I've acted with a lot of guys, and they've run the gamut from perfectly nice and bland to jerks with huge egos. Drew is one of the kindest men I've run into, and he's crazy about you. And if I've learned anything from working on a Tommy Crisante romantic comedy, it's that you shouldn't give up on love."

"You're right," I say as adrenaline starts to flow through me.

She leans in to give me a surprisingly warm hug, and then I run out the door and down the sidewalk.

"I have to get to the airport!"

The bell hasn't even finished jingling before the words are out of my mouth. Everyone in Nick's looks at me—not just Chloe, Don, and Tyler sitting at my usual table, but Nick and Tobin, and Gary, and a few other regular customers.

"All right!" Gary claps, then pulls on his coat. "Let's do this."

"Oh, I don't think you need to come, Gary," I say. "No offense."

He pulls his coat back off. "None taken."

"Feeling pretty dramatic today, huh?" Nick asks, leaning against the counter.

"Drew is there," I say to Chloe, still breathless from my run over here. "His flight leaves in"—I check the clock on the wall—"like thirty-five minutes, so I have to get there now."

Chloe stands up so fast she knocks her chair over. "Nick, I gotta go. Second family emergency of the day."

"What an urgent day you're having," Nick says drily.

"Don, Tyler, you're coming, too," Chloe says. "We need emotional support."

"I'm actually pretty tired," Tyler says, and she does look exhausted. "Would you mind if I take a nap at your house?"

"Of course, that's fine," Don says with such tenderness in his voice that I'm shocked. He normally only sounds that way when talking to his collectibles or me.

Chloe looks around the coffee shop. "In that case, Nick, you're coming with us."

He raises his eyebrows. "Why is my presence needed?"

Chloe looks at him like he's being deliberately dense. "Uh, because this is a classic rom-com rush to the airport and it's, like, seventy-five percent less effective if we don't have a car full of people screaming as we run red lights."

"I don't run red lights," Uncle Don tells the shop. "I'm a very safe driver."

Nick looks skeptical, so Chloe runs behind the counter and grabs his arm. "Come on, Coffee Man, you're coming with us."

He puts up no resistance as he attempts to hold back a smile.

"Tobin!" Chloe yells. "You're in charge! Can you handle it?"

Tobin shrugs.

"Good enough for me!" Chloe yells.

"This is a terrible idea." Nick sighs. "I'm leaving my business in Tobin's hands."

"It's *finally* ambient whale sound time." Tobin double fist pumps.

"All right, people!" Chloe says to the room. "Annie's off to get the love of her life, so wish us luck!"

Everyone claps, and Gary even wolf whistles. "Is this what it feels like to play team sports?" I whisper to Chloe.

"Wait," Tobin says, raising a hand behind the counter. "While you're at the airport, can you pick up my mom and my stepdad? I think I was supposed to do it, but I can't remember."

We all stare at Tobin.

"Call your mom and dad, kiddo," Chloe says, and then we leave.

Chapter Twenty-four

DESPITE CHLOE'S INSISTENCE ON PLAYING "THIS IS IT" BY KENNY Loggins ("It's the perfect pump-up song!"), the drive to the airport is much less dramatic than it is in most movies, probably because we don't run into any parades, drive through any road blocks, or ramp over any bridges under construction.

"That was anticlimactic," Chloe scoffs from the back seat of the Prius when we pull into the airport.

"I don't care about drama," I say, tugging off my seat belt as our car moves forward in the drop-off lane. "I just want to talk to Drew."

"So what's your plan, here?" Nick asks, leaning forward from the back seat, his head between me and Uncle Don. "Because this isn't a movie from the early '90s. You can't waltz into the airport and talk to someone anymore."

"I'm going to buy a ticket," I say like it's obvious. "That way I can get in there and find Drew."

"Wow," Nick says. "You are . . . really invested in this."

Chloe smacks him on the arm. "It's called romance, doofus."

I look over my shoulder and memorize the exact way Nick is gazing at her, the adoration hidden underneath irritation, so I can jot down the precise details in my screenplay.

Later. I can focus on the slow build of their relationship *later*. Right now, I have to get in the airport, buy a ticket for Drew's flight, then get to him.

"I'll be right back," I call out as I step out of the car.

"I'll go wait in short-term parking," Uncle Don says. "Keep us updated."

"I'm coming with you," Chloe says, pulling off her seat belt and jumping out of the car.

"Why?" I ask as we walk through the doors, dodging a woman with a giant rolling suitcase. "You're not buying a ticket. You won't even be able to go very far."

"Moral support," Chloe says, linking her arm with mine. "And because I'm living vicariously through you. As soon as you leave, I'm right back to working and studying."

I squeeze her arm. Once inside, we quickly find the right counter and run to it. "I need to get on flight 1147," I practically shout, then try to rein it in because I'm not trying to look un-hinged, here.

The man behind the counter clicks a few keys and then looks at me, lips pursed. "Sorry, that flight just boarded and is about to take off."

"But it's still here," Chloe says, leaning forward.

"But you can't get on it. It's full, and it's about to take off."

Chloe's mouth falls open. "You can't, like, stick her in overhead storage or something? She's a small person."

"As a matter of policy, we don't store passengers in our overhead bins," the man says without smiling.

"Someone's lap, then," Chloe says. "One particular passenger's lap."

"Lap seating is only for children under two years old," he says, looking at his computer screen.

"She could fit on someone's lap!" Chloe shrieks.

"Chlo." I grab her arm and start to pull her away. "Drop it. I missed him, okay?"

"Wait." Chloe holds up a finger. "When's the next flight to New York?"

The man clicks a few more keys, then says, "In an hour and a half."

"What are you doing, Chloe?" I ask, getting nervous.

"Babe." She turns to me and holds both of my hands. "This is it. This is your romantic comedy. You have the sad backstory and the montage of ridiculous dating experiences and big career aspirations and the lovable family and, most importantly, the quirky and charming and super-cute BFF." She points to herself. "And now it's time for your grand gesture. Fly to New York and find Drew. Tell him how you feel."

"Oh, my God," I say as it slowly dawns on me. "You're right. I guess I always thought I would be the recipient of a grand gesture, but maybe . . . maybe I have the power to do the grand gesture myself?"

Chloe starts jumping up and down, and then I start jumping up and down. "You're your own Tom Hanks!" she squeals.

"Ladies," barks the man behind the counter. "Are you buying tickets or not? You're holding up the line."

I give Chloe an uncertain look. Can I really do this? Fly to New York, when I'm not even sure if Drew wants to see me, when the only contact between us all day was one measly text I didn't even respond to?

Chloe nods at me, and then says smugly, "Yes, sir. Oh, we're buying tickets."

Chapter Twenty-five

APPARENTLY UNCLE DON HAS BEEN WAITING FOR AN EXCUSE TO GO to New York because there's some forum friend he wants to meet who lives there and he's been "talking about Baldur's Gate with this guy for ten years!" I'm pretty sure he's referring to a game, but honestly, sometimes I don't know.

Chloe somehow convinces Nick he needs to come along with us, and that's how the four of us, after going through security, end up on our way to New York City. Paying for everyone's ticket uses up most of the money I made working for Tommy, which might be a reckless financial decision, but I remind myself that the course of true love never did run smooth. That quote comes from the original king of the rom-com, Shakespeare himself, and I'm sure that if he were here right now, he'd approve of my actions (but also he'd be terrified of airplanes).

"I still don't understand why Don and I are here," Nick says as we sit at our gate. Although, by the way he's looking at Chloe, I think he knows exactly what he's doing here. "And couldn't you have looked up tickets online instead of driving to the airport first? Also, how much did you have to pay for these tickets, because—"

Chloe turns to look at him. "Dude. Have you never seen a movie? Maximum drama means a ragtag group of supporters have to help Annie find her man. Her loving and kind uncle, her super-hot BFF, and some random guy who's there because it's funny."

"So I'm the random guy," Nick says flatly.

"You're certainly not her uncle," Chloe says.

We weren't able to get four seats together, so once we get on the plane, I sit next to Chloe. Don and Nick sit several rows ahead of us.

"You're doing it, Annie," Chloe says, squeezing my hand.

My phone buzzes with a text notification.

ANNIE. READ THE SCRIPT. LOTS OF POTENTIAL. LET'S TALK SOON.—TOMMY

"Oh, my God." I can hardly breathe.

"What?" Chloe grabs the phone out of my hands and reads the text. "Wow, he texts in all caps AND signs his name? He really must be ancient."

"That's what you're focusing on? Tommy Crisante thinks my script has potential."

"Duh." Chloe hands my phone back. "I haven't even read it yet, and I could've told you that. Speaking of which, when do I finally get to read it?"

I squirm a bit, and Chloe's eyes widen. "Wait a second, you don't want me to read it, do you? What, do you not trust me? Am I no longer your best friend? Did I or did I not make you pancakes this afternoon?"

She's getting frantic, and the various families and businesspeople shuffling onto the flight are staring at us. I don't want to get kicked off the flight for causing a scene, so I decide this is the time to tell her. "Keep it down, Chloe! I need to tell you something. The screenplay . . . it's about you."

She sits back, a look of confusion on her face.

"And Nick," I continue.

"Wait, what?" she screeches, and I put a hand over her mouth. Maybe this was a bad idea.

"It's just . . . you guys have perfect romantic comedy chemistry. You're the quirky girl who doesn't believe in love, and he's the gruff dude who's clearly obsessed with her."

"Nick isn't obsessed with me," Chloe says, giving me a steely glare.

"Agree to disagree."

Chloe smacks me on the arm. "This entire time, you've been writing about *me*? You showed Tommy Crisante a screenplay about *me*?"

I shrug. "I mean . . . yeah, sort of. Although in my screenplay you and Nick make out, which hasn't happened in real life, as far as I know."

"It certainly has not!" Chloe snaps, then hides her face in her hands.

"This isn't that weird!" I say. "Look at *The Big Sick*. Kumail Nanjiani and Emily V. Gordon wrote that about their real-life love story."

"Yeah." Chloe scowls. "But that was about their *own* love story. You're basically writing fan fiction about my life. What, did you call us Rick and Zoe?"

I don't say anything.

"Annie!" she shouts. "Change the damn names!"

I put a hand on her arm. "Hey. Are you really not okay with this?"

She eyes me warily. "You wrote a movie that's a fictionalized version of my life where I end up making out with my boss. You get that that's weird, right?"

For the first time, it hits me that . . . well, it *is* more than a little weird for her. To me, it was just writing, but she never signed up for Tommy Crisante to read a highly fictionalized version of her life story.

"Do you want me to scrap it?" I ask. "Because I can. Our friendship means a lot more to me than a movie."

Chloe's shoulders slump. "No, I don't want you to scrap it. I mean, Tommy Crisante is already showing interest in it, and that's a big deal for you."

"He said it has potential," I hedge. "A pound of raw hamburger has the potential to make a great burger, but that doesn't mean I can eat it without cooking it."

Chloe stares at me.

"Not without getting E. coli poisoning, anyway," I say.

"Stop trying to change the subject to tainted beef." She turns to face me fully. "This is the only thing you've been really passionate about the past few years, and I don't want to stand in the way of that."

"Chloe," I say, my eyes welling with tears. "You're the best."

I pull her into a hug, and she says into my shoulder, "But try to make sure someone really hot plays me, okay?"

"I'll do what I can," I say, releasing her. As the preflight video plays and the flight attendant makes sure we're all buckled in, it starts to sink in that I'm on a flight to New York. To find a man and . . . do what, exactly? Maybe I didn't really think this plan through.

"What am I doing, Chloe?" I ask in a tiny voice, and she turns to face me again.

"Remember in *The Wedding Singer*? Remember how Adam Sandler needed to stop Drew Barrymore from getting married to that total jerk, so he got on a plane?"

I nod.

"In that scenario, Billy Idol was there, and also Adam Sandler had written a really lovely song about Drew . . . you haven't prepared any music, have you?"

"I have not."

"Okay, so we don't have that, but everything else checks out. This is your big *The Wedding Singer* grand gesture, and air travel is the most romantic form of travel. Well, except for train, but that's not exactly an option right now. Anyone can send a text; you're going to show up in person."

I nod again. Chloe's right; this is a pretty grand gesture, and it worked in *The Wedding Singer* . . . Of course, as she mentioned, Billy Idol was there and Adam Sandler wrote a song. I look around the plane and I don't see even one celebrity, major or minor. I'd settle for a YouTuber right now.

"I'm nervous," I say.

Chloe pats my arm. "Of course, you are, but it's Drew. Just go over your big, dramatic speech in your head."

The plane takes off, and I immediately fall asleep. For some reason, this has always been my reaction to stress—if I'm facing too much or getting too nervous, my body's like, "You know what? Let's sleep this one off."

I open my eyes and see Nick reading a paperback beside me.

"Where's Chloe?" I ask groggily.

"Sitting with Don. She asked to switch seats because she wanted to sleep and you were snoring too loudly."

"Oh. Whoops."

He shrugs. "No problem for me. I don't sleep on planes."

I take in his rigid posture and the way his hands are fidgeting with the book. "Wait. Are you scared of flying?"

"I'm not scared of anything," Nick mutters so quietly that I can barely hear him above the noise of the plane.

"You are," I say, sitting up.

"I have an absolutely normal amount of apprehension about sitting in a metal tube and hurtling through the sky," Nick says. "That's not fear. That's called being reasonable."

In a low voice, even though there's no way she could hear us several rows over and asleep, I say, "You should tell her."

He eyes me skeptically. "Tell who what?"

I raise my eyebrows. "Chloe."

"That I'm afraid of planes?" he asks, his eyes darting away.

"I thought you weren't afraid."

"Yeah, well." He meets my eyes again and gives me a wry smile. "Maybe I'm afraid of some things."

"You're in love with her," I say, a statement and not a question.

"I'm not . . . Love is a complicated thing," he says, rubbing his hands over his stubble.

"Yeah, well, I'm flying to New York to confess my love for Drew. At least telling Chloe how you feel doesn't involve air travel."

"And yet I'm on a plane right now," he says. He narrows his eyes. "So you really like this guy, huh?"

I nod.

"Well," Nick says. "He didn't bring in a bunch of bodyguards who peed on the seat, and he didn't scare Gary with a rant about fluoride, so I'd say he's okay."

"To be fair," I say, "that's a pretty low bar."

I glance at my phone—it's late now, and the coffee shop has been closed for a while. "Have you heard from Tobin?"

"Oh, God," Nick says. "He probably forgot to lock up. I can't believe I risked my livelihood on that kid."

I smile and close my eyes, and when I open them, everyone's putting their seat belts back on. This is it, as the great Kenny Loggins would say. We're landing in New York City, a place I've never been, because I decided I had to end my romantic comedy with a dramatic run through the airport and a big grand gesture that seems more and more like a silly idea.

Nick grips my arm as the plane lands with a few bumps and skips down the runway, then pulls his hand back and clears his throat as soon as we're stopped. "Don't tell Chloe, okay?" he asks with a groan.

"I won't," I say, already imagining putting an airplane scene into my screenplay.

We disembark the plane, and one of the plus sides of traveling with absolutely no preparation or logic is that you don't have to worry about luggage.

"Okay, so." Chloe claps her hands together as we stand outside near the line of taxis. "Where do we go?"

"Um . . ." I haven't thought this far ahead. "I don't know?"

Nick blinks a few times. "You mean you—we—flew to New York and you don't even know where this guy is?"

"I don't know," I mutter. "I guess I got caught up in the moment."

And then I remember: *Good Morning USA*.

"What time is it?" I shout.

"Uh, it's like six A.M.," Chloe says. "And also chill. You're scaring people."

"He's going to be on *Good Morning USA*!" I tell her. "That's where I can find him!"

"Alternatively," Nick says, "you could text him. You know, like a normal person?"

"But there's nothing romantic about texts!" Chloe says.

"I don't know," Uncle Don says with a shrug. "I've sent some pretty romantic texts in my time."

I am zero percent prepared to hear about Uncle Don's sexting history right now. "You guys, focus. I need to get to *Good Morning USA*."

"Isn't that one of those shows where you have to start lining up at, like, four A.M. just to stand outside the window and wave a sign?" Chloe asks.

"Yeah, but . . ." I think for a moment. "They film outside sometimes, too. Like, they have a stage set up, and everyone stands around it."

"So either we yell at him from the crowd while he's on the outdoor stage, or we create an elaborate sign that will get the attention of the producers and/or camera people inside," Chloe muses. "I suggest something with a *lot* of profanity."

"Let's go," I say, and I march over to the first cab I see, forcing as much confidence as I can. "Sir? Can you take us to the set of *Good Morning USA*?"

He looks me up and down. "Are you hurt, ma'am?"

"What? No! Why?" I ask.

He points to my hair. "Because you look, well, like maybe you've been attacked."

I run my hands over my hair. It has, to be honest, reached previously unheard-of levels of unkempt, and that's coming from someone who spends most of her days alone. Perhaps this is not the best look to confess my love to Drew in.

As if she can read my thoughts, Chloe steps between me and the taxi driver. "No. *No.* You cannot back out now. We're in New York; we're minutes away from Drew. You can do this. He doesn't care what you look like."

I turn to Nick and Don. "Do I really look that bad?"

Nick politely looks away, and Don says, "You've looked better."

In a gentle voice, Chloe says, "You're wearing a leopard-print coat over a Pizza Slut T-shirt. It's not a glamorous look, hon. But Drew doesn't care, okay? He'll want to see you, not some lady in a beautiful dress. Like Yoda says, just do it."

"That's not actually what Yoda—" Uncle Don starts.

Chloe holds up a hand, still looking at me. "So not the point, Don."

"If you aren't getting in, move out of the way," the driver says, no longer concerned about me now that he knows I'm not escaping an attack.

"Okay, okay," I say, sliding into the back seat. "Let's go."

Our driver lets us out at the edge of a small crowd, facing the back of the outdoor stage, although we're about ten rows of people away from it. The crowd is contained within metal gates, and intimidatingly large men in shirts marked SECURITY stand around them, arms crossed.

"Is that him?" Chloe asks, her voice high-pitched and excited as she points to the stage.

"The one in the red dress?" Don asks, squinting.

"That's Teresa Perez, the anchor," I say. "Drew's the man beside her."

"Ah," Uncle Don says. "Okay, I see it now. Maybe I need to go to the eye doctor."

Although we can only see their backs, I'd know those broad shoulders anywhere. Drew is standing next to his costar, and someone is fussing with their mic packs and their hair, so the interview must not have started yet. I might have time to get to him before it starts . . . if only I can get through this crowd.

I climb up on the gate and yell, "Drew!"

A forty-something woman wearing an orange windbreaker turns and gives me an apologetic look. "Oh, honey, good luck."

"No, I know him," I say.

As she takes in my leopard-print coat and my disheveled hair, her apologetic look turns into pity. "Of course you do, sweetie."

"Ma'am." A burly man approaches me and holds out a hand. "I'm going to have to ask you to step off of the gate."

"But I need to get to Drew!" I say, getting frantic. By now, the woman in the orange windbreaker isn't the only one watching me— pretty much everyone in the audience is. I look toward the stage again and shout, *"Drew!"*

"I'm here to stop women like you from getting to Drew, okay?" the man says, grabbing me by the shoulders and effortlessly placing me on the ground like I'm an annoying insect he's swatting away.

"I have to tell him something!" I shout, and before the guard can stop me, I pull myself up on the gate again. "Drew! *Drew!*"

The burly man speaks into his walkie-talkie. "I'm gonna need some backup over here."

Aside from some murmurs and a few nervous laughs, the crowd is silent as they watch this scene unfolding. Things are so quiet that it's easy to hear when someone onstage yells, "Annie?"

The burly man has his arms wrapped around me as my feet pedal in the air when I see Drew onstage, looking toward me.

"Drew!" I shout again.

"It's okay!" he yells to the guard as he easily leaps off the stage and over the gate into the crowd. "You can put her down. I know her."

"I told you." I give Orange Windbreaker a smug smile, and she rolls her eyes.

"God," Nick says in awe. "He leapt over that gate like it was nothing."

"He's done a lot of training," I say breathlessly, watching Drew make his way toward me, taking selfies with every woman in the crowd first.

"It's very impressive," Uncle Don says. "Did you know he used to eat ten chicken breasts every day?"

"I literally couldn't do that," Nick says. "I'll just stay wimpy and skinny. It's fine."

"You're not wimpy," Don says, giving Nick a pat on the back. "Every body type deserves love."

"Oh, my God, you guys," I hiss. "I'm trying to focus on what I'm going to say to Drew, and I can't when you're having a body-positivity workshop behind me."

"Annie," Drew says once he makes his way to me. He hops over the gate. "What are—how did you—?"

I look at his face, at those soft brown eyes, his hair that's gelled a little more than usual to stand up to the slight wind today, those lips that I spent hours kissing, and everything I wanted to say floats away like a piece of paper in the breeze.

"I wanted to tell you something," I squeak. And then I clear my throat. I didn't fly all the way from Ohio to New York to give Drew some half-assed, weak declaration of *like*. I came here to make a declaration of love, dammit.

I look over my shoulder at Chloe, and she gives me a thumbs-up, which is all that I need to go on. Because I know that, Drew or not, I'm not lonely like a rom-com heroine. I have Chloe and Uncle Don, and I always will, even if eventually we don't all live on the same property.

I turn my face back to Drew, who's looking at me expectantly.

So I open my mouth and start talking.

"I wanted to have some big speech for this moment, because that's what this is supposed to be, right? Matthew McConaughey on a bridge telling Kate Hudson not to leave? Adam Sandler singing Drew Barrymore a song? Or Katherine Heigl interrupting a wedding to tell James Marsden that she's falling in love with him in *27 Dresses*?"

"Oh, I love that movie!" says Orange Windbreaker.

"It's underrated, right?" I say.

"*So* underrated," she murmurs.

I look at Drew, the confusion on his face, and remember what I came here to do.

"If this was a movie," I continue, "I'd have some beautiful, poetic speech that has that one really great line people quote years later. But what I recently found out is . . . this isn't a movie. My life is just my life. Maybe it doesn't have that perfect narrative arc or characters who are just lovably quirky. Maybe it has some people who have actual flaws, like the really big glaring kind. Maybe people are going to let me down, and I'm going to let them down, and things aren't necessarily going to end with a slow pan out and a sweeping instrumental score. And that's okay! Because what I'm trying to say is . . ."

I take a look around me. Orange Windbreaker is looking at me in wonder, her mouth open like everyone else in the crowd, including . . .

Oh, God, there are camerapeople here now. I look into the camera for a second and freeze, then shake my head. I have to keep going.

I look back at Drew and block out everything else—the crowd, the camera, my fear—and keep going.

"Maybe not everything about romantic comedies is real, and maybe Tom Hanks is just an actor playing fictional characters. But what they taught me about love, and about being honest, and about growing as a person . . . that feels pretty real to me. And I'd rather have you than Tom Hanks any day, because . . ."

I take a deep breath and say what I came here to say.

"I love you. It's ridiculous and we haven't known each other for long and I know there's a chance it won't work out, but I love you, all right? I'm ready to move out of Columbus, and not because I'm following you like a creepy stalker or an obsessed fan," I say, shooting a pointed look to the security guard, "but because I want to take a chance. I want to work in movies and I want to do scary things and I want to be with you."

Drew still doesn't say anything, and a bloom of worry blossoms in my chest. This was a mistake. He's going to turn me down and it's on camera and this is going to go viral. Now I'm The Girl Who Got Turned Down by Drew Danforth on Live TV, and this rejection is going to follow me around for the rest of my life.

But then I see that he's smiling—looking right at me and

grinning, the kind of grin someone has when they can't believe their luck. That Drew Danforth smile, the one everyone's seen a million times before, is real and it's mine.

"Annie," he says, and my name still sounds so much better coming out of his mouth, "that was the best speech I've ever heard in my life."

He takes a step and closes the distance between us. Drew puts his hands on my face and leans in, so only I can hear, and says, "I love you, too."

And if you've ever seen a rom-com, you know what happens next; he kisses me, and the crowd goes wild.

Drew pulls back, and both of us take in everything around us. The camera crew. Orange Windbreaker, who's looking at us with misty eyes. Chloe, doing a wolf whistle. Nick clapping and Uncle Don dabbing at the edges of his eyes with a tissue. It's not perfect, because my mom's not here, but like I told Drew, this isn't a movie. It will never be perfect, but at least it's real.

"I'm really glad you ran into me that day," Drew says.

And as he leans in to kiss me again, although I know it's not possible, I swear I can hear the music start to play.

ONE YEAR LATER

DREW DANFORTH ENGAGED!

by Steve Babbitt
for Hollywood Gossip

Well, we thought it would never happen, but it's true! Hollywood prankster Drew Danforth has finally settled down, popping the question to his girlfriend, screenwriter Annie Cassidy. Drew is set to costar in the upcoming *Frasier* reboot, while Cassidy's first film, *Coffee Girl*, is in preproduction. Congratulations to the happy couple!

Keep reading for an excerpt from Kerry Winfrey's
next contemporary romance . . .

NOT LIKE THE MOVIES

Coming soon from Jove!

Chapter One

I can tell what's going on by the way the customer looks at me. The concentrated stare as I pour her coffee, the anticipatory smile as I put the lid on. This isn't someone who's only here for the caffeine hit. No, this is something different.

"Have a great—" I start as I hand her the drink, but she cuts me off.

"It's you, right?" she asks, breathless, eyes wide. "From the movie?"

I am typically friendly—some might say *too* friendly—to our customers here at Nick's coffee shop. It's kind of my thing. And it's not even a problem for me to let gruff patrons or rude comments roll right off my back; not because I'm a doormat but because I'm genuinely not bothered by it. People have hard days, and while they definitely shouldn't take them out on their baristas, I know it's not about me.

But this . . . this is different. This couldn't be more about me.

"Um, yeah," I say, trying to keep my voice down. "It's me."

"There's an article about you on People.com," she says, the excitement palpable in her rushed words. "With . . . pictures."

I see her eyes dart toward my boss, Nick, who's tending to the espresso machine behind me. I wince before I can stop myself.

"Oh, is there?" I say, and before she can complete her nod, I finish with, "If you don't mind moving along, there are other customers I need to help."

She smiles and walks away, so starstruck she doesn't notice that there's no one else in line. I let out a long sigh, then immediately pull up People.com on my phone.

There it is. "The Real-Life Love Story Behind the New Film *Coffee Girl*!"

There's a picture of me, one that I don't remember taking and certainly didn't give to *People* magazine. And then there are a couple pictures of Nick and me here, at work, behind the counter. The saving grace is that I was wearing an especially cute cardigan that day, one with little embroidered flowers and bees, so at least I look good, but that doesn't take away the weirdness inherent in seeing a picture of yourself that you didn't even know someone took.

But why am I, Chloe Sanderson, resident of Columbus, Ohio, and no one all that special, gracing the pages of People.com?

Because my best friend wrote a movie about me.

Okay, so Annie maintains that the movie isn't *about* me so much as *inspired* by me, and she's right. But anyone who knows me and sees the trailer can see the similarities. The movie's lead character, Zoe (come on, Annie), has a stubbornly, almost annoyingly positive attitude, even in the face of rude customers or family tragedy. She works in a coffee shop. She takes care of her sick father, although Zoe's father has cancer, while mine has Alzheimer's.

But there are a few key differences between Zoe and Chloe. Zoe is at least four inches shorter than I am, with hair that has clearly been professionally styled. She has a team of stylists picking out her artfully vintage clothing, whereas I stick to the Anthropologie sale rack, where all the truly weird shit lives. Oh, and Zoe makes out, and falls in love, with her boss, Rick.

The names, Annie. You couldn't have changed those names?

"Put your phone away. You're working."

Nick is so close I can feel his breath on my face. He smells, as usual, like coffee and this aftershave I've never smelled anywhere else, something that feels old-fashioned (like a grandpa) but kinda hot (not like a grandpa).

I jump, startled by his proximity, and shove my phone in my apron pocket. Nick and I do *not* talk about the movie; it's like the elephant in the room, if that elephant were making out with one of its elephant coworkers.

There are a few people clustered around tables, but still no one in line. "Ah, yes, things are bustling," I say, gesturing at the nonexistent line. "I wouldn't want to ignore anyone."

"It's the principle of the thing," he says, staring at me for what seems like just a beat too long. Or maybe it isn't.

The thing is, this ridiculous movie my best friend wrote (wow, that sentence will never stop sounding weird) has really screwed up a lot of things for me. Things I never thought about before, like whether Nick is hot or whether he's giving me a weird smile or what his perpetual five-o'clock shadow would feel like on my cheek . . . All of a sudden those thoughts are in my head, and I don't like it. I'm just trying to work over here, you know? This is my job, the thing I use to make money for the business classes I'm moving through at a glacial pace.

A new song starts playing: "Steal Away" by Robbie Dupree.

"Chloe," Nick says, his voice a low growl.

I busy myself with restacking the already-stacked cups, trying not to let my mouth twist into a smile. "Yes?"

"Didn't I explicitly ban your yacht rock playlist?"

I tilt my head, thinking about it.

"Several times? With increasingly dire language?"

I shake my head. "It's weird. I don't remember any of those conversations. I just remember the vague sense of dread that overcomes me as I'm forced to reckon with my own mortality every time you play the depressing music you like."

Nick sighs, then gives me another one of those looks. It's kind of a smile but kind of a frown at the same time, which is a face he's really good at. I widen my eyes back at him.

This is the fun part, the part I love about work. I like arguing with Nick because it's not serious (I mean, I seriously do hate the music he listens to, but I don't actually care that much), but we both treat it like it's life and death. I don't even know if I'd like yacht rock half as much if I didn't have to defend it to him every day.

To Annie, a born-and-bred rom-comaholic, our playful banter means we're destined to be together. Because that's what happens in rom-coms, right? Two people who can't stand each other are actually just hiding deep wells of passion, and eventually all those pent-up feelings will explode in one of those make-out scenes where shelves get knocked over and limbs are flying and people are panting.

But listen, I get angry at Siri when she willfully misunderstands me, and that doesn't mean I should marry my phone. Sometimes people just argue and don't want to make out with each other, because life isn't a rom-com (unless you're Annie and you're marrying a literal movie star).

Nick shakes his head and points toward the back of the store. "I'll be in my office. Think you can handle it up here?"

I gesture once more toward the mostly empty shop. Business isn't due to pick up for another hour. "Somehow, I'll manage."

I lean over the counter and pull out my phone again, but between you and me . . . yes, I do look up to watch Nick walk to his office. It's like that old saying, "I hate to see you go, but I love to watch you leave," except that it's, like, "I hate the depressing AF music you play, but I love to watch you leave because *fire emoji*."

Although it pains me to admit it, Nick Velez is objectively hot. He's tall and thin, with light brown skin, dark hair that's not too long or too short, and the aforementioned persistent scruff on his face. I don't think I've ever seen Nick clean-shaven, and I regularly see him at five A.M. That's just how his face looks, apparently.

But, unlike my romance-obsessed BFF, I am not someone who gets carried away by fantasies of love. Sure, Nick is hot, and okay, maybe I've had a couple of daydreams where he pins me against the brick wall of the coffee shop and rubs my face raw with his stubble, but there are lots of hot people in the world who aren't my boss. And since I kind of need this job, and I really need to keep my personal life as drama-free as possible, I think I'll stick to dating people who aren't intertwined in any other area of my life. Because taking care of my dad is messy enough, and I don't really need anyone else's feelings to worry about.

As if on cue, my phone buzzes. It's Tracey, the receptionist at my dad's care facility.

"Do you think you could check in for a minute when you get a chance? Your dad's having an episode."

Chapter Two

I SUMMON NICK FROM HIS OFFICE AND TELL HIM I'M LEAVING. An-other reason why Nick is a great boss, despite his abysmal taste in music: he's always okay with me leaving, on no notice, to take care of my dad.

"Let me know how it goes, okay?" he says, one hand on my arm and concern in his deep brown eyes.

"Sure," I say, pulling off my apron, already out of coffee-serving mode and into crisis mode.

A short drive later, I buzz the door at Dad's facility and wait to be let in. The stress, the potential bad mood, is coming over me, so I take a deep breath. Inhale positivity. Exhale stress. I smile along with my exhale, willing myself to be Good Mood Chloe for my dad, regardless of what greets me on the other side of the door.

Because no matter what I find—no matter what condition my dad is in—this is my responsibility. It's not my brother, Milo's, be-cause he lives in Brooklyn in an apartment I've never visited, on account of I can't fathom leaving my dad that long. And it sure as hell isn't my mom's, considering that she bounced right out of our lives when she left us for some dude she met on the internet when Milo and I were ten.

It was the week before the fourth-grade Christmas pageant, aka the biggest event on my calendar at the time. Milo wasn't involved, because even back then he was too cool for earnest performances, but I was an angel narrator that delivered a lengthy speech about the importance of the baby Jesus's birth. (In retrospect, a public elementary school probably shouldn't have been putting on such an explicitly religious production, but what can I say? It was the '90s in Ohio, and anything went.) Mom was a fantastic seamstress who made most of her own clothing, and she promised to make me a costume that would leave all those donkeys and wise men in the dust, meaning that everyone in the audience would be unable to focus on anything but me, instead of the birth of our Lord and Savior. Mom might not have said it that way, but that's the way I interpreted it.

But then she left with some dude named Phil, and I wasn't about to bother Dad or Milo by telling them I needed a costume. Dad was shell-shocked, staring at the TV for hours, and Milo was alternating between preteen anger and sobs. The worst part was that online dating as we know it didn't even *exist* back then, which meant that her leaving us for a guy she met online was Super Weird and basically a school-wide scandal. Everyone, even my teachers, looked at me with pity.

So I got shit done. I tore the white bedsheets off my bed and, using the most rudimentary of sewing skills, fashioned them into a sort-of-toga, sort-of-angel-robe. I'm not saying it was the best angel costume the elementary school had ever seen, but it worked, and it was the first time I realized two things: I can only count on myself if I want to get something done, and I'm capable of doing pretty much anything.

I'm still smiling and deep-breathing as the door clicks unlocked and I walk through quickly, right to the reception desk where Tracey's waiting for me.

"Everything's *okay*," she says, hands out to calm me. "I just thought you might want to come see him."

Tracey covers the front desk at Brookwood Memory Care, but she's more than just an employee. She's sort of my ex—we went on a few dates, years ago, before it quickly became apparent that she was looking for a relationship and I was . . . well, not. But we stayed friends, and she was able to get my dad into Brookwood, which is a huge step up from his previous facility.

"What happened?" I ask, nervously pulling at my tangled blond braid. When it comes to my dad, an "episode" can mean just about anything. There was the time he was convinced that the entire facility was being taken over by "the Mennonites" and wouldn't stop yelling about it. Or the time he slapped another resident because he was certain he'd broken his television. Or the time he claimed to be "starving," despite the fact that he'd eaten dinner just half an hour before, and went on an hours-long rant about how "this hellhole" was starving him.

Tracey sighs, clearly not wanting to be the one to break this news to me. But I'm glad she is; I'm glad I can count on her to give me the full story.

"He says someone stole his watch," Tracey says. "He can't find it anywhere."

"And do you think someone really stole it?" I ask, even though I know the answer.

She shakes her head. "If you want to file a report, you can, but we'd have to involve the authorities, and—"

I hold up a hand. "No. I'll go talk to him. Thanks, Tracey."

I try to give her a look that says, "I value your friendship and appreciate you breaking this to me gently but also, man, this really sucks."

I'm extremely grateful for my friendship with Tracey, because here's the thing: sure, we didn't date for long, but we transitioned fairly seamlessly from "two people who might make out at any moment" to "two people who talk about feelings and get lunch sometimes and call each other for emotional support." I mean, I was there when she married her wife last year. But I've never—*never*—stayed friends with any man I've hooked up with. Just a week ago, a guy who took me out on two uneventful dates two years ago walked into the coffee shop, saw me, and turned right back around and left.

I resent that, because I'm a wonderful friend. Attentive, loyal, helpful, ready to drop everything and get pizza at a moment's notice if you need to have a lengthy, emotional chat over a slice of pepperoni. But apparently dudes can't realize that . . . which is, of course, yet another reason I only date people who aren't involved in my personal life. I can't assume I'm going to meet another unicorn friend like Tracey.

The TV blares through my dad's shut door. I knock three times, right on the name tag. Daniel Sanderson.

When he doesn't answer, I slowly push open the door. "Dad?"

There's no telling what I'll find when I open his door. I'm not expecting full-scale catastrophe, of course, because the entire reason he's here at Brookwood is so a team of nurses and other trained professionals can care for him around the clock. But I don't know what his mood will be, how agitated he'll get, until I see him.

Bracing for the worst, I find him sitting in his recliner, remote in hand. He looks up.

"Hi, sweetheart!" His smile is so big it just about breaks my heart, because it's him. There he is. This is a good day, or at least a good moment.

"Hey, Dad," I say, leaning over to give him a hug. "How's it going?"

He gestures toward the TV, which is playing a rerun of *Three's Company*. He may not remember what he had for breakfast or whether I called him this morning, but he definitely remembers how much he loves *Three's Company*.

"Just catching up on TV. You ever see this show?"

"Uh, yeah, Dad," I say, sitting down on the love seat as Jack Tripper concocts another sitcom scheme on screen. "Listen, I just talked to Tracey . . ."

He pauses, thinking.

"She works at the front desk," I say gently, willing him to remember.

"I know that," he says, an edge in his voice.

"She told me you think someone stole your watch." I observe his face.

He looks up and meets my eyes, instantly angry. "I don't *think* that, I *know* it. You're treating me like I'm a child, Chloe, like I don't know where my own stuff is. The people here are taking my things and I—"

I stand up and cut him off. "How about I look for it, okay?"

He makes a big show of shrugging. "You aren't going to find anything in here. I looked already and I can tell you, it's not in this room. Someone took it."

I suppress a sigh and look under the bed. Behind the toilet. In the shower. All places his things have "mysteriously" ended up before.

Finally, I check the fridge, and behind the half gallon of 2 percent milk, there it is.

I hold up the watch. "Found it."

Dad squares his shoulders. "I did *not* put that there. Someone else must have snuck in here and—"

"Dad!" I nearly shout, before I can stop myself. "Why would someone do that? Why would one of the residents or one of the nurses come in here, find your watch, and hide it in the fridge? What kind of sense does that make?"

Dad looks away from me, toward his lap, and the expression that comes over his face is instantly familiar to me. Eyes cloudy, unfocused. "I don't know," he mutters, staring at his hands.

"Hey." I cross the tiny room in three steps. "I'm sorry for shouting. I didn't mean it, okay?"

He shakes his head. "I'm sorry, Chloe. I'm sorry this is happening and I'm . . . I'm just sorry I'm such a burden."

This is the worst part, the part when he realizes what's happening. The part when he knows he has a disease, knows that his brain tissue is shrinking and his cells are degenerating, even if he can't say it in those words. I bite my lip and hold out an arm.

"You aren't a burden," I say with force, as if that will make my words stick in his brain. And I believe that. This is hard and it sucks, but if I have the choice between seeing this weird, shitty glass as half-full or half-empty, then I'm gonna pick half-full every time. Because my dad might be different, but he's still my dad. Both of Annie's parents are dead, and at least I get to spend time with one of mine.

"Come on over to the love seat," I say. "I've got some free time; let's find out what kind of zany hijinks Jack and the girls get into, okay?"

He smiles weakly and lets me guide him into the love seat, and I sit down next to him. We sit there, my head on his shoulder, and watch three entire episodes of *Three's Company* (apparently, this basic cable channel is having a marathon), and I try my best to keep the sadness at bay and take this moment in. Because as bad as this is—as frustrated as I get, as worried as I am—it's only going to get worse. Barring some sort of miraculous overnight medical discovery, he isn't going to get better. He's going to forget my name, then he's going to forget my face, and then he's going to forget everything.

A fourth episode of *Three's Company* starts, that iconic theme song playing, and Dad leans into me. "This is the longest episode of *Three's Company* I've ever seen," he says, and even though I feel like crying, I can't help laughing.

PHOTO BY ALEX WINFREY

Kerry Winfrey writes romantic comedies for adults and teens. She is the author of *Love and Other Alien Experiences* and *Things Jolie Needs to Do Before She Bites It.* When she's not writing, she's likely baking yet another pie or watching far too many romantic comedies. She lives with her husband, son, and dog in the middle of Ohio. You can find her on Twitter @KerryAnn, on Instagram @kerrywinfrey, or on her rom-com blog ayearofromcoms.tumblr.com.

Ready to find
your next great read?

Let us help.

Visit prh.com/nextread

Penguin
Random
House